A KILLING *in* NEW TOWN

A KiLLiNG *in* NEW TOWN

Kate Horsley

La Alameda Press
New Mexico

I thank Tim Cokey, Melinda Skinner, Joanna Hurley and Barbara Dicks for honest opinions and advice. I thank Cheryl Foote for her historical expertise; she is not responsible for my decision to alter a few events and their times to serve fictional themes. I thank Ivan Melada for his literary wisdom, especially concerning the West. I thank Cirrelda Snider-Bryan and Claudia Ramirez for help with the Spanish; and Wayne Shrubsall for his devoted knowledge of banjos. I thank Barbara Daniels for her writer-in-residence-who-lets-the-dog-out program. I thank JB for understanding what this book is about and Michael Reed for being the best editor on the planet.

Special thanks to Jake Guralnick; the blue ribbon gang at the University of New Mexico Press; Robert, Desireé, Edy; Tony Mares; and Sharon Niederman for support and assistance to the press.

The Western States Book Awards are a project of the Western States Arts Federation. The awards are supported by the National Endowment for the Arts and by Crane Duplicating Services.

ISBN :: 0-9631909-6-2
Library of Congress Catalog Card Number :: 96-84329

First Edition

La Alameda Press
9636 Guadalupe Trail NW
Albuquerque, New Mexico 87114

For Aaron

THE COMPLETION of the Atchison, Topeka and Santa Fe railroad is an enterprise of no small importance to the commercial world, especially that portion of it west of the Mississippi. It brings New Mexico within easy and quick communication with the older States, will pour into her rich valleys and mountains new business life and enterprise. The land of fandangos has been an almost unknown country, but the railroad will introduce it to all and carry into its borders an army of progressive spirits whose duty it is to make a garden of the wilderness. New Mexico has many natural advantages, a climate beautiful in its clearness and salubrity, valleys well watered and fertile mountains veined with gold and silver, and broad pampas where vast herds of cattle may be pastured the year round. This undeveloped wealth will attract the farmer, the stockman and the hardy miners and many a 'big bonanza' will be struck by those who have the industry and energy to stick. The railroad will open up a new existence, pouring new blood and life into the old veins of New Mexico and making her future full of golden promise.

Weekly New Mexican
Saturday, August 23, 1879

✦ONE✦

*W*ooden floors creaked. There were whispers. In a dark, small space, dim light showed the features of a young woman's face—beautifully Irish, freckled, a mass of red hair pinned on top of her head. The pillows of hair around her face sent off glowing, aberrant curls. In the background, a thread of music began to bind the dank air as the organist practiced the right hand of Mozart's *Mass No. 14 in C major*. Behind the ornate screen by the woman's head was another face, a man's long face. The woman spoke softly, in a melodic, working-class Irish accent. She was leaning toward the screen and cleared her throat often, yet delicately, in soprano.

"I've been accused of many sins, father, surely I have, too many to fill your holy ear with this fine morning. But may the Blessed Mother of God herself strike me mute if I am not a virgin. I don't care who says what."

"What do you confess?" the priest said quietly but with some impatience. His accent was French.

"Well, I have cursed, father, that I have, and I've learned enough curses to fill a sow's carcass working at the dancehall and all." She moved a little, rustling her skirts. "So, father forgive me for I have sinned. I have called me boss a bastard and mentioned his mother's character as well."

The priest shifted, scratching something. The woman raised one hand slowly to her mouth and coughed.

"I have unclean thoughts, father."

"Yes?"

She pressed her throat and then, deciding against speaking the original thought she'd had, said, "About Indians. I'm afraid of Indians and all this talk about them gathering up to slaughter the whole town, well, I've had thoughts of killing those heathens and thoughts of being raped and molested by a man with nothing more than a squirrel's skin covering his private parts." She leaned back and sighed.

"Do you doubt God's protection?" The priest spoke as though distracted, perhaps reading something while giving habitual responses.

"Well, father—I just sometimes wonder, what with all the gambling and cursing and fornicating going on in this place, if New Town isn't like Sodom and Gomorrah. I'm a virgin, father, but I see a lot of things you wouldn't want to know about, a lot of things that would turn me dear mother's head to cinders."

The floor creaked heavily. There was someone else nearby, restless with his or her own sins. But the place was cool and peaceful, with the smell of old wood.

"Father forgive me, for I gave into me rage. I exercised it upon a fallen woman from Colorado who implied certain things about me character. You're likely to read about the whole hodgepodge in the papers, that is if you read the papers, father."

"Was there any physical harm done?"

"Well, she left with fewer hairs on her dear head than she came with, I'll say that much, but I had not a thing to do with her hat, which she claimed was trampled on."

"Is that all?" The priest's voice was fading like the band of light that slowly moved along the church walls.

"Father, I feel...I feel that something is coming unwound inside me, unraveling like, as though someone had reached into me and is pulling a loose piece of yarn until there'll be nothing left of me." She whispered these words, and even the priest looked around as though he might be being stalked by some doom along with the dancehall girl, whom he had not wanted in his church to begin with. He did not like women in general, and much less those who had about them a reputation for sexual involvements.

She continued, "I get a feeling sometimes, aside from the sickness." Her balled fist pressed against her chest. "I believe sometimes that God is going to punish me. I don't know exactly what for, father, but I have the feeling that I've done something terrible. This place," she said shakily, "seems so forsaken...and sometimes I'm not meself, not the daughter me mother brought up."

The woman rested her head against the grille. "I've entertained meself by discussing fornication and adultery. Katie, who works at the dancehall with me and is a fine girl, though she does have another trade on the side which I won't be speaking of to you—she has a world of knowledge about fornication, father, and sometimes I become fascinated-like. Sometimes I can't help but think about the pictures she conjures, for instance of a woman sitting on a man and..."

The priest interrupted and absolved her, turning his head away from her eyes, which were the green color of a pond choked with algae in some wooded place. He was beginning to feel that she could infect him somehow with her disease or her dread.

In a burst of light and noise—horses' hooves; dust; people shouting; the train coming in, a steaming black beast, huge and noisy—people clattered over the boards of the sidewalk, a man guffawed. Bridie walked from the church into the town, New Town, New Mexico, that smelled like horses, coal smoke, newly cut pine and bacon grease. She stopped to rest against the wall of the Occidental Billiard Hall, on Railroad Avenue across from the depot, coughing uncontrollably; she put a stack of papers under her arm, took a lacy handkerchief out of her sleeve and hacked into it. She looked at the blood spots and muttered, "Jesus, Mary and Joseph."

In a room above the street, the blonde head of another woman turned to the window next to her and looked toward the sound of the train steaming. There was also the sound of a man's heavy breathing, occasionally turning into moans. The soprano note was the squeaking of the cot that they were lying on.

Down narrow stairs, in a dark room where sacks and jars and bolts of cloth sat stupidly, a tired woman stood and looked up toward the rhythmic squeaking. Spiritless brown hair stuck against her head and culminated in a tight bun on her neck. A grey figure in the murky room, she could be seen through a shaft of light jeweled with motes of dust. There was one jar of yellow candy in front of her. All the goods seemed scared of this woman; it was as though they were staying perfectly still in order not to be noticed by her.

Eliza, the woman upstairs on the cot, spoke one thought aloud: "Maybe the banjo strings came in on the train." Her mind was acting up, unruly. She was picturing herself playing banjo, singing an insulting song while people were tied up in chairs. She was wondering why she kept coming up here with this man. Why should part of Franz go into part of her? It was best not to think too much about it. Thinking would probably lead to some shame, not for her husband's sake—not for George. This shame seemed an inevitable obligation, the duty of any member of a Christian society. She was a married woman, after all. But she had to remind herself of this fact by committing adultery, since her husband was often miles away tending to his railroad crew.

Franz, who was now in a frenzy of movement on top of her—creating friction so intense that it boggled the mind rather than stimulated the body—was definitely not her husband, was the husband of that dark stick downstairs.

Eliza laughed out loud at an image of the cot she and Franz were on crashing through the floor and landing in front of the woman downstairs in a cloud of dust. Franz chuckled too.

"Ya, it is goot," he said.

"I've got to get on home, Franz. My kids have been alone for too long." For just then she felt a fierce need to be with her children, to be with any children, surrounded by their whimsical noise. The longing for her own son and daughter came over her suddenly like a gas pain and made her a little breathless.

"Ya, ya." Franz pushed off quickly and stretched, not looking at Eliza's face. He was barrel chested, round faced, red faced.

Eliza took her silver-rimmed glasses off the windowsill and put them on with her eyes closed. She felt for her bun and then with both hands let the straw-colored braid fall free and reassembled it into a fat knot with hairpins. One hairpin dropped in the crack between the window and the sill, such a simple sound, it made her feel ashamed of the complexities she created. Franz was speaking again, but Eliza listened to voices in her head and heard, instead, her daughter Ruthie who was five.

"What're you gonna do, Aaron? What're you gonna do with them ants?"

Eliza saw Ruthie swaying back and forth, her runtish little body confident and her long, brown braid swinging on her back.

"Ants'll crawl up your pants," she was telling her older brother Aaron who said, simply and wearily, "Shut up, Ruthie."

"Well, I don't like ants crawlin' on me," Ruthie's voice said. And Eliza saw Franz standing over her, mumbling, "Eliza, pull down your skirts."

Eliza looked up at him and felt a little sad that he was her lover. The first tryst was hard to conjure with any clarity. She'd had some drinks, a half a bottle of sherry at a church meeting—the Episcopal Ladies Charity Committee. Eliza had told herself that she wasn't going to have more than a glass or two, but someone had started talking about the war, and it just made her sick to have to keep her mouth shut listening to all their ignorant prattle. If she'd told them what she thought about a damn war that was twenty years over and their mindless notions about honoring the veterans, it would have gotten her into far more trouble than getting drunk. So she'd listened and drunk. And when someone had asked her what her father had done in the war—that relentless question—she'd lied. She'd said, "He was a colonel and got wounded at Leesburg—shot in the leg." A lie. But she was drunk by then and didn't care. And then she'd managed to start walking home and had run into Franz, who'd lived in Prussia until five years before. Blessedly, he had no memories of nor interest in the war; he didn't even know who Sherman and Jackson were. They could have been the names of dogs for all he cared. So Eliza got very merry with him, and then they were up above his store, mumbling about banjo strings while he took her bloomers off. He kept saying he was "all right." And she didn't find out until his second seduction that he meant he was sterile. For several weeks now they had been "looking for banjo strings" in the upstairs stockroom.

Franz, still standing over Eliza, said loudly, for the benefit of his wife downstairs, "Ya, vell, I don't guess doz strings are up der, Mrs. Pelham."

Eliza put her hand out in an impulse to touch his, to hold it and look carefully at it, to ask him something personal, to ask tenderly if he was sad about not having children.

Instead, she stood up and looked out the window; she saw the Irish dancehall girl, Bridie, on the depot platform. Eliza started to tap on the window to get her attention. Then she saw Clarence, the New Town idiot, running frantically back and forth in front of the train, waving his arms.

"What's he yelling?" Eliza chuckled. "Sounds like 'No trains today. No trains today.'"

"Ve'd better go down, now. Mrs. Schwartzchild…" Franz waved his hand at Eliza to hurry up.

But when they clomped down the narrow stairs and entered the main room, Emily was not there. The room's goods looked sheepish, except for the jar of yellow candy, which the sun illuminated.

Many men and a few women and children were getting off the heaving train. They moved slowly, looking around—at the moun tains to the west, dark and piney; at the plains to the east, flat and pale, dry looking with thistle and pale grasses with silvery tassels. Here was where two landscapes met without subtle transition. A playful giant could have stepped back and forth over the town saying, "Mountains, plains; mountains, plains." Bridie watched the people disembark with an exaggerated look of innocence on her face.

Those passengers fresh in from the East, a little rumpled and dry throated, tried to assess the town, which to some was the ugliest thing they'd ever seen that wasn't about to be buried. Brown it was, flat and dusty. Not a substantial-looking tree for blocks. In New Town these new arrivals were mainly looking at one long, wide dirt street on either side of the train tracks. A short cluster of buildings elbowed each other for the attention of new customers—buildings in the fashionable Italian style with two stories. The depot stood on the east side, cluttered with stacks of boxes, crates, trunks and carpetbags. A chicken was walking around on the station platform as one woman dragged a worn carpetbag along. Another woman in a brown satin dress pointed to a black trunk. A man poking his fingers into the pockets of his green vest pivoted energetically to get his bearings. People weren't outright saying they were horrified; no one admitted that he should have gotten off in Colorado or at Raton Pass up north, although one woman was weeping inconsolably.

Two foreign-looking men in ill-fitting suits were getting off the train. One lingered, still holding on to the handrail. His hand was earth colored, like brownish red clay. The hair on both men's heads was black and thick, shiny because it was heavily oiled. The shorter man still hanging on to the train wore his hair parted in the middle; the other's hair was slicked straight back from his face, which was geometric, straight lined with cheekbones that looked like flying buttresses. He turned to face his companion above him on the train steps. "I'll see you," he said.

"Don't get your shoes dirty," his friend answered, pointing his finger at the creased, black-laced shoes recently polished.

The men laughed. Then the tall one sat on the train steps and untied his shoes. He tied the laces together and put them over his shoulder. People behind in the train waited restlessly. He and his friend seemed to be moving in slow motion, in another time or according to different standards.

"I'll see you," the taller man said again. He walked off to the west, passing by several people who stepped back and commented upon his bare feet. A woman in a flowered dress cowered and held on with both hands to the arm of the man standing beside her.

A conductor came up behind the man who was watching his friend walk away.

"Go on, git, Geronimo. This is as far as the train goes. Now go on." He shoved the man forward, and a group of three salesmen who were waiting behind him clutching bags and coats stepped forward and out of the train.

Prominent, rampant among the travelers were the salesmen, called "drummers," referring to some ancient and eternal practice of beating upon something—making a loud noise—in order to get the attention and business of customers from as far away as possible. All these men of commerce were wearing hats, as though a hat salesman among them had exploited their camaraderie. Their heads were punctuated with straw hats, bowler hats; one small gentleman sported a beret.

They were also all equipped with the magical bags and cases and catalogs that promised transformation, convenience, luxury, relief. Their business was profound here in the territories, and they knew it. Though they showed their teeth and nodded their heads, there was a serious look in their eyes. Some rubbed their hands together; some stood with their bags between their feet and studied pieces of paper; some strolled; one group of three were conversing, finishing up jokes. These were just the sort of men Irish Bridie was supposed to be handing leaflets to, but she just stared at them, listening to one laughing, "Tee-hee-hee," as though he was a cartoon drawing in the paper.

Feeling somewhat sanctified and distant after her midweek confession, Bridie was leaning against the station wall, coughing gently. She was glad the Indians didn't walk her way and kept them in sight for a while, as though they were spiders she didn't want to suddenly find crawling on her. She was holding a bunch of leaflets that promised in large black letters, "A Good Time For All Ages" at Near and Anderson's, where that night there would be a performance of "Virginia or the Triumph of Cupid." Several drummers doffed their hats and stopped to chat and take a leaflet. A domestic waiting for her new employers to show up and take her to their ranch mumbled a greeting at Bridie and looked her over.

Bridie nodded, then a fit of coughing overcame her. She dropped the handful of leaflets. They fluttered across the platform and up against the slick, black hulk of the train; some dove down onto the tracks or flew up into the air, caught by a current of wind and sent out to the plains. One chased the chicken off the platform.

Bridie pushed herself away from the wall of the depot; the woman waiting for her employers was gone. With two salesmen strolling behind her, overtly remarking upon the plush appeal of her bottom, Bridie walked past Schwartzchild's store just as Eliza stepped out. The two women said "good afternoon" to each other as the drummers went into the store. Eliza walked on, feeling a headache coming on over her right eye. The town felt aggressive suddenly, overly stimulating to the point of being threatening. But Eliza turned to look back at Bridie, because she'd always considered Bridie to be the most beautiful woman she'd ever seen—so ripe and pink, whereas Eliza felt skinny, bony. She was fascinated with the idea that Bridie was a working woman—a woman at least in the proximity of open breaches of morality.

Smiling nonchalantly when she realized she was caught staring, Eliza faced where she was going and kept walking. She could hear Bridie's hacking and that annoyed her, drove the nail over her right eye in a little deeper. And then the incessant hammering, the sound that came to town with daylight and had for a while been lost in the arrival of the train, came back like an audible representation of Eliza's headache. In a mild sort of hysteria, her mind occupied itself with two phrases, repeating them over and over hypnotically: "What're you gonna do with them ants?" and "Eliza, pull down your skirts."

Eliza imagined going somewhere else to live, or shooting someone, or having a drink or two. She hadn't yet made friends with the constant presence of dread inside her; she refused to pander to its whining, couldn't have explained exactly what it was about even to herself, though it had to do with George, with the children, with the hammering and the irrefutable fact that New Town was ugly and getting uglier by the minute. Even as she walked away from it, New Town was like a bunch of tin cans tied to her skirts. It was painful to watch people get off the train pretending they didn't see what everyone knew—that this was one damned dismal-looking town. Eliza remembered when the emptiness was free, even beautiful, before the railroad, before the buildings in the Italian style, before George's crew finished their work there and kept building the railroad south toward Santa Fe. She kept walking north, to where some of the old landscape still had its dignity and the occasional adobe structures of Hispanic farmers and herders. She hurried her thoughts ahead to where her children were, imagining that place where she was Mother and could be close to Aaron and Ruthie's faces and smell milk on their breath. Maybe even George would be there. She brushed at the sleeves of her dress, as though she could tidy her life up that easily before presenting herself to George.

Behind her, in New Town, young boys and old men watched the train workers, who acted very sure of themselves, making jokes in Spanish. And on the west side of town, at the edge of the mountains, the man walking with his shoes over his shoulders could now hear the sound of a three-noted birdcall over the fading beat of the hammer. Eliza and the Indian, completely unaware of each other, shared the effort of pulling away from the central sound of hammering, as though pulling two threads from the belly of one spider.

✧TWO✧

*T*he Indian was thinking about the hammering for a while, wondering if he should have stayed in town and looked for work. But as soon as he'd gotten off the train he had assessed the scene and had known that he should just keep walking. He had seen no other Indians around, which meant that there were none, or that they knew better than to show themselves in public. "Just keep walking," he'd told himself.

Then he started thinking about the task of finding out where he was going to end up and what he was going to do—who he was, in fact. Not who he was in big terms, but according to very specific kinds of identification. For example, was he a man whose hair was long or short? Was he a man who wore shoes or went barefoot? Was English the language that his brain and his mouth should fill up with or that other language, the one his mother had spoken to him? Was he an angry man or a man who preferred to go his own way and not be bothered?

He looked at the skin on the back of his hand.

When someone asked him where he was from, did he say Philadelphia or did he point in a northwesterly direction to that range of mountains that looked like a darker part of the blue sky that had cracked and boomed down on the earth?

He understood that a man could not completely rely on himself for identification. The world outside of him had a big hand in the process. What his eyes saw, what his ears heard, what voices said could conjure up from a man's soul who he was—what he liked, what he hated. The world would then nurture or squash what it had helped to create.

He didn't know.

He didn't know for certain.

Some of the older boys who came to the school had said to him, "Don't forget who you are. Don't forget that you are Tinde—you are Apache."

What did that mean? Even those boys had had their hair cut and were made to wear suits that fit loose like an old woman's skin. Even they were beaten when they didn't speak English. But they spoke in secret to each other, angry, full of passion about something. In secret they made vows that the younger boys knew were sacred and doomed.

But he had been too young to be allowed into their confidence other than to be told, with intense seriousness, that he must not forget who he was. What a horrible riddle they had left him with, going on with their lives away from the school, leaving him to go it alone as one of the "good" boys, one of the boys who didn't seem to seethe with resentment and exotic power.

He sighed. He wished he could ask someone some things.

Maybe it was enough to know basic things, like that you were tired or hungry, or felt like laughing.

He looked around him. He was now walking among the big ponderosa pines, big scraggly trees with no vanity, just aspiration. There were some huge ones, much older than he was.

"You tell those saplings not to forget who they are," he said aloud. "One of them might just forget and turn into a piece of lumber—get made into a fine latrine polished by a rich man's buttocks."

A tune entered his head, a march he'd heard played at Fourth of July gatherings. It was the kind of music trees might uproot themselves and march off to in a dignified frenzy to some lumberyard.

He did a jig with his bare feet then scoffed at the tune, throwing it away with a stick he had picked up; he continued walking, now feeling the eerie but friendly presence of trees around him, aware of him.

So he spoke aloud more.

"A man's mother should be able to tell him something about who he is," he said. This was the start of a plan that gave him some peace. He had to spend some time alone first, to get the smell of hair oil off him. But soon he would casually begin to find out where his mother was, using some old memories, perhaps asking a few questions of some reasonable people in these parts. He didn't want to scare the poor woman. He would just appear one day and sit at a distance from her until she was ready.

He looked up. A tree branch was shaking where a bird had just flown off. He felt oddly certain that he was being listened to by something that had a heartfelt interest in what he was going to do with himself. Instead of sensing a large destiny pulling him forward, he sensed an omnipotent curiosity following him, sneaking down the path behind him with a grin on its face. He unbuttoned the starched collar that was now irritating his neck. Laughing, he dropped it on the ground and walked on, rubbing his neck.

"Indian man seen walking naked in mountains," he announced to his reading public.

⇥THREE⇤

Stirred up by all the activity at the train station, the wind swept the long grasses on the plains east of New Town, shaking the leaves of an old cottonwood that marked the halfway point from town to Eliza's home. It was the one tree in a stubborn landscape of low growth and huge sky. The branches came out at angles from a thick trunk as round and squat as a giant's barrel. The wind was playing with Eliza's skirts, lifting them, twirling the hem. A banjo tune she'd learned back in Franklin, Kentucky, from the negro man who worked in her father's dental office—"Jordan is a Hard Road to Travel"—had calmed her thoughts somewhat, eased the headache. In tinny intricacies the song reached a poignant pitch and the cottonwood grew taller, up and up to heaven like a steeple. Eliza stood and watched it, her skirts following the dance the grass was doing. Then she moved on, along the old cattle path and wagon road around a small hill to see the comforting and familiar line of cottonwood and box elder that sucked the subterranean water from a usually dry arroyo.

A black movement occurred to her right, near the arroyo, in which there was only a trickle of water. Eliza often had the sensation that someone was around, someone besides her children. At times she wondered if it was her father's spirit finally come to the Far West like he'd always dreamed of doing. She wasn't sure she wanted to see him or anybody as a ghost. In the territories there were stories all the time about ghosts—families massacred by Indians, women killed by lovers, ancient Apache warriors, men hanged so fiercely that their heads ripped off, a religious hermit stabbed in the back—all wandering, moaning, wanting something. What did they want?

She started to run home, and from a distance Eliza was a small figure flowing down the overgrown wagon road between patches of dry grass and thistle. Newly opened purple aster laced the dryness as grasshoppers threw themselves to the wind, crisscrossing in front of her.

Then a lean, black-and-white dog appeared, yards away from Eliza. It just stood there. Slowly the tail began to wag. Behind the dog was a meek adobe house backed up against a piñon-studded, rocky hillside.

"I'm a'comin' to eat up any juicy little children I find!" Eliza called out in a creaky witch's voice.

A crow answered, cawing or laughing from one of the cottonwoods on the left side of the house.

"Oh, be quiet," Eliza said.

The wind swept the crow away.

Eliza called out, "Ruthie! Aaron!"

Then she said to herself, "Damn trouble."

She stomped off to a meadow between the house and the arroyo. In the tall bluestem grasses she saw the colors of her children. Sometimes she wanted to have the little house, the trees with their particular geometries, and the sky wrapped around everything all to herself, but always, the first sight of her children was a simple ecstasy.

Ruthie popped up and called out, "Lizards!" with hysterical joy. "We got lizards, Momma. Two of 'em and Aaron says he's gonna give me one as a pet."

Eliza's skirt got caught on a prickly pear needle; she stopp̃e
to pull it off, then picked up her skirt and tied it around he

She continued stomping toward her children, her yellowed bloomers exposed.

"You come on now," Eliza yelled. "Can't I count on you to have some sense?" She asked this of the boy who was still crouching, studying the ground. "You were supposed to be doing schoolwork, showing your sister her letters."

Aaron casually flicked his yellow hair away from his face, leaving his head cocked to the side.

"We seed a snake near the house," he said, trying to squinch a grin off his mouth.

"I ought to beat you," Eliza muttered. "You come on now right this minute. You've got chores to do. Children who aren't in school are supposed to do chores. Did you clean out the chicken pen?"

"You don't ever beat us," Ruthie said a little sadly. "How come you always say you're gonna beat us and never do?"

"Shut up, Ruthie," Aaron said.

"We got lizards," Ruthie said.

The three moved in a line, meandering between the thistle, grass and purple aster.

"You're going to kill those poor things." Eliza spoke without looking back at Aaron or the poor things. "They're going to suffocate in that box."

"I couldn't poke no holes in it," Aaron explained.

"I ought to poke holes in you."

"Can we eat lizard, Momma?" Ruthie asked.

"No."

"Momma, your head looks awful round today." Ruthie kicked the ground. "What're we gonna have for supper?"

White dough was stuck to Eliza's hands as she stood over the table on which she had just finished making biscuits. A big black-and-red ant was crawling across the lid of the bowl and Eliza watched it. She had a vision of George coming through the door and licking the back of her neck and saying, "Salt!" the way he did.

She lifted up a porcelain teacup decorated with hand-painted wild roses and half filled with white liquor, the fumes of which were visible and delicious to her like heat waves above a flat road.

"Are you thinkin' about Daddy?" Ruthie asked, twisting her head around in a singsong kind of movement. She was sitting at the table writing huge "b's" and "d's" on a pad of paper.

Eliza sat down behind Ruthie on the bench, pushing her forward between her legs. She kissed the back of her neck wildly as Ruthie screamed, "No-eee, no-eee, no-eee." The noise of someone stepping into the house, through the doorway that was always open in the summer, made them turn around.

Aaron was standing there tying the cord that held up his pants. He looked solemnly at the two females and said, "I bet I just filled up that outhouse. Ruthie, why don't you go and smell it!"

Eliza stood up shaking her head.

Ruthie sneered and went back to her writing. "Nobody cares about your do-do, Aaron."

"Ca-ca!" Aaron whispered, putting his face close to hers and wagging his head from side to side.

"All right." Eliza slammed a wooden spoon down on the table. "You're giving me a bad headache. We're going to church on Sunday. You're turning into little heathens. Savages."

Eliza drained the teacup, and feeling her son's eyes on her, she nonchalantly retied the blue ribbon on Ruthie's braid.

Aaron went to his bed, a cot on the other side of the same room next to his sister's cot, and picked up the tin of lizards. He opened the lid and turned the contents out on the blanket. There were three dead skinks, two about three inches long and one only about one inch long. Their iridescent blue-and-green bodies were delicately striped with dark lines. They were limp and lying no longer concerned for their pale, soft bellies that were partially exposed. They had nothing more to worry about, death being the ultimate absence of vulnerability.

"I told you you'd kill them." Eliza came over to the cot. She touched the bellies of the lizards. "So soft." She turned to Aaron and said, "You go bury them. You've got to give them a good burial now, Aaron. You've killed those poor things that didn't do you any harm."

Tears stood in the boy's eyes.

"They're just lizards," he said, trying to be angry.

Eliza gritted her teeth and her lips parted slightly to let air out. She squeezed Aaron's upper arm and said, "You bury them and you pray to God in heaven to forgive you." She looked away from her son so he wouldn't pierce her with his skepticism about her religious conviction.

"Nobody acts like you," Aaron said, narrowing his eyes and jerking his arm away.

Ruthie was humming a tune.

When it got dark, all three drifted off to sleep since no one bothered to light a lantern. Eliza touched the children under their blankets, vaguely aware that they'd gone to bed sometime while she had dozed at the table. She lit a candle and carried it into the other room—the bedroom. As she took off her clothes, hearing the small sounds of buttons and limp cloth, she looked around, assessed the room, taking inventory not of the objects but of her ability to understand what they were and if they had any significance.

The bureau across from the metal bed had a random arrangement of silver comb and brush (slightly tarnished), frosted glass bottles (green and pink), and a cigar box full of photographs and buttons. There were two photographs stuck in the mirror above the bureau, postcard sized. One was of an almost bald man with clumps of hair above his ears and a high, stiff collar holding his neck in place. His thin lips were smiling. The other photograph was of a baby, pale, almost translucent, in a christening gown and lace cap. The baby's eyes in the picture were closed and the lips were smiling too wisely for an infant. This was a dead baby lying snug in a little coffin.

There were two ghosts Eliza was particularly determined not to encounter: one was the mournful little spirit of the baby, and the other was the confused and sad ghost of a boy she'd known in Franklin.

In a kind of masochistic ritual that often occurred when she drank alone at night, Eliza started thinking about that boy. He had been considered devilish; he was older than she and went riding with her, amused that she rode like a boy. She was thinking about straddling that horse with the boy behind her, kissing her neck. He had made jokes that she didn't understand but knew she shouldn't mention around her mother; he had made her think, for the first time, of what a man and wife did in their bed. The boy was dead now, killed outside of Knoxville by a Yankee sniper, which was an irony because the boy himself was a Union recruit; the bullet had shattered his jaw. He was brought into her father's dental office first, as corpses were when the undertaker was full up. This was another irony because there were no teeth left in what had been the boy's mouth. Eliza had seen him and knew who it was because of the way he had rolled up his pants' legs and the way his spatulated fingers looked, all flattened out at the ends. Everyone could just tell it was him. Her father had noticed her, her feet stuck to the floor, staring and pale, and he had moved her gently out of the room and closed the door. "That's what happens in war, Ellie," he'd said. And she'd said, "Will Henry have to go to heaven like that, Daddy?" Her father had taken her by both shoulders and said quietly in case her mother passed through the hall next to the office, "What God in what heaven could let such a thing happen to a boy?"

Eliza didn't know, still didn't know. Didn't want to think about it. She looked around for signs that she was in a completely different place, far away from the dental office, which her mother had turned into a Christian library after her father was gone. George had come along, a visiting cousin from Boston, just in time. She understood his jokes perfectly; and he liked to engage her in discussions about utopian societies.

Eliza sighed and got into bed, rattling the springs. She blew out the candle, shut her eyes and removed her spectacles. Around the room little things reformed themselves in the dark: a man's suspenders hanging on a nail, a tarnished cuff link on the floor, a moustache comb on the seat of the chair.

Words came out of Eliza with a long breath: "Dear God in heaven." She paused and got up, jostling the bed roughly. Cool air was rolling in from the door in the other room where the children were asleep. She got a long-necked bottle off the top of the stove and drank from it—held it up to a portrait of her mother that hung over her bed, a taciturn, sour-looking woman with flat, grey coils twisted around her ears—a woman who looked an awful lot like Emily Schwartzchild now that Eliza thought about it. The last time Eliza had listened to her mother with any attempt at understanding her was when she had said about the boy whose body lay in her father's office, "It's better that he's gone, Eliza." And Eliza had looked up at her stupidly, wondering what awful secret her mother knew that pointed to the benefits of a young friend mauled by war. It had been a moment of realization for Eliza, and a voice in her own head had said to her, "Keep quiet. Keep quiet and wait for a chance to get away from these crazy, dangerous people." And her mother had said, "Close your mouth, Ellie. You look like an ignorant animal."

Eliza took another swig out of the bottle and put it under the bed. When she stood up, she saw a woman's face in the glass of the one window in that room. She laughed a little because it was a reflection of her own face, but then it wasn't. The woman in the window didn't laugh. Her lips parted, but she didn't laugh.

Eliza pulled her long braid around to lie over her breast. She backed up, leaving her mouth open to shakily suck in air. When she got outside to look in the rustling darkness, there was no one. But the white-and-black dog, who lived there and never came close, stood up beside a cottonwood several yards away and lowered its front, stretching. Eliza and the dog stood looking at one another, the dog cheerful, the woman nervous.

"Who's out here, dog? Huh? Who's out here?"

The dog wagged its tail a little.

She touched the children in their beds before she went back to her own bed, feeling their hair, checking their skin for just the right warmth. Her mother had believed tenderness weakened children; physical affection was unwise, uncouth, something only negroes and poor whites would show. Sometimes, though, it was all Eliza wanted, to touch and be touched. God for her was a hope of someone very large and powerful enfolding her in his whole being with his great arms. She could sink into a warmth so reassuring, so eternal that pain and regret would be as small as fleas.

Eliza went back to her room, where there was no longer a face in the window. She sat on the edge of the bed and said, "Dear God in heaven, if you exist..." the same way she always started her prayers, "keep me and Aaron and Ruthie safe." She thought for a minute and then said, "Amen."

She fell back on the bed, her feet still on the floor, and turned her head to see a banjo without strings leaning against the wall. In a dream state, Eliza became certain of some absurdities, the way dreamers do—for instance that the woman whose face she'd seen in the window was really her own sinful and exiled loneliness looking in on her. This notion, perceived as fact, metamorphosed into a dream about George trying to undress her.

⤝FOUR⤞

*T*wo things wound around the edge of New Town, separating it from another settlement to the west: these two things were the railroad tracks and the river. The river was not what you could call raging, except once in a while, maybe. People from the East like Eliza had a hard time calling it a river rather than what it would have been called back in Kentucky—a crick. But after a while, after you'd been in New Mexico for a while, it became to you a river, and damned grateful you were for it, too.

West of the train depot and across the river was the old settlement with its own plaza and structures made of dried earth. It was close to the mountains amidst the beginnings of ponderosa pine and juniper, but focused on the bleak aspect of a treeless plaza made of packed dirt and surrounded by two-story, columned commercial establishments. In the middle of the old plaza was a spindly, tall windmill over a dried-up well—looked like an unfinished steeple. The windmill had found its purpose in life as a gallows, so frequently used that, during preparations for the celebration of the railroad's first arrival, the townspeople almost forgot about the horse thieves that were hanging from the structure. Someone suggested that the corpses might dampen the spirits of the revelers in the train passing by on their way to the New

Town depot. So the hanged men were removed and replaced by evergreen boughs.

The adobe homes west of the river, some eroded and sunken into cottonwood, chamisa bushes and Apache plume, were once the original town, now referred to as Old Town. It was here that all important things were to happen and be sanctioned, where roots went deep and held the people, their ancestors, and their children to come together; where many things were to come and go, many languages, many ideas, many incarnations, but the notion of community and of the families that made it up would stay like a plant continually reseeding itself.

It was in the original Mexican town, in the slightly sloping plaza, that Colonel Kearny had stood and announced the great new day for the land of New Mexico. He had said that now all people were protected under the superior government of the United States of America. No longer Spanish, no longer Mexican, they were Americans. The colonel, who had stopped just outside of town to change into his most impressive uniform and comb his hair, had a man with him who translated his speech into Spanish for the people. The translator told them in Spanish about how the United States government was going to protect them from the "Índios bárbaros," and this seemed like a good thing because the Comanches, Apaches, Kiowa and Utes were a pain in the neck. The people just hoped that the American government understood the difference between good Indians and bad ones, between the Pueblo people of their mothers and the rogues that raided and thieved. Then the translator told the people that the new government would give them rights, like freedom of religion and the separation of church and state. And some of the people looked at each other and said, "¿Cómo?" They wondered why a government would separate itself from the Church unless it was in alliance with the Devil. And who in his right mind would consider it a privilege to leave the Church, to exercise his freedom to worship without the priests, the pope and the Holy Mother of God? "Oh, well," they thought, only in Spanish, "what can we do? There are many soldiers with a lot of ammunition behind those congenial grins."

The weeping mother was there, the woman who had been there from the beginning, even before Cortés came to the south and seduced her. She enjoyed fornicating with a conquistador. His penis and hands were powerful, and he let her fondle his crosses and guns; he told her about God the Father, the pope, the king of Spain. And she lay down for them all. But slowly, with great remorse and shame, she began to sense that the men she allowed between her legs had sickening weaknesses. She was somewhat amused by the horrible rash Cortés and his men had on their groins from wearing quilted cotton padding in the jungle. But the slaughter of eight hundred Aztecs in one afternoon was not funny, though the soldiers laughed about searing the wounds of their horses with the fat of the dead Indios. As La Malinche, she realized her part in the death of her people and wailed for them, crying, "Mis hijos, mis hijos," night and day. Three hundred years later she came north, stumbling through the Jornada del Muerto. The people changed her name to La Llorona and said that she drowned her own children for the sake of a man who considered her little ones a nuisance. And there she saw the coming of the Americans and she wailed again, from her hiding place in the arroyos, "Mis hijos, mis hijos." And still she wailed years later when fences went up around fields and cultures. The people heard her moaning at night and warned their children not to go near the arroyos or the witch La Llorona would drown them as she had drowned her own children. They called her a bruja, but she was still the weeping mother, more like them than they dared to consider.

On this morning the steam whistle in New Town, which awakened the people of Old Town to come to work, came into Deputy Salas's dream as the piercing scream of La Llorona. But his wife was standing beside the bed with his cup of café con leche. And he remembered. He remembered about New Town and its whistles, its hammering, its courthouse, its train depot—the one that was supposed to have been built in the original town when New Town was nothing but flatness. Odd, but the train did not come to Old Town as it was supposed to, even though Señor Aguilar, a man of dignity and means, had built a fine hotel near the spot where the original railroad survey had plotted the tracks and the depot. Odd, but the only thing the railroad ended up bringing to the people of Old Town was a whistle that woke them up to come to work, turned farmers and ranchers into laborers. Mysteriously the train route had been revised and did not stop in the established Hispanic town, but a mile to the east, where Americans with uncanny foresight had bought up huge tracts of land and were already building matchstick structures: restaurants, hotels, gambling houses, dance halls, pool halls, stores, a depot. New Town, unlike Rome, was built in one afternoon, the buildings connected like a set of uneven false teeth. Deputy Salas remembered that the men of Old Town were not made rich by the railroad after all, but were made laborers, workers in the livestock pens in the trainyard, pushing with their hands at the haunches of sheep and cattle.

Salas was the deputy sheriff in New Town, a position which gave him respect on both sides of the river. But he, like the other men who left their homes to work, felt a sickness in his muscles because they were not working the land, because they were not doing what his great grandfather had vowed his family would do until the end of time, vowed to the king of Spain. But the king of Spain, though sanctioned by the pope who was sanctioned by God, was replaced by grinning men who chewed on cigars and slapped a man on the back as though he was a child. What did it matter to them that these Mexicans fought in the War? "That my brother-in-law fought for the Union at Glorieta and died; that I was an officer in the Union Army?"

"Ave María," he said to himself. The anger—every morning the anger.

Manuel, his youngest son, walked with him to New Town across the fields holding his father's hand. His father carried a gun—

a Colt 45 Peacemaker—that made a soft noise against the pants leg with each stride. Manuel carried his father's lunch, a few tamales wrapped in corn husks and placed in a bucket with a bottle of beer.

Before they crossed the bridge over the river, Deputy Salas stopped and said to Manuel, "Espera hijo. Llévate esto contigo. Se me olvidó que yo lo tenía. Llévatelo y no se lo enseñes a nadie. Después me lo regreses."

He handed the boy a small, white flour sack that had been in his pocket. There were two eye holes cut into it.

Manuel put it in his pants pocket and they walked on over the bridge.

For a while, Manuel hung around the jail doing chores, then pulling a piece of rope for the orange cats who lived there to chase. Clarence, who gave Manuel the heebie-jeebies, started hanging around the jailhouse, watching the boy play with the cats.

"Them cats got bugs in their ears," he kept saying with growing intensity. "You watch out, Manny. Bugs make them cats wooly wild. WILD!" And he ran around like a child pretending to be a horse. He stopped to pick his nose and looked a long time at his finger. "Yep, bugs," he said. "Let's go see the train, Manny."

As soon as his father had to go to the courthouse, Manuel told him he was going to his friend's house—"Mi amigo, Aaron." Clarence watched him walk down the road.

Aaron was helping his mother dump a wash basin full of water over the small vegetable garden on the right side of the house. Eliza said, "Hey there, Manny."

"Hey, Señora Pelham. What're you doing?"

"We're putting this wash water on the garden. It's so dry these days. No rain."

"It rains sometimes in the afternoon," he said.

"What do you want to do?" Aaron asked him. Aaron was shorter but sturdier looking than Manuel, who was tall and thin, almost elegant. Manuel seemed older than Aaron, but actually he was younger by about six months.

Manuel shrugged.

"Whatever you do, you take your sister with you." Eliza took the wash basin back into the house. "And if you're going into town bring me back some potatoes for supper."

Manuel leaned into Aaron.

"Si Ruthie viene con nosotros, tenemos que tapar la boca" He got out the flour sack his father had given him and pretended to tie it around his head over his mouth.

Ruthie stood in the doorway and said, "What're you gonna do to my mouth? You better not. I'll get a gun and shoot you."

"I don't want to take Ruthie, Momma. She don't shut up. She makes us looney."

Manuel shook his head and made a comical face, widening his eyes and opening his mouth in mock horror.

"Come on. Let's go up to the river and fish," Aaron said.

They walked away, the two boys, and Ruthie strolled behind, saying, "I don't like to eat fish 'cause they got needles in 'em. I ain't eatin' any fish."

Eliza walked fast after Ruthie, and when she caught up to her she bent down and held her by both arms. "You be careful, Ruthie," she said. "You do what's right no matter what those boys say, and don't think about going in that river and don't let them go in either. You hear?"

Ruthie looked painfully at the boys, who were lengthening the distance between them, oblivious to her.

"And Ruthie, try not to talk so much. You're just going to irritate them into some mischief."

When Eliza let go and stood up, Ruthie bolted, yelling, "You better wait for me."

Eliza sighed in that uncomfortable mind-set where she was glad to be rid of the children and wanting them to be with her at the same time; where she imagined that if anything happened to them, anything bad, no matter how or where, it would be her fault. Even if George were there, it would be her fault if they got hurt or died. Drowned in the river—Aaron's foot caught by a rock and his screams muffled under brown water, bits of things floating around his face, his hair a frantic current.

"Stop," she told herself. "Stop."

She knew she would let them go for only a few hours, that she'd go looking for them down by the river before noon, because she suspected that if God did exist He might be fond of irony and have her son drown like her father had. He might want to prove to her with such an action that He does exist and that He wants to make it clear who is in control. What leverage did an adulterer have against such lessons?

Eliza lay down under the cottonwood tree she sometimes shared with the black-and-white dog. The dog always left when she lay down, though, and in a friendly way took herself some distance off, checking the food plate for scraps, pissing near the side of the house. Eliza looked up through the cottonwood leaves, a lulling activity, calming, some might say lazy. The branches went up and up in many layers. The patterns of light on Eliza's face made it look like she was under water. And on the periphery were immense spaces, the immense blocks of form and color—the arroyo, dusty and pale, that bordered the oceanlike plains, the llanos, and the dark green of the mountains. Somewhere down the dirt road was New Town, but here, looking up at the cottonwood tree, Eliza could hear no hammering, and there was an isolation in which one's only company were things completely unhuman, undisturbing. This solitude and newness was what drew Eliza to the territories, why her father talked about the West as though he was an old horse and it was open pasture. It was people like her mother who put up the Italianate buildings that looked ridiculous in comparison to the mountains and who were teased and blinded by dust storms. Sometimes Eliza wanted to get a good horse and leave before she got hooked into some god-awful project like the Ladies' Episcopal Church Building Fund, or the Veterans Monument Committee. Then she could ride right out, maybe even down to Mexico. Leave the children behind. God no, take the children. Of course. The children were what made her worthwhile in this world. Take all the money and Aaron and Ruthie and live in a house by the ocean as a mysterious rica with a dark man as a lover who brought her big, red flowers.

"Excuse me, Mrs. Pelham?"

Eliza emitted a little sound of distress and sat up, clutching her throat. A man was standing over her, holding his hat in one hand against his leg and smiling. One of his front teeth was slightly green and bordered with gold.

She stood up slowly, trying to exhibit some control and dignity. She lifted her braid up and let it fall back against her spine.

The man nodded slightly and said, "I'm Mr. Ingram from Mr. Catron's office. I've come up from Santa Fe this morning."

Eliza nodded.

"If you don't mind, I'd like to just look around and take some notes."

"Well, my husband isn't here right now. He's down there near Santa Fe, heading up one of the railroad crews."

"That's all right. I just need to look around for a few minutes." He never stopped smiling.

Eliza continued her effort to shift from the images in her head to the fact of a man in a suit standing in front of her. Was his hat too small or some new fashion?

"What for, if you don't mind me asking?" she said, looking intently at his hat.

"Oh, no, that's fine! Of course! That's fine. Well, Mr. Catron just needs some estimates about the value of your property."

"I don't know much about my husband's business dealings, but I wasn't aware that this was our land."

"Oh, that's all right. I'll just look around and make a few notes."

He put his hat on his head and took out a little pad of paper and a pencil.

"Are we going to have to leave, Mr. Ingram?"

"I don't think so." He licked the pencil and turned toward the house, stepping high over the grasses in polished, brown shoes.

"We never bought this land ourselves." She was following him.

"Well, Mrs. Pelham, you've been here for three years, I believe?"

"Yessir, we have."

"Well, there's no one else been living on this land. I think Mr. Catron is operating under the assumption that you own it." He smiled benevolently.

"This Mexican boy that plays with my son," she pointed behind her in the direction that the children had gone, "he told me that his family and some of the other Mexican families use this land for their cattle. Cows come and go along here. I think his family really owns this land. Nobody used the house anymore. Cows come through sometimes."

"It's all right, Mrs. Pelham. Your husband understands about these things." He tapped his pencil against the paper and walked over to the arroyo.

"Water?" he asked, pointing to the arroyo with the pencil.

"Sometimes. But there's a pump." She uncrossed her arms to point to the pump, which looked rusty and embarrassed.

She watched him for a few minutes, then called out to him, holding errant strands of hair against the top of her head so the breeze stopped playing with them.

"I'll just go on back to the house. It's an old house," she said walking backwards. "Been here long before we got here. Can I make you some coffee?"

"Oh, no, no thank you, Mrs. Pelham. I'm going to be having lunch in town. I'll just take a few notes. You go on about your business."

She turned and walked to the house. Inside, she just stood looking around at the stove, the table, the cots, the trunk with the children's clothes in it, the door to the bedroom. She poured the rest of the liquor in the bottle into the teacup still out on the table from the night before. She began straightening up, something she hadn't planned to do, but something the man outside would expect. She picked up a couple of Ruthie's dresses lying on the floor, made the beds, set a pot of water that had boiled greens the night before beside the door to put on the garden later on, even swept the faded carpets that covered the dirt floor. She was going to clean the bedroom up a little, maybe get the cobwebs off the walls, but the sight of the banjo annoyed her. She sipped from the teacup and looked outside; the man was still there. Shading her eyes against the sun, she called out to him, "I'm going to fetch my children. They're at the river. I'll be back in a few minutes." He nodded and waved his hand with the pencil in it above his head. A breeze blew his hat off his head.

Eliza walked down the path that went the northerly, back way to the Old Town bridge. The dog fell in behind her about twenty yards back. But after just a minute, Eliza stopped. Ruthie was running toward her, alone.

"Criminy," Eliza breathed, her skin tingling. Ruthie was flushed with prissy anger.

"Aaron and Manuel are in big trouble."

"What happened?"

"They got caught in the morada."

Eliza looked up to the sky. "Where are the boys now?"

"Some man come in and took 'em by the arms and was speakin' in Spanish."

"Where did he take them?"

"I don't know, Momma. Manny showed me spots on the ground outside and told me it was blood from the men who go there and stab and whip themselves."

"Oh, hush up, Ruthie. You just hush up."

She shook her head, looking up the path and thinking.

"I guess I'm going to have to go get him in Old Town."

But she stood a few more seconds and Aaron appeared down the path, walking and whacking at plants with a stick. He seemed so casual Eliza wanted to kill him. She waited for him to get to her, then pushed him along the path in front of her.

The man looking over the property was leaning against the house, writing in his little pad. He looked up and smiled at them as the three walked by.

"Who's that man?" Aaron asked.

"The undertaker come to measure you for your coffin after I finish with you."

Ruthie chimed in. "You're in big trouble, Aaron. I told you you'd better not go in there. You're not supposed to go into a church without a grown-up."

"It ain't a church, you little mouth."

Eliza pushed Aaron down on his bed.

"You hush. That man'll think I've raised a devil. You be quiet. You just sit there. I don't know what's wrong with you, Aaron." She saw the tin on the floor under the bed. "Did you bury those lizards like I told you?"

"Yes. That's what we were doing. Maybe you don't know, but that's what goes on up there—they take care of burying people and other stuff. It was a good idea. Manny said so."

"Yes? No 'yes ma'am'? Why do other boys say 'yes, ma'am' and you don't?"

"I don't know."

"Well, neither do I."

"I'll say ma'am, Momma." Ruthie spoke from the table where she was swinging her legs against the bench.

"Go outside, Ruthie." Eliza kept her eyes on Aaron. "Did Señora Salas talk to you?"

"Yes."

"What did she say?"

"She said we had done something very bad, that the men could punish us and that I'd better go on home."

"Is that all?"

"She said Manuel and I couldn't play together for a while."

"Good."

"He's my only friend."

"Don't you know that people are being killed around here for all kinds of things?"

He picked at the blanket and then looked up at his mother, leaning his head to the side so that the hair fell away from his face.

"You cleaned up. Were you tryin' to make that man think you cleaned up all the time?"

Eliza's hands flew up, fingers spread in front of her face. She clapped them together and kept them clasped in front of her mouth, looking down at her son.

"I don't know what to do with you," she said behind her hands.

He lay back on the bed and Eliza sat down beside him.

He closed his eyes and his mother said, "Why don't you go on and see if the chickens have done any laying."

"Okay."

Ruthie was standing in front of the man, who was squatting down listening to her, face to face. She was talking directly to the green tooth, which fascinated her. He stood up when he saw Eliza in the door.

"Well, I guess I'm done here. You've got a mighty smart little girl."

"I'll tell my husband you were here."

He touched his hat and nodded.

"Now don't worry too much about the children, Mrs. Pelham. These Mexican superstitions won't last much longer. They're beginnin' to see the light. Why there's a Mexican family belongs to the Methodist church in Santa Fe."

"I'll tell my husband you were here."

"Anyway, the land where that morada is doesn't really belong to them. They're just going to have to understand some things, hard as it may be to let go of the old ways."

Eliza just stood and watched him stepping backward.

"Progress, Mrs. Pelham!" He waved. The dog watched him walk down the road. He had a jaunty step until he stumbled over something on the ground and ended up stepping on his own hat.

❖FIVE❖

*M*any beautiful days went by, late summer days in which the sky's intense and large blue was matched by the depth of green in the dark ponderosa pines anybody who looked up out of New Town could see. Wild flowers and grasses changed like chameleons into surprising hues: oranges and yellows, dusty purples, whites—not to blend into their environment, but to create one. It was in such a quiet determination to be beautiful that the world motivated Bridie to order a pair of black-lace, Italian gloves and Eliza to engage her children in the effort of scrubbing down the chicken coop. There were three chickens left and a rooster whose crow was not quite right, sounding like a rusty swing. The coop was out of sight of the house, on the east side of the little hill and closer to the arroyo. Three edifices made up the Pelham's little homestead: the two-room adobe home, the outhouse, and the chicken coop, all of which had been there before the Pelhams. George had begun to build a corral for horses to the west of the house, among the bigger cottonwoods. A semicircle of fence posts was all that got erected. Looking at those posts made Eliza's head hurt because she knew that George knew that she wanted a horse. Why did George have time to visit with Mr. Near down at Near and Anderson's Dancehall but didn't have time to finish a damn corral?

George betrayed their pact—to find a place where they could be away from people and do what they wanted, maybe find a utopian community that wasn't run by a rabid preacher. George went into town all the time whenever he was home. When Eliza thought about that, she always remembered that odd night, when George came back home and got into bed with her and asked her to do something he'd heard about. He asked her in the dark so she couldn't see his face. He wasn't drunk. He was extremely sober. He asked her to lie on her stomach and let him lie on top of her, like, well, like some animals did, so he could see her naked, plump backside squirming against him. She hesitated—not because she found his suggestion disgusting, but because she wondered who down at the dancehall was talking to him about such a thing, or showing him. Carefully, Eliza said that there were things they needed to talk about, things they had put off talking about for a long time. George saw no connection between talking and having sex with his wife from behind. He succumbed to that dangerous combination of irritation and embarrassment and got up in a fury so forceful that it made the room warm. He never brought up such a subject again, but for many days it hardly ever left Eliza's mind.

At first she imagined just the thing he had described, even lay on her stomach with her nightgown hitched up when he came to bed. But it seemed that with George various utopian ideals dissipated in the face of his lack of willingness to be a fool of any kind. So George had conjured up tasty images and then left her alone with them. She considered mentioning them to Franz when they first went "looking for banjo strings," but Franz was no substitute for George. He had no smoldering fires. He was more useful as a discouragement against lustful imaginings, like the kind of cold-water treatment given to coupling dogs in a tittering schoolyard. Being with Franz seemed to underscore the mundane nature of sex.

Eliza stayed away from town for a few days, sending Aaron in to get a bottle of whiskey from Near and Anderson's and some bacon from the meat market. Sometimes the wind brought the sound of hammering, but those days of isolation medicated Eliza to where she didn't think so much about George. No one ever came out; cows walked by sometimes. Eliza took care of the children well, even getting them to read out of *McGuffy's Eclectic Reader* and teaching them both to sew. Actually, Ruthie sewed better than Eliza. Eliza admitted that; but she had no respect for the McGuffy's reader, which she openly scoffed at as being full of candied notions in stories teaching grammar as well as American values. Eliza felt certain that these notions were connected to the same nonsense that caused a person to say about dead boys, lost children, old villages, old cultures, old trees, "It's better that they're gone."

Inevitably, things were going to change. Just recently people had been building neighborhoods, bringing in spindly looking elm trees and planting them around fine homes with Victorian gingerbread trim. One day, Eliza figured, she'd look outside and see her squat little adobe home surrounded by a landscape from Peoria. It was such an image that popped into her mind when she heard a wagon pull up outside the house; perhaps she'd slept for ten years and the neighborhood civic association had come to suggest that the demolition of her home would be a benefit to the community.

Eliza finally opened her eyes at the sound of a wooden creaking outside and the faint snort of a horse. Her thought now was that George had come, but she heard several voices, including a woman's.

"I don't believe this," she muttered, because in all the time she'd been living there, only her own family and Manny had come out to the place—until that Mr. Ingram a few days ago. And now what? Her deepest fear was that it was the ladies from the Episcopal Church Building Fund, whom she'd taken great pains to avoid recently.

She sat up and grabbed her glasses off the table. They dropped to the floor so she had to bend over the side of the bed to get them. She saw the half-full bottle of corn liquor under there, considered it for a minute, then pounded the cork in tighter with her fist and got up. When she walked into the other room, rebraiding her hair, the children were in their cots and a big fly was buzzing around the table. Now the voices came up to the doorway—a woman's delicate but rich laugh and then a cough.

Wrapping a shawl around her shoulder, Eliza pushed the wooden door with her hip to open it more widely. Sunlight crashed through, and in this blinding light she saw three figures walking toward her.

"Mrs. Pelham, then." Bridie, dressed in black skirt and shawl and a white, high-collared blouse, stepped up to the door and touched Eliza's arm. Bridie was carrying a small hat with a mangled feather on it in her left hand. The feather was black but gleamed greenish in the morning sunshine.

The two men hesitated behind Bridie. One was wearing a bowler hat, and the other, a short man, was wearing a French beret. The latter held his hands behind his back and swayed back and forth. The man in the bowler hat stood very still, holding a carpetbag.

"Bridie," Eliza said calmly, but not with any noticeable warmth. She picked a strand of hair away from her lips and stepped back into the house.

"These gentlemen asked me to show them about. They're drummers from the East." Bridie's eyes sparkled and she nodded and coughed into her fist quietly.

"That's fine," Eliza said. "Let me put something on."

"We don't mean to inconvenience you, Mrs. Pelham," the little man said from outside, leaning his head to the side to address her demurely without looking at her.

The other man held his bag with both hands in front of him and looked around.

"That's all right," Eliza said. "You come in, come in and sit down here." She was talking from her room. "I'll just get dressed and make some coffee. Please come on in. People don't usually come around. Excuse the condition of things. Aaron, go fetch some water."

The visitors slowly clomped in and looked at the children in their cots. Ruthie and Aaron were sitting up, staring at the three people who stood by the table—two holding hats in their hands, one wearing what looked like a round pot holder on his head.

From the other room: "Aaron, you help your sister up and go on outside and get some water."

In a few minutes they were all sitting at the table with their hats in front of them, except for Mr. Bagby, the man who kept his beret on. The tall salesman smashed a fly with a thick catalog.

"Momma, that man killed that fly," Ruthie said.

They all laughed.

"His name is Mr. Smith," Bridie said. She was sitting straight with her hands in her lap.

"Mr. Smith is the finest drummer in the country," the bereted gentleman said.

"Now, Mr. Bagby, I'm just a man who loves this country and the people in it. I love to make people happy." Mr. Smith lifted the catalog. The fly was stuck to the underside.

Eliza was staring at Mr. Smith, a little dazzled by his solid and confident bearing.

Bridie cleared her throat and said, "We'd surely be bereft without you drummers, wouldn't we, Mrs. Pelham?...still making our own soap and all instead of having such a lovely variety of things."

Eliza stared at her coldly with undisguised irritation.

Mr. Smith started flipping through the catalog past pictures of women in underwear, men hooked up to electric devices, hats, stools, tie-up shoes, baby bonnets. He showed Ruthie the drawings of dolls, wide-faced babies with tiny mouths. Ruthie was more interested in examining the dead fly.

"He's awful flat," she said.

"Don't you like dolls?" Mr. Smith asked in a cooing kind of voice.

All the grown-ups looked at Ruthie. She said, "Yea."

"Yessir," Eliza corrected.

Ruthie knitted her brow at her mother and looked back at the salesman.

"You have two fine children here, Mrs. Pelham." Mr. Smith smelled like medicine when he spoke. He had brownish red hair that lay flat on his head but ended just over his collar in thin curls. His most distinguishing feature was his voice, which resounded like an orator's.

"Come over here, son," he said to Aaron. "You like good knives?"

"Yessir," Aaron said, standing up and looking at his mother.

Mr. Bagby laughed and nodded, "What boy doesn't!"

"I bet your daddy is proud of you," Mr. Smith said, putting his arm around the boy's back and showing him the catalog pages full of life-sized blades realistically rendered in ink etchings.

Eliza's annoyance at this intrusion was growing. She didn't know what was expected of her and hated trying to figure it out before she was ready to be out of bed.

"His daddy is a foreman with the railroad," she told everyone there, smoothing out the brown skirt of the dress she was wearing.

Mr. Bagby nodded and smiled.

Mr. Smith jerked his head in Bridie's direction and said to Eliza, "Your friend here has ordered a very nice pair of gloves, genuine black lace from Italy, the thing every woman in Europe is wearing to church these days." He spoke as though he was terribly proud of Bridie for what she'd done.

"We were just wondering if you were in need of anything, Mrs. Pelham. I specialize in art supplies," Mr. Bagby announced. "I've got some out in the wagon if you'd like to take a look."

Mr. Smith lifted Ruthie up onto his lap and continued to turn the pages of the catalog to show the children.

"You got any banjo strings?" Eliza leaned back and smoothed out her skirt again.

Mr. Smith looked up.

"Well, here's someone who loves music like me!"

"Can you stay for supper?" Ruthie turned her face to the man whose lap she occupied.

"Ruthie, these gentlemen have a lot of business to attend to."

"You can always order from the catalog, Mrs. Pelham," Bridie said. "Oh, there are all sorts of fine things in there."

"I don't need much," Eliza said.

Mr. Smith lifted Ruthie off his lap and stood up. His head almost touched the ceiling. He gave a small speech:

"I am often impressed and awed by the simplicity of life in these parts. I am amazed at what people can do without. But we are, after all, Americans. We're all Americans wherever we live and so have the privilege to live better than any other people on this Earth. We are the world's models of success and Christian prosperity. God has given us this great land to prosper on and humble men, like myself and Mr. Bagby here, are just servants, Mrs. Pelham. We are merely servants of progress."

Bridie's mouth was slightly opened; she looked dazzled but thoughtful.

Eliza was mesmerized by the man's crotch, which she could have sworn displayed the tight outline of an erection. She wondered if she had aroused him by being found earlier in her nightclothes.

Ruthie said, "I want to have a tiger. How much is a tiger?"

Mr. Smith looked sheepish and sat down.

"I'm sorry. I get preachy sometimes. This isn't a lecture hall. You ladies must forgive me." He patted Ruthie on the head as she was trying to revive the fly by pushing it a little.

"Oh, no, Mr. Smith." Bridie put her hand out toward him. "You have such a fine voice and I agree with every word you said. Where I come from, why people are begging and all such thing just to get over here. Why there's no imagining the suffering of

51

people in Ireland." She looked down at the table and then at Eliza. "Though I must admit that I do get homesick now and again. Me family is still there, you know. And some mornings," she looked now at Mr. Bagby, who might understand melancholy since he sold art supplies, "I ache to smell the salt water. I have to bite me lip sometimes at dusk to keep from weeping. I start thinking about the sound of the cuckoo in the woods near Clonakilty, a sound so peaceful and sweet and so sad, too, if you know what I mean."

Mr. Smith was glaring at her.

Mr. Bagby said, "I may be able to get a cuckoo clock. German. Fine work. I know a fellow in Pennsylvania who imports them." He grinned, looking at everyone at the table.

"I don't want a clock that makes noise, Momma."

Now everyone stared silently at Ruthie as though they were all in some trance.

Finally Mr. Smith said to Aaron quietly, but in a voice that still resonated, "Why don't you show me around, son. I'd like to see what's around here."

"There's nothing Mr. Smith can't get or sell," Mr. Bagby said when his colleague was out the door.

"What's on your head?" Ruthie asked him.

Bridie said to Eliza, "There are many fine things. You should take a look in the wagon. Surely you can't let these two gentlemen leave town without buying something."

"I need some banjo strings."

"Mr. Smith can get you a fine new banjo, five-string S.S. Stewart."

"I just need strings."

"Mr. Smith can get you as many sets of banjo strings as you need."

"Just one set." Eliza stood up.

Bridie stood up, too, and leaned into Eliza to say, "I surely do love those gloves, Ellie, and Mr. Bagby and Mr. Smith said that if I helped them out a bit and showed them around to some customers, they'd give me the pair outright."

Eliza stepped away from Bridie. She had always been tall, but next to Bridie she felt like a gangly giant. Bridie winked and tapped the hat against her leg so that the feather shimmered.

Eliza touched the table with her fingertips because she was feeling shaky for some reason: she'd gotten up too fast, maybe, or she hadn't eaten; and these people had made her think, for an instant, that George had come home.

"It's not your place to call me 'Ellie,'" she said, fully aware that this would change the atmosphere significantly.

Mr. Bagby walked outside humming. Ruthie pulled at her mother's skirt with both hands and asked, "What's he wearin' on his head, Momma?"

Bridie bent over and touched Ruthie's cheek. "You help your mother now, young lady," she said. "She misses your dear hardworking father. Don't be under your mother's feet now."

Eliza took Mr. Smith's hat off the table and held it out to Bridie.

"There are other women in town. Take them on to Mrs. Boggs's house or over there to widow Anderson."

"Well," Bridie began to speak, but then just put her hand over her throat and walked out. Ruthie went beside her and took her hand. Aaron and the salesman were outside.

"You ought to get yourself an icebox, Mrs. Pelham," Mr. Smith called in to her.

Eliza smiled very stiffly and replied, "Where would I get the ice?"

Mr. Bagby and Mr. Smith exchanged a merry look.

"Well, "Mr. Smith said, "Mr. Sweeney is setting up an ice business. I was just talking to him this morning."

"Well," Bridie said, "we'd best be going on, then." She did not look at Eliza.

Ruthie ran out after them and grabbed Mr. Smith around the legs. He laughed and picked her up; holding her, he tousled Aaron's hair. Eliza couldn't help but smile, and then she felt bad about Bridie, who was sitting on the wagon seat telling Ruthie that they would have to sing together again some time like they'd done the last Fourth of July. Eliza wanted to touch her, to embrace her as a sister, to say to her, "Stay and have coffee. Let the men go on. I don't want to hear about being American. It makes me feel lonely. Do you ever feel lonely? I'm going to put a little whiskey in my coffee; here, you have some too."

But Eliza just watched as the horse pulled the wagon around through the grasses on either side of the path. Eliza said to Aaron, "That wheel looks like it's about to fall off. It makes me dizzy to look at it."

He came up beside his mother, enclosing her hips in his arms, and watched the wagon wobble out of sight.

"Should I run and tell 'em?"

"Tell them what?" Ruthie called out from inside.

"Naw, they'll get to town okay, and with all his big talk about prosperity and progress, I guess he can get a wheelwright to help him."

"He asked me to show him the outhouse," Aaron said.

"Well, don't you think a drummer's got to relieve himself just like everybody else?"

"He said, 'Your momma ain't gonna buy nothin' is she?"

"And what did you say?"

"I said, 'No, sir, she ain't.'"

She held his head against her chest and kissed the top of it that smelled so sweet and sour at the same time.

"But I did order some banjo strings."

"I told him we mostly trade for what we want and that we got credit at Schwartzchild's, and he said, 'That ain't the American way.' He told me maybe we could go huntin' together some time like father and son. I think he felt sorry for me 'cause Daddy ain't here. He gave me this."

Aaron held out his hand and showed the rusted iron ball in it. He closed his fist up around it again and smiled.

"He said it was a musket ball got out of a Confederate's skull."

His mother looked at it and then put her finger on it and pushed it gingerly in Aaron's palm as though it was something alive.

Then she told him, "You go on and see if there're any eggs. And, Aaron, see if there's enough to take one or two to Miss O'Doonan—the woman that was just here."

"I know," he called back. "Down at the dancehall."

The dust from the wagon was still swimming in the air. Eliza went back inside, tired of looking at that road. She could tell this was one of those days when she was going to feel tired in her eyes.

⇢SIX⇠

A quiet man stood at the counter in Schwartzchild's store. At first Eliza strolled in; thinking that he was just another customer, but Emily looked odd, shrinking into the shadows of the shelves behind her, listening to the man. He was talking with a Spanish accent. Eliza could see the dark hair trembling against his stiff collar.

Emily kept pulling her head back, but stood in the same spot. She looked so furtively at Eliza that the man followed her gaze and saw the other woman standing beside a barrel of scrap wood.

The man's face was red; there were tears in his eyes. Eliza picked up a piece of wood and examined it.

"You cannot do this," the man said. "Tell your husband that we are men, that we will do what men have to do."

He backed up a few steps and then turned to pass by Eliza and out the door. He nodded to her politely as he left.

Emily stayed still and changed her focus to Eliza with no alteration of her stunned expression.

"Mrs. Schwartzchild, are you all right?"

"Ya, I am fine, Mrs. Pelham. I don't know about dis business among men. Der are hoodlums, dos men vearing sacks over der heads und killing cattle. He is one of dem I'm sure—all dos

Mexicans are criminals." She turned the jar of lemon drops a bit to the right. "Mr. Schwartzchild has gone to da lumber yard."

"I was just getting some ham for dinner over at the meat market. I wanted to tell him not to bother about the banjo strings. I ordered some from the salesman, that big fellow with the theatrical voice."

"Ya, Mr. Smith," she smirked. "He told me."

"He told you what?"

"He told me about da banjo strings. He vas making fun, Mrs. Pelham. He don't like to make such a puny sale." She brushed one mote of dust off the counter with her whole hand.

Eliza felt as though her face was steaming. She stepped up to the counter and said, "Give me a nickel's worth of those lemon drops. I'll take them home to Aaron and Ruthie."

Emily kept her eyes on Eliza while putting the lemon drops on some brown paper and folding them up in it.

"A nickel, please, Mrs. Pelham," she said.

Eliza stared. "A nickel?"

"Ya, a nickel, Mrs. Pelham."

"Can't you just put it on the bill?"

"Ve don't give da credit no more, Mrs. Pelham. I been tellin' everybody today and nobody vants to hear. Dey all tink you can get someting fer noting. Mr. Schwartzchild has decided to call in da credit and you'd tink da sky vas falling in. Ve aren't a charity."

"Well, I don't have any money with me right now. I'll just put them back." She wanted to throw the candies against the wall right behind Emily, who was sighing.

"No, Mrs. Pelham. You go ahead. I'm sure dat Franz vould let you haf da credit."

Before Eliza turned away, Emily said, "Haf you left your children alone, Mrs. Pelham? If I had children, I vould never leave dem alone in da middle of dis crazy place."

The door opened and two men came in loudly, stirring up dust with their boots, laughing at some joke that had been finished outside.

Eliza put her packet in a canvas bag over her arm and left. Music came from Near and Anderson's, a merry tune on the piano. A man selling a horse on the edge of the trainyard was showing the animal to a gathering group of people. The wind gusted and an empty flour sack blew against the horse's front leg, spooking it. When the piano stopped, the sound of hammering came in clearly from the north.

Eliza saw the Hispanic man who'd been in Schwartzchild's store talking with two other men by the bank; then she saw Mr. Smith walking down the sidewalk in her direction.

"Mrs. Pelham," he said without smiling. He nodded and just touched the brim of his hat. "I won't forget those banjo strings. I'll be here for a few days more if you think of anything else. But don't dawdle, now. I'm getting restless here. Too much violence. Have you read the paper today? Why, there's another killing, a man up there at the Miller place, some poor soul working up there got shot in the head last night. Everybody knows it was a Mexican. A bunch of them were riding up there last night wearing sacks over their heads. You'd think they'd realize they live in a civilized country now."

"I believe I ought to just go home and stay there, Mr. Smith. I believe when my husband comes back we'll just move on where I can get some peace. I don't even like coming into town anymore. It's my fondest wish to be somewhere quiet, away from wars and trains and guns going off. My husband has talked of starting a community somewhere—a utopian community."

Mr. Smith waved at someone across the street and said to Mrs. Pelham, "Well, now, I wouldn't be in such a hurry, Mrs. Pelham. I hear your husband is about to make quite a bit of money."

"Where did you hear such a thing, Mr. Smith?"

"Why I believe Mr. Anderson was telling me that he and your husband were in with some other gentlemen on some land deal. He and Mr. Pelham were talking about it a few nights ago—the day after I was at your place two or three days ago."

"My husband was here talking to Mr. Near?"

"That's right. That's right." Mr. Smith laughed. "Mr. Anderson's dead. It was Mr. Near."

Eliza looked over at the dancehall, which was quiet now; all she could hear was the hammering and some clinking sounds and conversation in the billiard hall.

"Well," she said to Mr. Smith, "a lot of things are happening all of a sudden around here. And since I've run into you like this, I might as well just tell you now to forget about those banjo strings. It just isn't worth your while to get something so small, and they bust real easily out in this dry climate."

Mr. Smith scratched his chest and laughed, showing small teeth.

"You're absolutely right, Mrs. Pelham. It's not worth my while. I'm beginning to wonder just how to make a living in this godforsaken sinkhole."

Their eyes met. He nodded and touched the brim of his hat again before walking on. Eliza could hear a horse, the one being sold in the trainyard, whinny. Then an Indian man with long black hair rode by on the horse, which he had just bought. The animal's hooves shook the whole earth as both horse and rider flew out of sight. They left behind them a brilliantly blue sky and a stillness that had not been there before. Eliza walked slowly down the line of buildings to the one where piano music trickled out in starts and stops.

She and Mr. Near, the owner of the dancehall had, a few years past, had a brief flirtation, until Eliza found out that Mr. Near had flirtations of varying lengths with every woman he met. His face was as smooth as a boy's, his eyes blue. They hardly every blinked, which was a disturbing distraction to Eliza whenever she spoke to him. She came across as very muddled, perhaps flustered, when she spoke to him, because she often paid more attention to whether or not his eyes were going to blink than to what she was saying or hearing. He was half listening to her now; he had gained a reputation for being preoccupied, since there were six new dancehalls in New Town and four more under construction. Whereas he used to see women solely for their potential to entertain and flatter him, he now saw everyone for their potential to benefit him financially.

The dancehall girls were hanging around; dressed as young ladies during the day, they fancied themselves helpmates, each one certain that she was more respectable than the next, each one certain that marriage to Mr. Near was a possibility. Bridie was behind the bar wiping glasses and humming the tune the girl at the piano was playing with one finger—an Irish ditty called "The Black Velvet Band." Two of the girls were whispering to each other; one was talking to a table of men, one Hispanic and two red-faced gringo cowboys who kept calling their companion "Pancho," though he kept telling the girl that his name was really Julian. They were eating apple fritters and drinking ale, the foam of which clung to the moustache of one of the cowboys.

Eliza, putting a full bottle of clear liquor into the canvas bag, was saying, "I've just talked to Mr. Smith, that salesman, and he said that George has been here. He told me that you and George are in on some land deal."

Mr. Near didn't speak until a rolling chord banged out of the piano. "Shut up, Mary, for godssake."

The piano noise stopped. Mr. Near studied Eliza, looking often at her chest. One of the girls softly laughed.

Slowly, Mr. Near said, "He was in just yesterday—had to pick some things up at the depot and head back."

Eliza just looked at him. A chair scraped on the floor.

"I guess he doesn't remember that he has a family," Eliza said.

Mr. Near's eyes narrowed very slightly.

She spoke more loudly, with her arms folded across her chest. "I guess he doesn't know that people are getting shot up here and animals and fences and whatnot getting all cut up."

"It's just Mexicans, Eliza. Ignorant Mexicans. They think you can have land sittin' around that nobody owns. Don't worry about it."

"I'm alone out here with my two kids, Will," she whispered. "I don't like all this. I think you men are causing a damned lot of trouble with all your deals and schemes. It doesn't seem like there's any laws or anybody watching over all these goings on. It seems like people are just doing whatever they want to do and that what men want to do is cause trouble, and women just have to sit back and take whatever comes."

"You want me to come out there and stay with you?"

"No, I don't."

Behind the bar Bridie coughed into her hand. The back of her head could be seen in the brown-stained mirror. Mr. Near turned and glared at her.

"Damned Mick," he said, smoothing his thick hair back. "Consumptive. She's going to have to go." He turned back to Eliza and said, "People won't come in with somebody coughing like that. She says she isn't sick, but I know damn well she's consumptive. She had fever two days ago and I told her to go on until she got better. Showed up this morning swearing she was better. You don't get better with that sickness. You can slow it down, but you don't get better. I don't want that around here. It scares people off. And that fracas with the whore from Colorado...excuse my language, Eliza."

Eliza watched Bridie, who avoided looking back.

One side of the double doors to the dancehall creaked open and a man strolled in—an Indian dressed in cowboy clothes.

"I'll give you a drink, son," Mr. Near said to him, "but you take it on outside."

The cowboy with the moustache called out, "You mean to tell me, Mr. Near, that you'll serve a Texan but not an Indian?" He shoved his sheepish companion in the shoulder and everybody laughed, even the Indian, who shrugged.

"Next time you see him," Eliza said, "you tell him I'm taking the children and going back to Kentucky."

Mr. Near looked puzzled; he hadn't finished grinning over the joke about serving Texans. Then he said, "Oh, you mean George. Sure. I'll tell him."

"Tell him I'm taking Aaron and Ruthie and moving down to Mexico."

"Mexico," he said. "Your skin's so fine, Eliza, I'd like to go on down there with you. You've got the finest skin of any woman I've seen." He moved in closer and said, "I'll leave all this behind and we'll run off together."

Eliza patted his cheek. "Okay, Will, I'll meet you around six tonight, me and the children. You can be their daddy. Be sure to bring all your money and a good horse."

He laughed but she didn't as she brushed past the Indian, smelling sage on his clothing.

"Why don't you stay for a drink," Near called after her.

Eliza smiled back this time and said, "I'm a wife and a mother, Mr. Near."

Stepping outside, she saw the whole town—with its hammering and pine smells, signs and hitching posts, good women, bad women, that tan dog that was always in the road and Clarence—the forty-year-old man with the mind of a three year old—wagons, dust, entrepreneurs, pieces of the daily paper blowing in the wind.

Bankers were meeting, committees were discussing new projects; the wind was uselessly turning the windmill about a mile away in the Old Town plaza.

And in the mountains to the west, beyond the noise of the town, the man who had walked away from the train depot a week ago was looking down at a disheveled mining camp—a little tent town in a small canyon. He held up one hand, palm up, and tossed some coins up and down.

SEVEN

La Llorona wails, wails, wails. She trudges along the arroyos and irrigation ditches, vomiting her sorrow and shame in wretched moans that curdle the leaves on the quaking cottonwood. People say that long ago she made a big mistake, a horrible mistake, because of her obsessive desire for a man's face and hands. She drowned her children, held their heads beneath the water because her lover did not want another man's children; and they did not struggle. That is what haunts the woman who wails by the arroyos at night, calling for her children who quietly, sweetly, trustingly allowed her to do this strange thing: to take them by the hands down to the arroyo; to lead them into the brown water rushing by with bits of blackened wood in it; to sternly push their faces down into the brown, gritty flow and hold them there while the angels sang. They waited to see what their beautiful mother was doing. It did not occur to them to think that she was drowning them. She was so beautiful, so much fun, smiling and childish herself—an angel who smelled like roses, cinnamon, and fertile ground.

The man faded, erased from the woman's mind by her sin, by her own realization of her godlessness and by her horror when she looked at her own hands. These hands had caressed his penis, his face, clutched his back. They had held her children's heads beneath the brown water. The man had gone on, changing the landscape where he stepped, putting his hand up women's vaginas and pulling out gold.

Forget the man—how small the man turned out to be, compared to the death of her soul. Now she wails—sometimes in Spanish, sometimes in a more ancient language—calling her soul and her children back. And she cannot hear them; they don't cry out. But the silence she hears is clearly them, watching, feeling the pressure of her hands on the backs of their little necks. Sometimes the silence is broken by the wailing of other women. As women walk by her, sometimes she wants to touch them, to ask them to speak with her about their sons and daughters. Sometimes she wants to caress them, to care for them, to sing to them. But they call her a witch, because she is dangerous, because she knows how they sin.

Mourning doves sang slowly and sadly to each other as Eliza walked home holding the shawl to her with both arms, hugging herself and talking to herself. She stopped beside a hill of tiny pebbles swarming with red-and-black ants. The sunlight rolled down from the mountains and stretched out on the plains.

The white-and-black dog came out from the copse of cottonwoods near the house and wagged its tail with its head lowered.

"Aaron? Ruthie?"

Some crickets tentatively began to chirp. It was still afternoon, but some of the shadows had the feel of evening in them to the crickets. The interior of the house looked secretive in the dim light. The table and chairs were arranged as they had been that morning when the three had eaten bread pudding together.

"I don't like them not being here so late in the day," Eliza said aloud. She looked into the other room.

"I'd be a good mother," she heard Emily Schwartzchild saying.

A thread of light lay across the silver brush on the dresser.

"Criminy."

Eliza walked outside. She shaded her eyes with her hand and examined the scraggly fields of sage and cactus where Aaron and Ruthie pursued lizards, horned toads, and orphaned meadowlarks. But there were no children there. Eliza waded through the prickly growth to the arroyo.

"I'm too tuckered out for all this," she said. She huffed in irritation. "I don't have time for this nonsense."

There was no visible life in the arroyo until a dark brown piece of it turned into a jackrabbit springing away in winding, manic fashion along the dry bed as though evading death.

Eliza stood with her hands on her hips watching it, annoyed at its emotion. She then gazed at the sky and located a pale half moon developing in the blue.

"Where are you?" she whispered.

She ran back to the house; a cholla cactus reached out and grabbed the bottom of her skirt, and she ripped it pulling it away.

She went into her room and looked under her bed. There was a big box along with dust and the stub of a candle—no faces peering out.

Then she sat in a chair at the table with the uncorked liquor bottle in front of her, watching the light fade, slumping and then straightening, staring at the table surface, listening. A tiny scratching noise came from somewhere around the stove. A breeze rustled the dried herbs that hung outside the door. A bird trilled from varying distances, melodically covering a large territory as the day slipped off and the prairie became luminescent, as though each blade of grass was lit from within.

Schwartzchild's store was dark when Eliza got there. She peered through the window and saw the spill of light from the living quarters in the back. Her pounding rattled the window. Finally a light moved toward her; then a lantern followed it, carried by Emily Schwartzchild. The woman's face floated on the window in the light of the lantern, a horrible, sallow visage. The face stared at Eliza and did not move.

"Emily, let me in. I've got to speak with you. Please, Emily."

The sky behind Eliza was orange. The piano music from Near and Anderson's had broken out and was boisterous now around people laughing and conversing, swearing and flirting.

Emily did not move right away, then she stepped to the side and opened the door.

"Are you looking for your children, Mrs. Pelham?"

"Yes, yes."

"Dey vas vit da drummer, Mr. Smit."

"What?"

"Yah, Mr. Smit, da drummer."

"Where? Where is he? Over at Mrs. Boggs'?"

"No he left town, Mrs. Pelham. Took da wagon."

"What? What do you mean? Where are Ruthie and Aaron?"

"I told you, Mrs. Pelham. Dey are vit Mr. Smit."

"Well, I don't know anything about this. Nobody told me anything about this."

"Vel, I don't know den. He said he had talked to you about dis, but you veren't der ven he come to pick dem up."

"What?"

Eliza's hands were shaking.

"Where are they, Emily? Where did he take them?"

"I don't know, Mrs. Pelham. He bought some tings for hunting, said he had a scheme to hunt da coyotes und sell der skins back east. Said he vas gonna give dem children some faddering und let dem help vit da hunting."

"What are you talking about? Ruthie is five years old. How can she help?"

Eliza pushed past the thin woman. Franz was at the counter in the dark, empty store. He seemed to have been standing there for a long time, waiting.

"Franz, have you seen George? Did George take Aaron and Ruthie?"

The slightest mist of dust in the air turned golden as it glided through the light of the lantern.

Franz spoke softly, kindly, "Ellie, dey're all right. Dey just vent hunting vit Mr. Smit."

"But it's almost night."

"Vell, dey probably vill be out for da night und come back tomorrow. You can probably go out and meet up vit dem in da morning."

Eliza imagined waiting for them, waiting for the last human beings on Earth that she felt connected to, during a godless, sleepless night.

"Maybe dey're on der vay here. Maybe dey'll come back tonight. Da moon's giving good light."

"Maybe ven dey come back you'll be happy und be a good motter," Emily said.

Eliza wanted to dump over the barrel of nails. She said to Franz, "You've got to do something for me, Franz." His eyes clicked over to his wife and then back at Eliza.

"Yah?"

"Send a telegram to George. I don't know how to do it. I never sent a telegram before. Send him a telegram telling him to come back here. If they're not back tonight, I'll just go on out and get them, and you can bet I'll talk to the sheriff about this, about anybody who knew about it, too. I knew you'd know something about it, Emily Schwartzchild, you old serpent. I just knew you'd know, just sitting here coiled up all day—you knew and you didn't do anything."

Emily placed the lantern down on the counter and said, "You'd better keep quiet. You vould be surprised, Mrs. Pelham, vot I know."

"Well, I won't keep quiet about my children; I won't have my children just taken off as if they don't belong to me. You have a terrible hate inside you about not having children of your own, don't you?"

Franz started to say something, but Emily interrupted him.

"I told you I vouldn't leave my children alone in a crazy place like dis."

"I don't want anybody messing with my children, do you understand? I don't want anybody touching my children."

Eliza swept the lantern off the counter and smashed it on the floor. Emily jumped and her arms froze stiffly, held a little out from her side. A harmless fire was burning on the little pool of kerosene on the floor. Franz ran to get the broom and beat at the flames with it.

Outside Eliza stopped and rubbed her forehead; then, looking to her left, she saw Bridie down at the dancehall, leaning against the wall and looking back at her. Her grey form was a contrast to the light, music and laughter coming out of the hall. She had her hands behind her back and was pushing off the wall with them, leaning back, pushing out in the rhythm of someone in a rocking chair. Eliza and she just stayed looking at one another in the dim light of the moon and the dancehall. Finally, Eliza walked to her, shaking.

When they were close, Eliza could see the flush on Bridie's face and that it was misted with perspiration.

"That drummer you brought out to my house has gone off with my children," Eliza said. "For all I know, he's shooting them in the head right now, or sold them to some Indians."

Bridie coughed and stayed leaning against the building.

"They'll be all right," she said.

"What do you know about all this?"

"For one thing, I surely don't know a holy thing about your children or Mr. Smith or anything else. And for another thing, did your mother teach you to speak rudely to people, Mrs. Pelham? I've been wonderin' for a time now just why you're so rude and all. You're the angriest woman I've ever known in me life, angrier than a cat in water."

Eliza stood against the building beside her.

"You know Ruthie," she said closing her eyes. "I can't stand her being without me. I don't think they knew they were going to be taken away like this. Ruthie is so little."

Bridie leaned out and looked inside the dancehall. The lanterns around the little stage shone in eerie patches on the heavily made-up face of the singer—red lips and red cheeks. Behind the bar, Mr. Near was running his hands through his hair and watching the customers.

Bridie clucked her tongue.

"Oh, she couldn't sing a song if it came and jumped into her throat. The only reason people listen to her screechin' is because of her big bum."

"I guess they'll be all right," Eliza said. "It isn't right that they just took off, no message left or anything. If the town was like it used to be, if there weren't so many people coming in and you don't know what they're like, and these old soldiers still wanting to use their guns. I wonder if Mr. Smith fought in the war. He's Yankee isn't he?"

"I don't know. But he's a wonderful man, Mr. Smith is. A fine, patriotic gentleman, so fierce about progress and so helpful and all. That he is. He's been as kind to me as though I were a queen." Bridie spoke seriously. "He doesn't put on airs, you know—no, not at all—believes in the equality of all people to have fine things."

There was a sudden burst of laughter in the hall because of something the singer did.

Bridie clucked her tongue again.

"Probably showed her bum, or sat it on some poor, unsuspecting storekeep who'll be crippled by the weight of it. Pah—she can't sing a single note."

Eliza stood away from the building.

"Leaving, Mrs. Pelham?"

They stared at each other. A pair of men walked past and doffed their hats. "You can call me Eliza."

"Well, don't worry about the children. They'll be all right. Maybe if they don't come back tonight you could go on out there and meet up with them. It's right lovely in the mountains, I hear, away from all this dust and noise—lovely they say, all full of trees."

"Maybe I'll just borrow a horse and ride on out to meet them. I wish George was here with his horse. Damn George. I ought to have a horse of my own to use."

"You're going out all by yourself and all?"

"Well, I suppose so, depending on where they went. Somebody's bound to know where they went—maybe that Mr. Bagby. There aren't too many places they can go in a wagon."

She looked at Bridie, who leaned over a bit and pushed herself off the wall.

"Well, you know, Mrs. Pelham, it's a funny thing and all, but I think I heard them discussing where Mr. Smith was planning to go, to do some hunting I think he said. I could ask Mr. Bagby about some of the details."

"I just better go on home. Maybe they're there. I just do not understand. I don't like not knowing where they are."

A man came along taking sloppy, jovial strides. He ran up against Bridie and said, "I just wrote a piece about you for tomorrow's paper, Miss O'Doonan."

"No doubt," Bridie muttered, looking away. "So long, Ellie," she called out. And the drunk journalist also said, "So long, Ellie," and continued on down the sidewalk.

A thought came into Eliza's head that it was her peculiar and cold lot to have all her children taken from her. All of them dead. All of them gone.

✦EIGHT✦

*M*illions of grains of grey light were taking the shape of the table, the chairs, the walls, the windows. Eliza was sitting at the table, still dressed. The house was still. Eliza's eyes shifted to the corner of the room where the children's clothes were kept in a lidless trunk. She got up, and hands shaking, she picked through the items: overalls, corduroy pants, woolen smocks. She smelled them and, in the dim light, continued to dig through the clothes.

In New Town the *Daily Optic* was coming off the bulky, mahogany press, brought from Pittsburgh by covered wagon some years ago. There were the usual stories and announcements. There was a plea for the federal government to pay more attention to its outlying territories, especially because there was a need for more troops to fight renegade Indians, derelicts ungrateful for the gift of reservations. Reliable sources had informed the editors of a conspiracy brewing between some of the Kiowa to the east and the Apache and Ute from the reservations in the northwest: raiders, rebels, heathens who wanted to savagely plunder the town as though they could eradicate civilization.

There was also mention of a man hanged in Hillsboro for stealing another man's horse along with his new hatchet. He was to be sentenced by a judge but, as the paper put it, was "out of luck" when armed citizens took him out of jail and hung him: "Early in the morning, Hillsboro was startled at the ghastly spectacle swaying in the wind, and many while gazing on projecting eyeballs and distorted face resolved that horse stealing was unprofitable."

And the shootings: "On Monday night Jose Seccon was shot and dangerously wounded by Guadalupe Campos"; "A party of Texans were camped on the Seven Rivers near the Hogg ranch in Lincoln County when a quarrel arose about a horse trade resulting in the death of one of the party. The man who did the shooting went before the justice of the peace with witnesses to prove that the shooting was in self-defense, and was discharged." According to the paper, one man who had disappeared some days before was found dead with bullet wounds in his head and his heart: "An inquest was held on the body after it was brought to town and the jury returned a verdict of death by suicide." Such was the profoundly unique and mysterious nature of the great western territories that a man could commit suicide by shooting himself twice, in both the head and the heart.

There was also the social news in the *Daily Optic*, some bits about visitors and new businesses opening and a little humorous piece about the dancehall girls at Near and Anderson's, who got a visit from one of the parsons as they were doing their wash outside on Sunday. He implored them, according to the reporter, to go to church, especially Bridie O'Doonan, so recently involved in a "hair-pulling fight with one of Colorado Spring's most notorious entertainers, who implied that our Bridie was partaking of the hot springs in order to cure a disease of their trade." Bridie had, it seemed, taken offense to this implication that she was a fellow syphilitic whore, and rather than appreciate the wealthier woman's sisterly tones, she jumped her.

And there was Bridie herself, standing in the doorway of Eliza's little home, the dawnlight making her hair all the more orange.

"There are clothes missing," Eliza said, still kneeling in front of the trunk, grabbing and dropping clothing. "Hair ribbons—all her hair ribbons. I don't know why everybody just thinks having children taken off is a perfectly fine thing."

"Well, you know there are a ton of things happening that seem a sight more serious, people waving guns around and killing and thieving in a dangerous manner. Sit down, Ellie. I'll make some coffee."

Eliza didn't say anything as Bridie opened three tins before finding the coffee. When she got down the cups usually used for the children's water, Eliza didn't say anything then either.

Finally, holding the steaming cup with two hands, she said, "I have to get a horse. I guess I'll ask the sheriff. He's got one or two extra. I just can't sit around waiting."

Eliza looked at Bridie through dirty glasses and asked, "Why are you here?"

"I thought I'd go with you."

A crow landed just outside the door, cawed and flew off.

"Maybe I'd better wait for George."

"I thought maybe we could make an outing of it. Take along some food, a fine, healthy outing and meet up with the children, surprise them like."

"I don't know exactly where they've gone."

"Well, I'll just bet that that other gentleman, the one with the beret..."

"Mr. Bagby."

Bridie pointed her cup at Eliza. "Sure, sure and he'll know like I told you. I heard them talking and all. We can go and ask at Mrs. Boggs's."

Eliza turned her face away. Her nose was stinging. She felt nauseated by the tears being drawn up into her eyes. What was wrong with her, she wondered. Why this sudden weakness when no one else thought there was cause for alarm?

"You don't have to go with me, Bridie. It's probably nothing."

Bridie set the cup down on the table.

"I've a mind to get out of town," she said. "Things are a little discomforting these days."

"You're not coughing so much."

Bridie coughed softly and smiled.

"No. I'm feeling all right in that way. And you know the doctors say that outings are good for the health, the clean air in the mountains and all."

Eliza slumped.

Bridie took the almost empty bottle of liquor off the table and put it up on top of the stove. "You just haven't gotten enough sleep. You'll be better, relaxing out in the mountains. You'll see; it'll be jolly, and the children will be all jumping and yelling with joy to see you and tell you all about their adventure."

"I just don't understand why he'd take them off like this..."

In town, getting the horses and getting information from Mr. Bagby at the boardinghouse, Eliza kept several paces in front of Bridie. But it was Bridie who got the sheriff, a man with a long, Rip Van Winkle kind of beard, to loan them the two horses. Deputy Salas advised against such a loan, but the sheriff dismissed his logic in favor of Bridie's pink cheeks. And it was Bridie who picked out the pastries at the New Era Restaurant and Bakery— four crossed buns to go with a loaf of bread and a big slab of ham. Bridie kept smelling the ham and remarking that it might be turning, which began an irritating dread in Eliza that Bridie would somehow ruin everything with her concern for unimportant details. They got four apples at Miller's Grocery where the proprietor let Eliza buy on credit. The bank teller who gave Eliza five dollars from her account reminded the two ladies to take water with them, so they got some empty bottles from Near and Anderson's and filled them up at the pump in the back. Bridie wouldn't go in until Katie, one of the sisters from New Jersey, told her that Mr. Near wasn't in—had, in fact, gone to Santa Fe.

When Bridie and Eliza left the dancehall, three ladies were walking down the sidewalk in their direction. They strolled in a swarm of children aged two to eight, belonging mostly to the woman carrying the parasol. She was arrogant due to the fact that she'd given birth to eight children and had lost none of them. But she had domestic help, too. Another woman beside her, who was mother to three of the swarm, modeled herself after the parasoled matron but had a sickening look of fatigue on her face all the time. She had no domestic help.

"Criminy," Eliza muttered. "Get on back inside," she hissed to Bridie, who just stood frozen for a second, then stepped backwards just inside the door.

One of the women saw Eliza and asked, "How d'you do, Mrs. Pelham?"

"Just fine, thank you," Eliza answered.

"We are certainly looking forward to some of your peach bread tomorrow night."

"Well, I'll do my best to get some baking done. But I have to do some traveling today."

"Where are your little ones, Mrs. Pelham?" the parasoled woman asked.

"Oh, they're on a little outing in the mountains with their daddy."

"Well, isn't that just fine," they all said, concluding that the new hotel that was going up in the mountains would bring in many tourists to partake in the healthful hot springs and fine air of the mountains. And no doubt some of those tourists would be Episcopalian, and wouldn't it be fine to be able to show them the plans for the new church.

They walked on, parasol twirling. One of them looked back and smiled; the children skipped and pulled and pointed.

"She drinks," the parasoled lady said, loud enough for Eliza to hear.

Bridie stepped out, her arms having lengthened by the weight of the water bottles she was holding in each hand.

"What's Mr. Near going to say about you not being at work?" Eliza asked her.

Bridie was quiet, sulky. "He doesn't give a plump fig. And besides, he's been spouting off about letting me go."

Eliza clomped down the steps and was untying her horse when Bridie said, "I think I ought to tell you something."

"What's that?"

"I've got a terrible fear of Indians."

Eliza checked all the paraphernalia on the horse, touching several times the bulge made by the bottle of corn liquor she was taking along.

She said, "Well," as she maneuvered the horse next to the steps and leaned her back against its side, "I guess there's always a chance we'll see one; might see snakes too." She hoisted herself up to sit sidesaddle, the left leg bent around the saddle horn. She watched Bridie jam the water bottles into her saddlebag with a folded tablecloth between them. Then Bridie went through the same process getting herself up into the saddle.

"So, Mrs. Pelham, would you like me to wait five or so minutes and follow you out, so that no one will see that we're riding together? I'd be the last person on God's green earth to want to ruin your fine reputation."

"Did you bring the hats?"

Bridie patted two straw hats tied onto the back of the saddle.

"All right, then, keep up with me."

Eliza pulled the horse around and walked then trotted it out the southwestern part of town. Eliza's horse was a caramel-colored gelding with a dark mane; Bridie a few yards behind her was on a dark brown mare with a black mane. The two riders crossed the bridge to Old Town plaza, where several people stopped to watch the women on horseback pass through the shadow of the windmill that was creaking like an old man laughing. In response to information given to them by Mr. Bagby and Deputy Salas, they were heading for the Royene mining camp in the nearby mountains. When they were at the outskirts of town beside several Apache plume bushes about eight feet high, Eliza swung her left leg down, sitting with her legs on either side of the horse, and pulled her skirts up.

"Well, I'm glad you were the first to do it and not me," Bridie said also changing from sidesaddle to the way men rode.

"We'll follow this road south like it goes, and we're supposed to turn west at the mining road. There'll be a sign. It's about twelve miles down and four or five miles over kind of along the river." She extended her arm to the west.

Since they'd stopped, both animals were ripping at the tall, pale grass around them.

Bridie had a little coughing session and Eliza rolled her eyes and yanked the reins, pulling her horse's head up. Bridie's horse turned around in circles before she could get it headed in the right direction. Eliza laughed at her.

"Come on," she said, suddenly gleeful. "Let's see how fast they can go."

As they rode off, the horses kicked up dust and the women's skirts fluttered around their knees. Bridie screamed and laughed, and Eliza was bent over the horse's neck like a jockey, grinning.

✧NINE✧

*A*fter several hours on the road, the women started to get powerfully hot and had to stop to put on the hats. There was no shade. They could see a trail of trees about a quarter mile away running parallel to the road they were on. Those trees—box elders, cottonwoods—marked where the river was running from the mountains down between Old Town and New Town. They were using the road that miners, people visiting the hot springs and the workers building the resort hotel used. Mercilessly unshaded, the road led up to the mountains, the closest ones gardens of ponderosa and juniper, the more distant ones soft purple bruises in the background.

The land Eliza and Bridie went through now was a dry carpet of clumps of grasses broken only by the oasis of the river. When trees began to appear beside them, they'd come to the area around the hot springs, touted by health seekers and entrepreneurs as an American version of a Swiss spa. They saw the beginnings of the future resort, but there were no workers there, just cleared land behind two huge ponderosa pines and a pile of lumber.

"You ought to go there, Bridie, when they get it done. There'll be lots of lungers in that place."

"And they'll be rich ones at that," Bridie said. "You don't think they're building a charity house now do you? Supposed to be bringing in things from France—curtains and chairs and gilded this and that. No, I won't see the inside of that place unless I get work as a chambermaid. It'd be awful nice to see it, though. Amazing to think of it, supposed to have a hundred rooms."

They were both silent, seeing edifices matching their private fantasies. In Eliza's mind the place glowed with horses, the best horses, corralled and running behind a white fence with a plantation-like mansion in the background. Bridie's picture was of a stone house with gables and stained-glass windows. But really there was nothing there yet. There was only a pile of lumber, only a barren place.

Bridie and Eliza crossed a wooden bridge over the river that was then adjusted to their left side. They slipped onto a part of the road more mysterious for its lack of use. Shade was now available from taller pines, from which an occasional vulture careened, high up enough to seem a majestic bird rather than one with a long, naked neck adapted for carcass cuisine. All in all, it was a pleasant ride which the women took at a walk, allowing the horses to consider the grasses but not to taste them. The road stayed wide enough for a wagon but got steep and started curving along the edge of ridges. Around noon their horses were walking side by side with the river far below them, the two women were eating apples and conversing.

"I've never been out this far," Eliza said. "It feels good, nobody around; the sky looks bluer out here." She let the horse walk without her guiding him, as she rebraided her hair beneath the hat. "It's good to be out of town," she managed to say with the apple core held in her mouth.

"How'd you come out here?" Bridie asked.

"We came on a wagon train a few years back, before the railroad got this far." She bent over to give the horse the apple core. He tossed his head, looking wildly behind him, not at all comfortable having food come to him from behind.

"Oh, calm yourself, "Eliza said, patting the animal hard on the neck. "My daddy raised horses. I learned to ride when I was four years old. My mother had a fit, made me ride sidesaddle. This is a pretty good one." She patted him again and sat back. "We lost all the horses about a year after the war started. I was about eleven, I guess. Soldiers took them. We weren't sure whether it was the Confederates or the Yankees. My mother said it was the Yankees. My daddy said it didn't matter; they were gone no matter who took them."

Bridie shifted in the saddle and asked, "Did you have Aaron and Ruthie with you coming across?"

"Yes," Eliza said. She kicked the horse forward. She stopped a few yards up and said, "I think this is where we're supposed to turn in. It's the first stream bed with a bit of a wagon trail beside it. Kind of steep, though, and there isn't any sign. Deputy Salas said there was a sign. Do you see any sign?"

Bridie said, "No."

"You don't look so good," Eliza said. "You look like you can hardly get your breath. You want to stop for a while?"

"Maybe we'd better go on and look for a sign up ahead."

But after a few minutes, Eliza stopped the horse again and said, "I think we should have turned back there."

Bridie coughed.

"You shouldn't have come out here," Eliza yanked the reins. She turned the horse around and headed for the canyon where she'd first stopped. They both rode in a way and got off the horses.

The hills around them sparkled with grasses. Grey boulders that had been poised there for centuries seemed about to fall or speak. A thin, trickling stream ran along the middle of the little canyon for as long as they could see; then the canyon curved up and out of sight between the hills turning into cliffs. Bushes and young trees danced raucously in gusts of wind that shot down the canyon. They looked like many squat creatures waving their arms in alarm. And indeed a bird called out some frantic message from the top of one of the large ponderosas. Both women were silent, experiencing some of the loneliness and dread people can feel when there is so much out of their control, so much oblivious to them: wind, plants, animals, sky. Bridie sighed, her back curving as she let the breath out.

"I didn't think this was going to take so long."

Without looking at her Eliza responded, "Don't start whining. If you start whining, I'll leave you behind and you can find your own way."

"Well, that's terribly civil of you, Mrs. Pelham. I don't think I should be faulted for observing the pure and simple fact that women don't naturally find themselves in the middle of the wilderness with no one to assist them."

"Didn't you come out here from the East? Didn't you have to haul water and pick up manure and cross rivers? Or did you and the other women you knew just wait for the trolley?"

"I came out on the train," Bridie said.

"The train," Eliza practically spit. "At least my children have learned how to survive without trains." She looked up at the cliffs.

"You're even worse away from town; your irritable nature hasn't improved one bit."

"Perhaps you've forgotten that my children are missing."

"They aren't exactly missing."

A bright strip of red fluttered and tumbled in some sedge above the stream, pushed by the wind. Eliza dropped the reins and ran after it as Bridie stood with the horses. She ran, reaching for the ribbon, which kept being pushed farther and farther by the wind up above the grassy stream banks to where the ground was covered by brown pine needles and little else. A coyote was standing on one of the larger boulders at the top of the eastern ridge. He was looking at the foolish woman stumbling after a red ribbon.

Eliza's hand finally grabbed the ribbon and held it up toward Bridie. Her face contorted to call out: "Ruthie's! This is the right way! It has to be!"

"Well, it doesn't have to be," Bridie muttered so only she and the horses could hear. "Surly bitch."

The two women walked toward each other, Bridie leading the horses. The coyote backed out of sight.

They looked up the canyon at the jagged geometry decorated with trees and shrubs, the landscape becoming darker as it went up, pulled up by the sky—up into the yellow, bilious clouds that circled the sun.

"There's a nice meadow just up ahead."

Eliza looked all around. "We can stop here. I think they'll have to come down this way."

They walked the horses up the stream bank without speaking until Eliza turned around and said, "He couldn't possibly take a wagon up here. Look, the road across the stream gets steep and narrow."

Bridie didn't have the breath to speak. She kept walking the horse, trudging up behind Eliza.

"Look, Bridie, you can't tell me that a wagon could get up this far."

The caramel horse tossed its head, pulling at the reins.

"Let's stop and let the horses have a drink of water. Look here, mine's pulling like a dog to get at it." Bridie bent over with her hand on her chest.

"Not much of a traveler, are you? Well, I'm here to meet up with Aaron and Ruthie. I want to keep my eye out for that wagon."

"I know you do, sure you do, and we'll find them surely."

"If we have to spend the night out here, I don't know what we'll eat."

"Spend the night?" Bridie took off her hat and pushed the hair up with the back of her wrist.

Now there were two coyotes looking down on them from a bunch of boulders shaped like giants' heads leaning against one another.

"I think it would be wise and all to kneel down right here and say a prayer."

"Say a prayer?"

"Yes, say a prayer."

The two coyotes stepped backward as the two women went down on their knees. Bridie's head was bowed over clasped hands. Eliza's hands were clasped, but she was looking around and suddenly tapped Bridie on the arm and pointed. She saw the wagon, a grey, crooked, man-made thing tucked into some scraggly bushes close to the mouth of the canyon. They must have passed it and not seen it. One back wheel was off. From a distance, from above in the mountains, three gunshots cut the air all the way to the women and beyond.

Bridie said, "Jesus, Mary and Joseph"; Eliza stood up.

"He's hunting, Ellie," Bridie said from her knees, her hands still clasped in front of her. "They'll surely be down before nightfall, surely they will."

"What are we going to do?" Eliza crossed her arms over her chest and looked down at Bridie.

"Well, like you said, they've got to come back down this way. We'll wait here, Ellie. It's a glorious day. We'll refresh ourselves and the children will be here soon. They'll be here before nightfall."

"And why should they have to come back here if the wagon is busted?"

More gunfire.

Eliza muttered, "What could they be doing?" She rocked back and forth on her toes and then slowly walked around to face Bridie, who had started to sing "His eyes they did enchant me" while she undid the buttons that flowed down the blue-flowered cloth of her dress.

"What are you doing?" Eliza asked.

Bridie finished the line, "He swore he'd be my true love," and answered, "I'm getting ready to bathe in the stream, like the ladies taking their cure in the spas, only this doesn't cost the farm. It's free, God's gift to the poor and wretched invalids of this world. Come on— you might as well refresh yourself if we're waiting here."

"What if they come down now?"

"We heard the shots way up there. We'd have at least a half hour or so before they'd be here. That's what I'd guess. I'm not coming all the way out here and not bathe. That's what people pay all that money for at those fancy places." She pointed down in the direction of the unbuilt hotel. "And here I am to partake of the same thing for not a penny. I'm sure I won't be out here soon again, and I might as well get all I can out of it."

Eliza looked upstream at the horses, who were relaxing in their way, lips to water, eyes assessing grass.

"I'd better tie up the horses. The sheriff would skin me if I lost his horses."

Eliza took the opportunity to get a bun to share with Bridie and have a taste of the corn liquor, which was unpleasantly warm. She took the bun to the spot on the stream where Bridie's feet could be seen through the glassy water.

Both women undressed to their underwear, secretly glad to see that neither had anything to boast about in the upkeep of their lingerie. Bridie's camisole had lace edging and little pearl buttons, though the middle button was missing. Eliza's camisole was plainer but clearly newer. Both had the straight bloomers that tied with a drawstring and were more yellow than white. Bridie's stockings were far grander than Eliza's; they were black silk, and she displayed them on a rock with the pretense of caring for them cautiously, while Eliza balled her green, woolen leggings up and tossed them on the ground away from the stream.

"I'd better unsaddle the horses," Eliza said.

Bridie watched her step gingerly around on bare feet to tend to the horses in her underwear. Eliza took a longer drink of the liquor and walked back carrying the bottle. Bridie noted, like a connoisseur, the elegant lines of Eliza's shape—her long legs and straight shoulders, and how the braid came down directly in the center of her back, which she held straight. Bridie tried to straighten up, but then slumped a bit, compensating for the weight of her ballooning breasts, which she usually appreciated but which made her feel awkward next to Eliza.

"You look like a pagan goddess," she said when Eliza came to where she was sitting still dangling her feet in the stream but bringing some of the water up to sprinkle on her arm. The drips sparkled. "Like that Diana, the huntress."

Eliza laughed. "Well, you look like something far more interesting—like a grown-up cherub."

"Achh," Bridie said and kicked water toward Eliza. "Now, who would want to look like a grown-up-sized baby!"

Eliza sat beside her and studied her.

"Well, more like those women in paintings about bathers, all plump and beautiful, kind of ripe and…"

Bridie coughed and looked away. Then she started singing with dramatic flair, spreading her arms wide and putting the back of her hand against her forehead with the line, "And she died of a broken heart."

She dipped her hand in the water and then dripped it on the back of Eliza's neck. Something moved amongst the trees, different from the pattern that the breeze made in them—a darkness that slid in a semicircle around them from a bit above in the canyon wall.

Eliza handed the bottle of liquor to Bridie, who took a couple of delicate sips and handed it back.

"I don't think I want to spend the night here, Ellie," Bridie said, shuddering and looking around her but seeing only trees, bushes, seedlings.

"Well, we might have to."

Bridie started to sing again, and Eliza moved her toes in the water to keep rhythm.

"I'm not going back without Aaron and Ruthie," she said as Bridie kept singing; Bridie leaned against Eliza and put her arm around her. Her breast was warm against Eliza's arm. They shared the bottle until Eliza held it up and said, "I want to save some. It gets cold at night."

"I am a virtuous maid and true," Bridie sang, and then she stopped and said to Eliza, "Now you sing, 'I will not trifle with your heart.' And then I sing, 'I could not wish for more than you,' and you sing, 'Then never shall I part.' "

"I'm the man."

"Right you are, the man himself."

They sang these four lines a few times, and then Eliza said, "Let's add a verse." And she came up with, "But you're going across the ocean wide/ Yes I will find our home/ Then take me as your legal bride/ And never more I'll roam."

"That's a fine bit of composing, I should say," Bridie grinned at her.

"I wish I had my banjo here."

So they performed the two verses with a flourish. Eliza started pretending to make love to Bridie as she sang, scooping up water and soaking Bridie with her caresses. Bridie won the game by standing up to deliver her line and then kicking water all over Eliza. Eliza stood up, still singing, and clutched both of Bridie's hands in mock affection but with enough force to keep her from running as she kicked water all over her. Laughing, they ended by clasping hands, leaning toward each other with one of their feet raised up behind them as in some theatrical picture. They batted their eyelashes and then, the song over, they kissed, still laughing. A bird screeched loudly and flew off. Bridie's lips were so warm that Eliza stepped backward in some alarm.

"You're feverish," she said in an irritated tone.

Bridie shrugged. Then a coughing fit hit her. Eliza just stood and watched. Bridie's coughing frightened Eliza more than anything so far; it reminded her of disaster and death. She wanted Bridie to disappear. She wanted to trade Bridie for her children, hand her over to whatever horrible fate hungered for tragedy and snatch her children away in exchange. She would run and run then. Run all the way back to New Town and hide in the little house for years. She would hold her children in her arms tightly and not give a damn if people laughed at her, if the drummer laughed at her for being so worried. The drummer would go away, everyone but her children would go away and leave her alone. Then maybe something huge and safe would descend on and enfold her forever.

"I guess he just wanted to take them hunting," she said aloud.

"Maybe we should just go on back," Bridie finally said. "I thought we'd just be out for the day and all. We've been out long enough."

"Long enough for what?" Eliza said, shivering. Her eyes narrowed.

"Just long enough. We don't know what we're doing, Ellie. They'll be back in New Town soon enough. The drummer has all his things at Mrs. Boggs's, you know. He hasn't run off with them at all."

"I told you I'm not leaving without Aaron and Ruthie. I don't like that some damned drummer came and took my children like they were orphans."

Eliza sat down hard and then Bridie sat down, leaning her back against Eliza's. Eliza began singing "Somebody's Darling": "Who'll tell his mother how her boy died?" The clouds looked very white passing slowly over the tops of the tallest pines. Most of the sky was still blue, a thick blue that seemed to be able to hold things, birds and milkweed seeds, like it was some kind of gelatin. Eliza was welcoming the effects of the liquor, which caused her to think with a floating mind.

Bridie said, "It's been almost twenty years since that war and people still talk on and on about it, like me father and brothers talking about the British—on and on like, never a moment's peace about it."

Eliza continued to sing.

"Did your father fight for the North or the South?"

"Neither. He didn't believe in war."

"What do you mean he didn't believe in war?"

"He thought all the killing was cruel and wasteful."

"Well, there's times and reasons..."

"My mother wanted him to fight—for the South. She's a good Christian woman, and like a lot of good Christian women she figured that the Bible said 'Thou shalt not kill except when you can get people together to do it in uniforms."

"You go to the Episcopal church?"

"Sure I do. Why shouldn't I? Just because I'm not sure about the Bible or Jesus or God—at least not the God that everybody says is on their side when they're shooting each other's teeth out—that doesn't mean I can't go to church like everybody else. I just don't say much, that's all. Maybe there's others that don't say much either and feel exactly the same way. My daddy used to quote somebody all the time who said the only church he had was his mind. I go to church anyway. I don't see any harm in it."

"Did your father get into trouble for not fighting and all?"

"He was the only dentist in town, so they didn't bother him too much. My mother nearly died of it. He got into more trouble because he talked about the war being a terrible horror, brother killing brother for unworthy causes. People called him a coward. Called him indecent because of the things he said about religion. But he drowned."

"Drowned?"

"I was fifteen. The newspapers said that he was bathing in the river and some ladies came down to bathe and he drowned himself 'from motives of delicacy.' "

There was a silence in which both women heard the creaking sound of insects. Then Bridie laughed.

"I'm sorry, Ellie, surely I am, but you can't mean that your father, bless his departed soul, drowned himself in order not to show his private parts?"

Eliza sat away from Bridie and twisted her head around to address her.

"My father was a decent man—a good, decent man. He never wanted to upset anybody. I guess he just swam away too far." She saw the people standing around his pale body, bloated but clean, so much cleaner than the other dead she'd seen, boys lying in her father's dental office with dirt and blood and yellow mess on them, their faces blackened and split. How good and right it was, remembering him so clean and smooth, like a rock at the bottom of a stream, polished by the movement of water.

"Oh, you don't mean to tell me that you believe it?"

"Believe what?"

"The newspapers saying he drowned himself 'from motives of delicacy'?"

"Why shouldn't I? That's the kind of man he was. You didn't know him. Even my mother finally understood what a decent man he was. I always knew it. It was my daddy who told me to go out west; he said he would've gone out west himself if he were younger and if mother had been for it. He told me I should go out west because I acted like a boy so much and didn't want to learn anything my mother wanted me to."

Bridie kept shaking her head and stood up to face Eliza.

"You don't think your father might have had in mind to drown himself for other reasons besides delicacy? A man will do strange things when he loses his honor and the respect of his neighbors."

"I'm just telling you what the newspaper said, and I never had any reason to doubt it. My daddy wouldn't have left me on purpose. He just wouldn't have done that."

"Well, then, what you're telling me, Eliza Pelham, is that you don't believe in God who cures the sick and raises the dead, but you do believe in newspapers and journalists?" Her face was very red and she leaned toward Eliza with her hands on her hips. She spat, as she'd seen the whores at the dancehall spit. "I'd say your faith is a bloody lot bigger than mine. The Bible talks about God, but there's nowhere in it that I know of that talks about newspaper men."

"What's got into you? I think a fly has flown up your bloomers." Eliza threw a stick into the water.

Bridie stomped off down the stream, splashing and stumbling.

When Eliza caught up with her they were in a clearing of pine needles and some young trees spaced apart from each other. They paced around, sometimes in a dance, sometimes kicking at ground. Wind swayed the upper branches of trees.

Bridie was thinking and then said, "I could be a singer, a dancer. A man in New York told me. Then he set me up to come out here. I was right shocked to see Near and Anderson's the first time, it not being at all grand like I was told. But, Mr. Near says that he means to turn it into a real theater. Already there've been great actresses performing there—like Miss Diamond who came through. I know I can sing for certain as well as that woman, as glorious as her costume was, and she's flatchested as a dog."

Eliza lay down with her hands behind her head and her eyes closed but still able to see the pattern of sunlight between the tops of the trees. Bridie sat down beside her, her legs sprawled out in front of her, and she continued to speak.

"It's not such a bad place. I'm able to make a good living without compromising meself as some of the girls do. And even those girls aren't so bad." She laughed, letting her head fall back. "Some of the things I've heard from those girls. Oh, we start laughing, and any man comes in we just can't help but roll all over each other laughing, thinking about what we'd just been saying." She crossed herself, still laughing. "Oh, it's a sin, and me mother would have me head in the wash tub." She looked sideways at Eliza, whose eyes were still shut. "They say that a man's Johnny looks like a bearded man with a long fat nose and two bulging eyes." She nudged Eliza, who didn't even smile. "And Katie, you know, one of the sisters from New Jersey, she told me that a woman has these moments of, well, like a man, that a woman has something happen down there that's like a kind of ecstasy. Only, you know, I have no desire whatsoever to put a man's part inside me—none whatsoever. I've seen what happens. I've seen me mother, looking eighty if she's a day, always bent over something, scrubbing or cooking and children hanging off her like she was a Christmas tree. Jesus, Mary and Joseph, I want no part of it."

Eliza's eyes were open, looking at Bridie.

"Katie told us that this feeling didn't happen so much when she was with a man, mostly with other women, all curled up together and cuddling warm and nice—only some men knew about it and wanted it to happen. She said she had to pretend with some men who wanted it to happen. She showed us how she pretended."

Bridie lay down next to Eliza and closed her eyes. She waited a moment, gathering inspiration and concentration, and then her mouth fell open and she breathed out softly, "Oh, Oh, Oh." She bent her knees up and waved her hips from side to side. The "Oh's" got louder, until at the end she uttered a prolonged, sighing "Oh." She coughed, rolled on her stomach and grinned at Eliza, who was shaking her head.

"You're not right, Bridie. You're as bad as those other girls, the things you talk about. It's not right to talk about those things."

"I'm an angel compared to them. You don't know what goes on, what people talk about and what they do."

Eliza rolled onto her stomach and said, "I think I've had that ecstasy."

"With your husband?"

"No, a horse. Riding a horse."

Bridie's eyebrows went up, "A horse is it?"

The two women laughed, Eliza nodding her head.

"It can't happen riding sidesaddle though," Eliza instructed.

"No, I suppose not."

Eliza closed her eyes. "I wish George were here. Sometimes I think that I'd be all right, that everything would be all right if George held me and I could just sink into him, all warmth and quiet. There's so much we've been through. He wanted to find a place to live that was perfect, people doing for each other."

Both lost in thought, they listened to the wind and watched a thrush bobbing from branch to branch.

"I wonder if we'll go to hell," Bridie mused.

They thought more.

"I don't see," she continued, "as how hell can be much worse than me mother's life. I'll have none of it, I'll tell you, not if I have to beg for me supper, I'll not end up like her."

Eliza stood up and brushed damp twigs and bits of leaves off her legs and hips. "It's getting late and they're not back. We'd better eat that food and decide what to do."

Bridie stood up but had to lean against a tree for a minute. Eliza came to move her along but when she touched her arm she said, "You're burning up with fever. You had no business coming out here. What am I going to do with a sick woman out in the middle of nowhere?"

Bridie abruptly looked up above them, to where a bird took off from a tangle of bushes on the canyon wall.

"Someone's watching us," she whispered. "Fairies, maybe. They'll do mischief."

Eliza put her arm around Bridie's shoulder and led her back to the horses. She could see the wagon still there, untouched, looking older and older, as though some spell had been put on them and they'd been gone for a hundred years. "Maybe," Eliza thought, "after a hundred years the world won't be so dangerous and mean." She just hoped that her children were also under the same enchantment and not dead like so many other children in this world.

→TEN←

A hand comes down—a big hand, wrapping itself around the upper arm of a boy. His eyes are dark, smoky quartz. He lets tears stand in his eyes and spill onto his face, making shiny tracks on his cheeks like the silver trails left by snails. His lower lip is trembling. A man laughs. A woman says something, words that have hard sounds but are gentle. In English they say, "Be a brave man. Go out and see what is in the world." The boy doesn't speak; he closes his eyes as though to allow the gods to direct him. But he tries one more time to ask his mother to let him stay. He only has to say her name; she will understand what he wants. The back of her hand wipes away the tears on his face, and she says again, "Go out and see what is in the world. Come back and tell us what we can use."

The hand around the boy's arm pulls him away. With his eyes closed he is seeing the mountains. He is hearing the things he was taught to hear, a quail's cry, the panting of a mountain lion, a deer's tongue lapping water, silence—the silence of his own mouth, because if it were not silent it would shame him; he would call out for his mother until he couldn't speak. He would tell the white man that he smells bad, that his food tastes like wood and sand. If he is not silent, the words will come over him and flood him and back up in him, and he will never again be able to hear anything, even the sound of that woman coughing, coughing, coughing so that everything in the mountains is listening.

Bridie was lying on her side, her front illuminated by the fire, her back in the darkness, facing lumpy shapes that were trees and bushes and the demons of her imagination. A loud pop spewed orange sparks into the air, and she coughed again, bending forward over her fist.

"How did you get so ill?" Eliza asked.

"Well, there was sickness everywhere on the boat, when I came over—a pitiful lot of sick folk, coughing and even dying. One baby girl sounded like she was choked to death, and two old men—brothers from Skibereen just down the road from me home—both died—just run out of breath, gasping like they were underwater."

In the firelight her face and hair were rich—an arrangement of orange-colored blossoms.

"I was sent to America by me parents. They only had money for one of us to go, and me brother, who was meant to go, got taken by soldiers and put in jail. We heard not one word from him for weeks until me father went all the way to Cork to find out what had happened and come to find that he was going on trial for threatening a man with a pitchfork. Then the newspapers said that he was a rowdy, frequently rampaging and speaking out against the English. Lies, pure and simple."

She was having some difficulty breathing and talking at the same time. She stopped to catch her breath, then lay back. Tears were coming out of the sides of her eyes. Eliza saw them and looked away, rattling the fire with a stick.

"I wish I'd never left. I wish I was there now. When I close me eyes sometimes I can hear things and see things. I sometimes find meself glad when the fever comes on, because it brings me close to home. I can hear me father whistling just outside the door—just as he's coming in and about to stomp the mud off'n his boots. I can hear the cuckoo, just at dusk, making his rounds in the trees beyond the yellow gorse. The gorse, so yellow I want to pour it on meself to keep warm."

She had to sit up to keep from going into another coughing fit.

"Sometimes, when I look out at the grasses, you know, as you can see them at the edge of town by the depot, it reminds me of the ocean," she continued, breathing as though having run through brambles. "Oh, I used to love the ocean, and still I do, but it scares me, now. I don't take it for granted so, and I'm glad to be away from it for a while. The boat I was on seemed a right tiny thing going on and on forever on that water, a great grey-green mass of never-ending water, the depths of which no one could even imagine. And some days there were waves like hills, rolling on and on, and I wanted to die before going on anymore. And there was always the sound of a baby crying or someone coughing as though to retch their very lungs out— noises in the dark like hell. Surely I know what hell is like—I'm sure of it like I'd had a vision from God Himself saying, 'This is what it'll be like for you, Bridie, me girl, if you're not minding yourself'—all darkness, complete and total darkness, with nothing but the sounds of people suffering around you and the endless rolling to where you no longer want to have a stomach or a head. And you don't know when it will end, and you can imagine that it will never end, and scream though you may, there's no one to come to you, no one to help."

A yip burst out from the steep hillside above them that made a scalloped line against the sky. Further up were clear stars, polished, shining as though about to burst.

"You can't think about things like that," Eliza said. "You just can't." She threw the stick into the fire.

"Well, I prayed. I prayed all day and night, I did. And that's all I had to go on." She sat up looking dizzy and disheveled, her face shiny with perspiration. "I don't see how you could've left all your kin and come out, and you scorning God the way you do—all alone in the world."

"I wanted to come out here. It was my idea." Eliza put her chin on her knees. "My daddy would've come with me."

"I just wish we were back in town. I don't think we should be out here like this."

Eliza stood up and brushed off her dress.

"We'll go back tomorrow morning if they're not here. George will have gotten word by then. He'll have to come out here and fetch them." She looked toward the wagon, now just a shadow like everything else. "I'll leave a note in the wagon if they don't come down before we leave." She nudged a leather pouch that was lying on the ground. "We've got a couple of apples left. We're going to just have to be hungry for a few hours getting back."

She sat down again and put her forehead on her knees this time.

"Maybe we should say a prayer" Bridie said.

"You go ahead."

"Surely you need God's help."

Eliza looked up at her but said nothing.

Bridie crossed herself and stared at Eliza shaking her head.

Interrupting her own prayer, she said, "You know, Eliza, there was a miracle happened in a town just five miles away from me own home, in me own lifetime, when I was a child. I heard it like you hear about the weather—like a real thing from a real person and all."

She put her hand on her chest to quell an urge to cough—to tell the urge to wait a minute this time—and continued.

"Well, it was Mrs. Doohig, who never said a strange thing in her life—as trustworthy as an iron pot, she was. And one day she saw the baby Jesus in her garden, standing between rows of cabbages just as real as me or you. She was going out to pull some carrots, and he spoke to her, just as plain as you please."

"How did she know it was Jesus and not some little one wandered off?"

"Well," Bridie explained sitting up with excitement, "he was all aglow like." She fluttered her hands around her body to indicate a light, an aura.

Eliza narrowed her eyes, "Could have been the way the sun was, or a reflection on water."

Bridie brushed angrily at her skirt.

"Do you want me to tell you or not?"

"Go on."

"Well, he said, 'Mary'..."

"Wait." Eliza put her hand up. "This is a baby talking just like a person—a little infant, only he's standing and talking?"

"Well, yes. So, he says, 'Mary, go and tell the father that there's a leak in the church roof on the northeast side, about to burst.' And sure as I'm sitting right here, the next rain, the water came pouring in the church, right where he said."

Eliza shook her head. "Some baby standing in some woman's garden talking about a leaky roof just isn't my notion of a miracle. I don't see the point in it if the roof went ahead and burst anyway."

Bridie held her breath and then let it out in a long sigh.

"There's no use at all trying to talk to you. I don't know what I'm doing out here with a woman who's scorned the very God that gave her life. And who everyone knows worships the bottle. Yes, disgracing yourself with drink more than once. You don't understand a thing, Eliza Pelham, not a thing. Did you ever behind those sad spectacles of yours consider in your head the possibility that God was waiting for you to show some respect and repentance before He gave your children back?"

Eliza sat up and bent forward so that her face was wallowing in the firelight.

"If God makes children suffer just so people take notice of Him, well then, I'd rather keep company with the devil himself." She stood up, walked around in a little circle and sat down again in the same spot.

"Jesus, Mary and Joseph," Bridie said. "You call the devil up, then you deal with him. I need God, Eliza Pelham. I'm a sick woman, as far away from home as a body can get. And you, keeping so quiet in town as though you were a Christian woman like the rest. Well, you can't hide your love of drink." She held her legs and looked around, fear glistening in her eyes as she coughed. "It's like the devil was right here watching us."

Something small, like a nut or a pebble dropped on the ground in the dark between their camp and the stream.

"I hope it doesn't rain," Bridie said.

Eliza looked up at the sky.

"Not a cloud. Clear and deep, and look—no ring around the moon. It's real wondrous, the sky. I wish I could live out here. Nobody around."

"If there was music, maybe..."

The wood and ashes glowed, no longer flaming.

Bridie gazed at her own hands and held them toward the waving heat of the embers.

"It gets cold at night," she said.

Eliza stood.

"I'm going to sleep before you keep me up all night with one complaint after another. That's what's wrong with you people who came out on the train—no notion of taking care of yourself without a nice chair to sit in."

She picked up the liquor bottle, which had only a thin line of liquid left in it and said, "Here, drink the rest. It'll quiet you, help you sleep. I don't need it like you do." But she watched the last of the liquor with a haunted eye, wondering about the thoughts she'd have to contend with during a long night.

Fidgeting uneasily with the blankets, the women settled down, listening to little noises and the lulling sound of the stream until they fell asleep, Bridie seeing the face of a hobgoblin receding into the trees, and Eliza having the sensation that someone kicked a chair out from under her. Then a woman's voice, sweet and whispering, said into her ear, "It does not matter. Go to sleep." And the words fell down the coils of her ear until they become a sound in the center of her. Using a dream as their landscape, Eliza and the woman cried out together, wept for their mistakes and careless innocence.

A man, dark, with a wide band of black across his eyes, stood above the two sleeping women in the first light of day that was muted by the veil night still trailed behind. The sky was pinkish along the eastern horizon and the moon still had light in it. The man's black hair shot out in tufts around his head. On the ground, close to Eliza's glasses, his feet were bare. Bridie moaned and tore at the cornflowers on her dress. Her plump breasts moved as though something was beneath them, trying to claw its way out. Eliza was silent and still with illuminated hair. She was lying on her side, her grey sleeves against the ground, her mouth slightly opened. The man stood still, a current of air playing with feathers tied around his ear. He was carrying a rifle in his right hand; it hung forward so that the barrel pointed to the ground. He had on an open vest but no shirt, and over his shoulder was a satchel made of elk skin. Moving just his eyes within the black band, he looked toward the horses. Then he pushed Eliza's glasses with the end of the rifle. They made a clicking sound and he waited. But neither of the women moved. Then he pointed the barrel right at one of the lenses.

✦ELEVEN✦

*W*hen Eliza woke up, Bridie was propped up on her elbows. Her hair was chaotic, and she was looking down at her feet as though wondering what they were.

There was moisture on the sedge and grass that covered the ground. Eliza picked up a fistful of mulch and smelled it. She put her glasses on and stood up, letting the blanket fall. She walked to the horses and rubbed their rumps. Then she untied them and walked them down to the stream. As the horses drank, occasionally looking upstream at some shifting shadow, Eliza splashed her face with water and took sips of it out of her palm. She could see the wagon, still there, more permanent than ever. She pressed her face into her hands and allowed two sobs to mix tears with the stream water. She came up with the question, "Why doesn't the world just leave me alone?" She hadn't asked for any trains, or drummers, or consumptive dancehall girls. She hadn't asked for any damn thing. It was George who had wanted a perfect life—some kind of heaven on earth—at least up until the baby died. Eliza had just wanted to keep moving, away from her mother's Christian library, away from old battlegrounds, away from thinking about anything—until maybe some precious thing, the intimacy with George or maybe a new and marvelous landscape, would wake her up to a beautiful warmth. Eliza walked back up to Bridie, leaving the horses on their own but in sight.

Bridie was moving oddly, like everything had to be thought out carefully, even the lifting of her hand to smooth the hair back. Eliza shook out her blankets and watched Bridie.

"I don't feel too right this morning," Bridie said quietly, and she coughed once. Eliza could see her elbows shaking as she tried to hold herself up.

"Eat one of the apples."

There was gunfire far up the mountain, crackling, and then the sharper crack of gunfire close by.

Bridie began to cry.

"I'm doing poorly, Ellie. I can hardly move without thinking that I'm going to faint right out. And me chest feels terrible bound up."

Continuing to fold the blankets, Eliza said, "You should never have come out here. It wasn't my doing."

More gunfire.

"Jesus, Mary and Joseph," Bridie whispered. She looked up at Eliza like a lost child. "Indians. It's Indians, Ellie. Surely they'll find us and do horrible things. And I couldna get on a horse and ride if I had to or die. I saw them around here last night; I could hear them talking to each other all night long and I couldna move a muscle."

Eliza tossed the folded blankets on the ground.

"There's not an Indian within ten miles of us or more. It's just Mr. Smith hunting, and there's a mining camp around here somewhere. I've been a lot farther out than this."

Bridie lay down again, shivering and holding the blanket to her with both hands.

"Criminy," Eliza said. She sat down next to Bridie and straightened the blankets out around her. She covered Bridie's feet, which were vulnerable in little brown shoes frayed where the leather attached to the soles. Eliza sighed, looking up the canyon, down to the horses and back at the wagon.

"Damn you," she whispered. And she stroked Bridie's forehead, gently lifting off hairs that were plastered in sweat and laying them back with the others.

Gunfire and Bridie's eyes opened wide.

"It's all right," Eliza said. "It's all right. I'm just thinking. That's the gun starting all my thoughts to running around and around." She made a circle in the air above her head with her finger. Eliza held Bridie tight and felt a shift inside her as she comforted Bridie, rocked her like a child. She got a taste of a restful surrender as she mothered Bridie with intense tenderness.

Bridie looked puzzled and closed her eyes again.

A brown bird landed very close by on the sedge, and Eliza stared its little eyebeads down until it flew off in some distress.

✧TWELVE✧

*A*s Eliza was tying the horses up to a little aspen near the stream, she heard Bridie scream—a hoarse and frightening scream that might have come from someone being dragged down to hell by Beelzebub. Bridie was sitting up, the blanket clutched in both hands around her chin. Near her feet lay a dead rabbit. The wind blew its fur, exposing a soft, light undercoat. The two women stood over the rabbit's corpse, which had suddenly appeared before them.

Bridie crossed herself and looked at Eliza.

"Well, don't let me be the one to point it out to you," she said, a mess of sweat and red-rimmed eyes wide and chaotic, "but here's a miracle if I ever saw one."

"How did it get here?"

"Fell right out of the sky it did."

Eliza looked at her fever-crazed companion, then around at the sides of the canyon. She pushed the limp rabbit with her toe, and it flopped back to its original position. Bridie just watched Eliza's face as the latter squatted down and lifted the rabbit up by the hind legs. It was long and grey with some brown in it. One hind foot was missing.

Woozy and swaying a bit, Bridie said, "You're not going to tell me, then, are you, Eliza Pelham, that a rabbit just happened to jump into where we've camped and lay down on the ground to so kindly, if you please, die for our benefit? It's a miracle. God works miracles as sure as I'm standing here, and He worked one for you to see."

"Well, I guess God needs luck. He took the hind foot here." Eliza turned the carcass around. "And I guess God's got a gun, because this rabbit's been shot through the neck."

Bridie squinted her eyes and leaned forward.

"There's someone watching us," Eliza said, "and he's got a gun. Maybe it's that salesman—I don't know. I don't know why he'd leave us something and not show himself or let Aaron and Ruthie come on with me." She lay the rabbit back down and stood up. "Well, I guess I'll fix it up and we can eat it. It'll be good for you to get some meat in you. And then I'm going to walk on up and find them myself." She put her hand on Bridie's arm. "You can just stay here. Don't worry; you can just rest here."

A cool wind whipped around, kicking up dead leaves and grabbing the women's skirts.

"It's clouding up," Bridie said.

The air had a pouting feel to it, like a child before it resorts to tantrum. Breeze had become wind.

Bridie lay down, letting Eliza fiddle with the fire and start skinning the rabbit.

"I was getting better. I was better," she said with her eyes closed and the back of her forearm over her forehead.

"You'll be all right. We'll have a good meal and then you'll be strong enough to go on back. If I don't find Aaron and Ruthie,..." she cleared her throat of the slightest trace of a sob, "we'll ride the one horse together, me holding you and leading the other horse behind." She looked up the canyon and back at the wagon.

"They'll be all right, Eliza," Bridie said.

"I don't know why he hasn't come back to the wagon. Maybe they went on back some other way, all three on the horse."

The wind blew hard, bothering the horses, who jerked back on their tethers.

Bridie could eat little more than a few bites. Eliza ate a good deal of meat just when it was cooked and still hot, peeling the greasy strips off and sucking her fingers after. They squatted there, eating with no concern for appearances, reduced, some might say, to a state resembling savagery. Eliza chuckled to herself. Then she jumped up and kicked at the liquor bottle, which was resolutely empty. Gusts of wind were bending the young trees by the stream now, turning them inside out and blowing ashes out of the fire.

"I don't think we ought to try to ride out in this," Bridie whispered.

Eliza sat back down and gnawed on a frail bone. "We'll wait until it blows over." She looked up at the sky in all directions. "It's coming in from the east. It'll be by us in a few hours."

A gunshot reverberated in the sky above the mountains.

"I hate that sound," Eliza muttered. She stood up again and tossed the bone into some bushes. "I'm going to walk up the canyon a ways. You stay here and rest."

A massive, blackening cloud covered the sun. Behind the peaks of the mountains was a bank of these clouds, spying on the world like minor gods.

"I don't know what I'm doing," Eliza muttered as she tied her skirts around her waist and trudged up a vague trail beside the stream. "George should be out here. I want Aaron and Ruthie for godssake."

Then she got the idea to climb up the wall of the canyon and take a look around—maybe locate that mining camp or see some signs of the salesman and the children. She wound around trees and boulders, stopping when she heard distant rumbling, then moving on.

At the top she realized she was only on one side of a shallow saddle and that the next canyon had to be on the other side of the next ridge or farther. But she could see up the stream fairly far— the tops of the trees and bushes in various hues of quivering and swaying greens. She could see Bridie and their little camp, too, and as she looked down she saw someone with Bridie.

"Dear God in heaven," she breathed as she crouched down.

The man was dark with disheveled black hair and the remnants of a suit—just the pants and vest. He was carrying a rifle and a leather satchel. Bridie had stood up and was swaying terribly, stumbling over to a tree to lean against it. The man followed and stood across from her. Eliza was no longer able to see both people clearly, only the man and pieces of Bridie.

The sound of gunfire cut the air behind her. She, Bridie and the man looked up the canyon. When she looked back down, Bridie had collapsed against the tree and the man was bending over her.

Eliza ran in a sideways fashion down the slope, her little shoes, seeming worthless now with their nickel buttons, caused pebbles and dirt to slide down before her. She fell, bounced on her backside, then got up again and fell, finally resolving to go down the side of the hill sitting. She strode up to the Indian, who turned around to see her as he lifted up his rifle. Bridie was looking up at both of them with her hair pushed up by the tree and falling into her eyes. Her hand was poised in an effort to cross herself.

Eliza pointed arbitrarily up the canyon and said, "Go!" as though speaking to a dog.

Bridie's hand moved to her forehead then down to her stomach and stopped there.

"Go on. Go. You go," Eliza said, flailing her arms. "Go."

"He doesn't understand, Ellie," Bridie breathed. "He's a savage; he doesn't understand English!" She was outraged and frantic.

The man lowered the rifle and pointed it at Bridie. Calmly he said, "This woman is very ill, consumptive, I believe. You should take her back to town. There's a big storm coming and she shouldn't be out in it."

Eliza narrowed her eyes.

"What?" she said.

"She has a fever. Are you ladies lost out here?"

"I know she's consumptive," Eliza said, pointing to Bridie. "What do you want?" Eliza's eyes focused on the horses for an instant.

The man saw where she looked and said, "You have two fine horses."

"They aren't for sale. I think you ought to just go on."

"You're with the man and the children?" He jerked his head toward the mountains.

"Yes. They're my children and that's my husband and we're waiting for them. They're coming down to meet us."

The man nodded and said, "Hmmm."

The wind was now churning branches and bushes. It blew pieces of Eliza's hair that weren't secured in the braid. She watched the man's face for a long time, and then she asked, "Do you know where they are? Have you seen them?"

He waited a few seconds before answering, then said, "Yes, I've seen them. He has a strange way of hunting. He is the children's father?"

Eliza placed her hand over her stomach and closed her eyes. When she opened them again she said, "Did you leave the rabbit for us?"

"I had more than I needed. I was actually getting a little tired of rabbit."

"We're grateful to you—we thank you—but you'd better go on now. My husband doesn't like Indians."

He nodded and walked away, passing by the horses, whose tails and manes were frantic in the wind.

"He better not take our horses," Eliza muttered.

Bridie stood up and got very close to Eliza with her warm breath and fevered eyes.

"Surely there are worse things an Indian can do to us than take our horses, Ellie. We've got to be careful and watch him every minute—and for godssake, woman, look at your skirts—they're tied up around your waist, showing your underwear. You'll drive the heathen out of his wits with lust." She said the last in a loud whisper.

Eliza angrily untied her skirts and said, "Never mind. He probably saw us dancing around yesterday halfnaked."

"Jesus, Mary and Joseph," Bridie said.

"Be quiet, Bridie. He's going off anyway."

"Going off to come back, I'll bet my father's fortune. She leaned back against the tree. "We've got to go. We've got to go on, storm or no storm."

"It's raining. I felt a couple of drops."

Bridie started to sob; it sounded like a laugh at first as she grabbed Eliza's arm. "I want to go back, Ellie. I shouldn't have come out here. I want to go back. I'm frightened out of me mind. I'll go crazy if we stay here. Something terrible is going to happen."

Eliza sighed angrily. "This is a discomforting mess. I want you to be quiet for once in your life so I can think."

Bridie sank down and put her arms around Eliza's skirts which were getting splattered with rain.

"Please, Ellie. Please take me back."

Eliza looked down at Bridie and knew that here was a woman who was a victim, pure and simple. Bridie was a choice put before her. She could have sworn that a dark woman stood behind her, amused, arms folded over her chest saying, "Well? Are you going to fall down there with her; are you going to kick her? What are you going to do?"

Then Eliza bent backwards, holding her face up to the sky so that rain plopped onto her glasses. She howled with her own voice but in unison with the dark woman behind her, "Aaron! Ruthie!" Then she cupped her hands around her mouth and yelled, "Aaron! Ruthie!" Thunder rumbled as though the gods were moving chairs around to get good seats for what promised to be entertaining.

✦THIRTEEN✦

*I*n the false dusk made by the storm, one tree had the shape of a sad old man; a coyote howled, answered by two others. Another tree was bent over, gathering its own fallen leaves; two coyotes howled, disharmonious wails that met and separated. The silhouette of the ridge and the mountaintops made a corrugated line of black, frilled by the shapes of leaves. To the east, one faint patch of blue pulled down the whole sky, which was rumbling as though the biggest god was stirring and irritable. Gusts of wind lashed the trees and bushes, making the two horses step nervously around the place where they were tethered.

Staring at a small lick of flame, Bridie and Eliza sat beside one another, Bridie shivering.

Eliza threw little pebbles over the fire. "You don't have anything to write with, do you? A pencil?"

"No."

"Well, I'll write with the charcoal from the fire on something." She looked around. "What can I write on?"

"I'm getting terribly cold."

"Put another blanket on."

Raindrops hissed in the small fire.

"Why are those coyotes howling so much?" Bridie asked.

Lightning flashed, and one of the horses stamped and pulled back against the rope. And then the rain fell harder. The fire smoked out, and the steady rain made the horses' eyes go wild.

"God in heaven," Eliza said.

The rain was soaking them. Bridie stroked the wetness off Eliza's face with the back of her hand. Warmth—warm hand, warm breath, lips like little pillows of warmth.

Eliza took the blanket off her shoulder and held it above their heads.

"We'll just wait. We'll get through this and go back. At least we know we're only a couple of hours from town. I remember times like these when we were days from anywhere."

Something suddenly ran by, vibrating the earth.

Bridie whimpered.

They flipped the blanket off and saw the caramel-colored horse galloping down the canyon, the rope flailing the air behind it as though the animal was being ridden and whipped by a ghost. It took them a few seconds to admit to themselves that they had seen what they had seen.

Eliza stood up, completely drenched, standing now with rain streaming over her head, spotting her glasses. Through the droplets she saw a man beside the other horse. The wind and intermittent coyote cries mixed in with the now steady pounding of rain. Eliza screamed, "Don't take that horse. Don't take that horse, you devil!"

The remaining horse's eyes were wild, whites showing. It whinnied and reared up, rain sliding off its back. Eliza ran up and grabbed the man's arm.

"Move!" the man yelled, "Move!"

Rain streamed down Eliza's and the man's faces. Bridie ran up screaming, a wet, long-haired cat with her orange billows of hair flattened and dripping.

"Get away from him, Ellie. For God's holy sake."

"He's stealing the horses," Eliza yelled above the sound of the rain. The dark horse bolted and got free, running, tail arched, away from the mountains.

"You devil!" Eliza pounded the man's shoulder hard with her fist. He grabbed her wrist and bent her arm back. Bridie sank to the ground, covering her head.

"Come with me," he yelled.

"You devil!" Eliza screamed as she struggled to get her arm free. "We've lost the horses. We've lost the damned horses."

Bridie cowered down further, trying to sink into the earth.

The man dragged Eliza by the wrist down the hillside. Bridie staggered to her feet and followed, calling out, "Let her go."

Everything was now water, their clothing, their hair, the blankets. Everything had darkened and become water.

They stopped by the litter of the old fire, saddlebags, two drenched hats, rabbit bones, the empty bottle of liquor, which made Eliza sick to see. The man nodded toward the bags, and Eliza picked them up.

"Come on," he said. Bridie just stood by, watching them and chewing on her knuckles in the rain.

"What do you want with us? Why don't you just take these things and go?" Eliza whipped her elbow away from his grasp.

"Come on. You're going to kill her if you don't get somewhere dry."

Eliza turned to look at Bridie, who was terrifyingly limp and dazed. Then she turned with wide eyes to the man and said, "My children. Do you know where my children are? Are they still out here?"

"Come on," he said again and walked to the stream and crossed it. On the other side he looked back at the two women and waved them over. They were just standing there like pictures in a catalog selling wet clothing.

Eliza turned and put her arm around Bridie's shoulder.

"Let's go, Bridie. Come on with me."

"You've lost your feeble mind, Eliza Pelham. That man is a savage who means to do us harm. I will die out here, I'll be struck by lightning before I'll go with the likes of him, a godless savage." But it was easy for Eliza to move her forward, and they followed the man up the slick hill. He turned beside a dripping bush and disappeared into a small cave made of rocks leaning together.

One person could stand in the middle of the cave, but the three of them had to bend against the rock walls. The two women slid down and sat close together, staring at the man, who was pressing water out of his hair and shaking it off his hands.

"What do you want with us?" Eliza said.

He looked them both over, squinched his eyes and his mouth, rubbed his beardless chin like a man considering a purchase.

"Well, I could be your guide."

"Guide?"

"Clearly you don't know what you're doing. I don't mean any offense, but you didn't tie the horses up very well. I could see that right away. I figured they'd run off in the rain if you didn't tie them up better."

Bridie shivered and clung to Eliza, putting her face into Eliza's arm.

The man squatted and lifted a blanket off a pile of sticks. He gave the blanket to Eliza, who put it around Bridie.

"Why do you want to be our guide?" Eliza asked.

"For money," he said, sitting back and dragging a leather satchel closer to him. "You know—money."

"We don't need a guide. We know exactly where we are and just how bad things are."

"I understand," the man said. He emptied the leather pouch of its contents. There were six small apricots, a brown book, something wrapped in a greasy piece of cheesecloth and some bullets. His long fingers picked up the fruit and handed one to each of the women.

"Fruit?" he said twice like it was some hilarious joke he was trying not to laugh at. Bridie just looked at hers and put it down on the ground.

"You don't speak like an Indian. He doesn't sound a bit like an Indian, Ellie."

Eliza tore the apricot in half and ate it.

"You know where that man has my kids?"

"Your husband you mean?"

Eliza didn't look away from his eyes.

He stood up and straddled the fire, shaking out his pants.

The rain outside sounded like animals stampeding.

"This is a bad storm," the man said. "Even the coyotes are acting strange."

"They sound mournful," Eliza said. Then she added, "He isn't my husband. He's some drummer who took my children when I was gone. I want them back. I think I'm going crazy thinking of them up there now with this storm. I don't know what I'll do. This has gone much too far. I knew something wasn't right no matter what everybody was telling me. It just isn't right having your children taken off like this. Dear God in heaven—out in all this rain. I thought I'd seen the worst. I thought I'd seen enough bad happen to me already."

The man put another stick on the fire.

"Maybe there's nothing bad happening."

Bridie lifted her head and looked around the little cave as though it was someone's parlor, then she saw the man standing and waving his arms to push the smoke from the fire out the opening.

"What's he going to do to us?"

"I don't know," Eliza told her.

They both looked at the man, who widened his eyes again in exaggerated ferocity and wildness.

"Is that the Bible?" Bridie asked, pointing to the book on the ground beside his satchel.

He picked it up and tossed it to the ground by her legs.

Eliza picked the book up and read the binding: *The Confidence Man*, by Herman Melville.

She gazed at the man's face as he sat down against the opposite wall.

"I went to school in Pennsylvania," he said. "I just got back. My name's Robert Youngman." He held out his hand to the two women, who just stared at it. Finally Eliza took it and shook it. Bridie sat up and felt her hair, discovering what a mess it was.

"I'm Mrs. Pelham and this is Miss O'Doonan."

"Pleased to meet you," Bridie said. She looked so discombobulated that Eliza laughed.

Robert smirked and said, "How dee do!"

"I haven't got much money with me," Eliza said.

"And just what kind of an Indian are you, anyway?" Bridie asked.

"Tinde," he said.

"Is that the good kind of Indian then?"

Robert shifted and poked at the fire with a green stick he had peeled the bark off of.

"Apache," he said. "Jicarilla—my people lived with the Mescalero for a while, but we're from up north and west of here, on our very own reservation, I'm told."

"Apache" was all Bridie heard. She had clutched her dress collar in her fist and was looking at Eliza with silent messages sparkling in her eyes.

"Apache," she hissed. "Those are not good Indians, no indeed—I'll tell you that, Eliza. Surely you've read about Apaches and Utes and those others in the papers—why they're the ones supposed to be planning some awful massacre."

"Yes. My mother is a huge woman and has plans to sit on every white person she meets. She has bad gas, too. And there are old men and hungry children too—many dangerous elements. They will try to whip you to death with their blankets."

Eliza eyed Robert, who was waving at the smoke again, this time with just one hand.

"The papers said..." Bridie began.

"I thought you didn't believe in newspapers, Bridie—Miss O'Doonan."

"Well, some things are just fact, plain and simple."

She coughed, softly, then gave way to a fit of it.

"Lay her flat on her stomach," Robert said. "Put the blanket under her head like a pillow."

Bridie tried desperately to watch Robert vigilantly, but her eyelids seemed to melt over her eyes.

When Bridie was fitfully asleep on her stomach, Eliza said, "I don't know what we're going to do now without the horses. I'd pay you something to round them up for me."

"There's a mining camp just over the south ridge there, about a mile, maybe less. You could probably buy a couple of horses there, though they aren't as good as the ones you had. I bought my rifle there."

"They weren't even my horses. And what makes you think that I've got all this money that you keep talking about?"

Robert shrugged.

"I'll get your children for you," he said.

"For how much?"

"A hundred dollars."

"What?" Eliza drew her head back as though smelling something foul. "What do you want money for, anyway?"

"I don't feel like making pottery. Pottery is very boring to me," he said, picking up the book and looking as though he was starting to read.

"Well, I'm sure not going to pay you one hundred dollars for doing a Christian deed."

He looked at her over the book. "How much will you pay for a Christian deed?"

"Twenty dollars."

"All right."

He read again.

Bridie started talking in her sleep about Albuquerque.

"What's she keep going on about Albuquerque for? What's down there?"

"I have no idea," Eliza answered. They both looked at Bridie.

"She looks like something dragged up from the bottom of a river," Robert said.

Eliza gave him a sharp glance.

Robert shrugged and went back to the book.

Eliza sighed. "When are you going to get them?"

"After it stops raining. I don't like to get my hair wet." He touched it lovingly, a mass of blue-black spikes.

Eliza let her head fall back against the rock and closed her eyes. Robert read. It kept raining, changing intensities.

"I'm going to wait until later," Robert said, still looking at the book, "because that man is crazy and I don't want to have to deal with him. I'll get your children back when he's asleep. I'm glad you decided he's not your husband."

Eliza lifted her head.

"What do you mean he's crazy?"

"He talks loud, even for a white man. You shouldn't have let him take your children off."

"I didn't let him take them off."

They stared at each other.

"I don't want to hear what you have to say," Eliza said. "If I'm paying you, I just want you to get my children."

They both stared outside, looking at the rain.

"I wish those horses hadn't run off. They weren't even mine."

"They might go back to town on their own."

"Maybe. What about you? Where are you going? Are you just going to live up here?" Eliza asked.

He put the book down, the way people do when they know there's no use trying to read.

"I don't know. My father and his family are dead."

"Killed by soldiers?"

"No. Utes. My father worked for the army. Worked for the Union army as a scout. He was rewarded for his service, honored at a ceremony in which his family received not one but two bags of white flour—only a few bugs."

Eliza thought about this for a moment. Usually, when people told what their fathers had done in the war, she dreaded the inevitable question, "What did your father do?" But Robert didn't ask, and she got the feeling that he really didn't care.

"What about your mother?" she asked.

He could see his mother's hands, but not her face. He could hear her tell him to see what was in the world.

"She's with the others, back in the mountains northwest of here."

Bridie suddenly sat up in a panic.

"I can't breathe," she said.

"It's all right," Eliza told her. She moved Bridie around so that she was sitting between her legs, leaning up against her. "Here. I'll plait your hair. Such beautiful hair."

Robert picked up the book again. When Eliza finished plaiting Bridie's damp hair, she squirmed a bit to relieve her numb buttocks and dozed off to the rhythm of Bridie's soft snoring, telling herself that she was not really sleeping, that if the man did anything funny, she'd be awake like a cat. She calculated into a dream the time of day it must be, though it was almost dark outside. In the dream, it didn't matter what time it was; what mattered was that the Indian man from Pennsylvania wanted to serve her some French brandy.

Robert finally put the book down. He had been reading the same paragraph over and over again since the women had come in. He still didn't know what it said. He'd been thinking about everything else but what his eyes were scanning. He was thinking about how much money he could get from this woman. He was thinking about how oddly he'd seen that white man act with the little girl and boy. He was thinking, of all things, about Mozart; he had become mesmerized by the fugues and the powerful sound of the organ in the great church in Carlisle, Pennsylvania. He had been sent out into the world to come back and bring what was useful. Was Mozart useful? He wasn't sure. He looked at the rifle. A gun was useful. Money was useful; money was the future. If he could bring money to his people, lay it down at their feet, hundreds and hundreds of dollars, he would have done something worthwhile; he would be giving his people, his mother, what they would need for the new journey that his great uncle had told him about, a journey that started with a little boy going to Pennsylvania and ended who knew where or when. It was to be a dark journey, full of confusion and noise and loss. But the strong, those who understood where power came from and how to use it, would make the journey and live to heal themselves.

These two women, he was thinking as he looked at them, were very pathetic. He thought about the whores in Philadelphia, who ended up liking him; he thought about finding a real woman, one his mother might pick out for him, whose skin would be rich and who knew how to laugh. He had considered trying to have sex with one of these white women. He had to admit that. But he was not ashamed of himself for such a notion. Being ashamed was a great waste of time for a man who had done nothing wrong. What he wanted was to keep carving himself out of the block of stone he'd been chipping away at. He needed details.

He looked at the details on the women, the buttons on their dresses, the texture of their hair, the shape of their lips, the dirt on their fingers. If he were going to do it, he'd have sex with the tall one. She seemed limber and someone who had once laughed a lot. But he was put off by her ferocious resistance to something; he couldn't figure out what. She had a dangerous hardness about her, like she was protecting something inside her and would do great harm to anyone who poked at it, would make a lot of noise. He was looking forward to being with a woman, though, one who smelled like wood smoke and playfully bit his ear, one whose long, brown fingers he could watch caress her own belly with his child in it. He would make sure that his children knew who they were.

He picked up the book and read again.

✦FOURTEEN✦

Something was up with the coyotes. They howled so plaintively, Robert couldn't keep his concentration on the book. He often looked above the pages at Eliza, who moved and sighed in her sleep. She finally woke up and said, "Ruthie?" She explained to Robert that she thought she'd heard her little girl crying.

"Coyotes," Robert said. He handed her a chunk of meat. "Rabbit."

Then Bridie sat up straight and opened her eyes wide and started talking to them as though she was in the middle of a conversation. She sat away from Eliza and spoke to her.

"I would wear the gloves with the black dress, the one with the pleated front, you know." Her brow was wrinkled and she stared at the ground, trying to figure out how to organize her thoughts. "And he'd give me enough money to go down to Albuquerque to the sanatorium there where all the rich people from the East are going." She looked up at the two in the cave with her and explained, "People pay good money to come out here for the cure, and me being already out here but without a penny, without so much as a penny to get just down to Albuquerque. I don't want to die on the streets, Ellie. That's what happens if you're poor and sick and you haven't any family to go to. The man was asking about you. He said he knew how much I wanted the gloves."

"You're not making any sense, Bridie. Try to make sense. Are you talking about something that has to do with me?"

"Who's he?"

"Mr. Youngman."

"Jesus, Mary and Joseph, the Apache."

Bridie touched her hair and looked puzzled when she found it plaited.

"I need a drink of water," she said, so Robert got a tin cup by the little woodpile and held it under the trickle that came down the rock behind him. Bridie wiped the rim with her skirt and drank, coughed, and drank the rest.

Eliza had been staring at her.

"What were you talking about just then? You were talking about someone paying you to go down to Albuquerque."

"You don't know what it's like to be sick," she whispered, as though she could keep a secret in that tiny space. Robert just sat with one leg bent and his arm draped over it. The rain was still steady but lighter. It was dimmer outside because day was ending.

Bridie wanted to talk, as though all this time that she'd looked like she was asleep she was really collecting things she was going to say.

"You're not a real person any longer when you're sick and dying," she said. "You're the sickness itself. You think and act and breathe the sickness. You lose yourself—everything is tainted. You can't look at a room or a person's face without somehow thinking about your sickness. And there are good days when it doesn't ride you and you can pretend that you're all right, but you've seen the others and you know how it goes up and down, until one day there's no coming up again—there's just surviving hour to hour by the grace of God. And even if you do manage to fool yourself into thinking you're not dying of something that's in your body, feeding on your life, the people around you will let you know—walking at a distance, making sure not to touch you, telling you you're not fit to work anymore. And then what are you supposed to do? You're too sick to work and you need to get help, but if you're not working, you have no money to feed yourself, much less try all the tricks people try to sell you knowing you're desperate—salves and potions, elixirs in dark bottles that you know don't do a blessed thing but you take anyway, just in case one of them is the miracle. Because what you want more than anything is some hope. And it's only the rich can buy any real hope. I just want a little of it, a picture of meself lying in some clean room with people giving me good food and tucking the blankets around me chin, and a doctor to come and thump me on the chest and smile a little. That's all I ask for. I don't have any family here. I don't have a home." She placed her hand over her chest; her face was flushed.

"You dwell on it too much," Eliza said. She looked away. "Anybody could dwell on anything and feel pity for themselves. Everybody has some suffering to dwell on."

"Sometimes it overwhelms a person," Bridie raised her chin. "Sometimes it's more than a person can take. Sometimes the suffering is cruel, because there's hope given and then taken away. Sometimes you tell yourself you're blessed with what you've got, and the next day even that's taken away."

Robert leaned back against the wall and crossed his arms over his chest. He closed his eyes and listened to the women's voices like someone listening to music, an ironical piece of chamber music.

Eliza turned her head to glare at Bridie with the resentment of a child who's caught an adult in some hypocrisy.

"I thought you believed God would take care of you, Miss O'Doonan. You don't sound like one of the faithful to me." Eliza shook out the bottom of her dress. "I don't like listening to people complaining. Don't you think I could be complaining about my children being taken? Don't you think I could dwell on them being out with God knows who in this storm? There's no use thinking about what pains you."

Tears made Bridie's eyes glassy.

"Oh, I don't mean to trouble you," she said. "I don't mean to trouble anyone. But at least I have God, Eliza Pelham, and He'll forgive me for what I've done."

"What have you done?" Eliza asked.

Bridie looked down at her lap.

"If he gives me the money now, I won't use it for the sanatorium. I'll use it to go home. I just want to go home. I don't care how poor I am nor what scolding me family gives me for coming back with an empty hand. I want to go back, and I'll hang on 'til I'm at the door and me father says, 'Bridie, is that you, girl?' And I can see just green-and-yellow gorse and pink rhododendron and the road winding down the hill to the ocean. I'll hang on even in the boat going all the way back over the water."

Eliza and Robert exchanged glances.

"Who's going to pay you, Bridie, the drummer?"

"No, I don't know anything about him, Ellie, I swear it. Just some man who came into the dancehall and said someone was interested in making sure that you got out of town for a day. He said I'd be paid."

Eliza looked from her to Robert and then laughed.

She stood up and walked out into the rain.

When she came back in, she stayed standing, her head bent down under the rock ceiling.

"And just why did this man want me away from town?"

"I don't know. He said it were none of me business."

"Had you ever seen him before?"

"No, but he seemed familiar with Mr. Near. He seemed harmless. And a man of means, Ellie—not some ragamuffin or criminal."

"Was he American?"

"Well, I guess so."

Eliza walked back outside. Lightning flickered in the distance, illuminating the clouds from within.

She bent down to be heard inside the little cave and said to the man, "Are you going to get my children for me? It's almost dark."

"I don't know," he said.

"I'll pay you. Damn, I'll pay everybody."

She came back in, looking scorn at Bridie.

"You're a pathetic sight, Miss O'Doonan, and you have yourself to blame for your troubles. You won't get pity from me, pretending to be my friend. I swear there's not a soul to be trusted on this earth. Not a soul. All I want is somebody I can count on. Just one damned person. But I guess I'll have to do things for myself. And that's just fine with me."

Thunder rumbled and there were flashes of lightning every now and then. Finally Robert said, "The storm's coming back around."

Bridie crossed herself and lay back.

Eliza looked down at her, watched her shiver for a few minutes. Then Bridie opened her eyes and looked up at her.

"Don't worry, Ellie," she said.

Eliza covered her with the blanket and sat down beside her.

"You're a strong woman," Bridie went on with her eyes closed. "I always sensed that when I saw you. 'There's a strong woman,' I'd say to meself, 'strong and mad at someone.' I figured that's why you drink, Ellie. Me father drinks for the same reason—mad at someone."

Eliza growled. "Why don't you get some sleep."

"Who are you so angry with, Ellie? Maybe you don't believe in God because you're so mad with Him. Maybe you think God will be like some lover and say to you, 'Aw, Ellie, don't be mad with me. I'll be good to you from now on, Ellie. Just don't be mad at me." She giggled sleepily, eyes still closed. "I can just see God standing there sheepishlike, finally beaten down by Eliza Pelham being mad at Him."

"Go to sleep, Bridie," Eliza said.

And Bridie did, after reaching out and taking Eliza's hand, holding it firmly. Her last words were, "When I pray, Ellie, I pray for you too. I say what I think you'd say if you prayed."

For a few minutes Eliza thought about what that would be, and the only thing she imagined herself praying was, "Please give my children back to me safe and sound." She squeezed Bridie's hand, suddenly wishing they were sisters who were having a feud. She slid her hand away, though, because the sister was ill, the sister was so needy. Eliza didn't want to think about illness and needs.

She looked at Robert, at his weird hair sticking out like spikes. He was lying back with his eyes closed, oblivious, it seemed, to her.

Then an acidy panic began to spread inside Eliza, causing her skin to tingle. Certainties crept into her mind with such force that logic seemed simple-minded and weak in comparison. These certainties were that the night was never going to end for her, that the blackness outside was permanent; and even if logic did mean that the sun was going to come up, it would be too late for her. She would be forever suspended in this predicament, forever waiting. She would be finally overwhelmed by the pictures she'd been keeping out of her head for the past two days: her children somewhere, afraid, suffering, believing that she did not care about them. If she had something to drink...If she weren't so tired, maybe she could keep resisting, but she could feel herself giving way, losing all sense of order and hope.

She began to pray inside her own head, not yet gone enough to give any outward signs of spiritual desperation.

"Dear God if you exist, please let them be all right. Please keep them safe and let them know that I love them, that I'm trying to get them back with me."

But there was that voice—the one she was so terrified of, the one, she now guessed, she spent most of her waking hours trying to ignore. It wailed and moaned. What did it want? And if she gave it what it wanted, would she get her children back? It wanted a drink right now; that was for sure. God, why hadn't she brought more liquor? If she could just have one stinging drink, she wouldn't have to worry about what she was going to do, about how she might do certain things, say things in front of this Indian and this damned consumptive dancehall girl. Without a drink she wasn't sure she wouldn't start crying herself, moaning and reaching out and asking questions that couldn't be answered and generally making a fool of herself.

"Oh, God," Eliza whispered, and she put her head on her knees and tried to sob quietly. The voice in her head was sobbing, too, saying, "What happened to the baby? Why isn't the baby crying?"

"I'm losing my mind," Eliza muttered.

And another voice, a man's voice said, "No, it's just very difficult to go without enough sleep for several days."

It was Robert, who hadn't moved, but his eyes were now open. He touched the book as though he might pick it up and read, but instead he sat up straighter and put another stick into the miniature fire.

Eliza looked at him, and her thoughts seemed to stumble and collide into each other, cursing and accusing in a heap.

"I wish I had something to drink. I'm a little chilled. You don't have any whiskey do you? No, I guess not."

She rubbed her arms.

"Fire water. That's what we Indians call it. Fire water. And no, I don't have any fire water. Indians can't handle it, you know, like white people can."

"You're a card, Mr. Youngman. I can see that. I don't think anyone in New Town would believe anyone like you existed."

"No, I guess not."

"I wish they were with me." Eliza sighed. She held her own arms and stared at Robert, finally saying, as though someone had dared her to, "I've already lost one child." She knew that for some reason if Bridie were awake she wouldn't be saying this. She needed to talk, though, mostly because her body felt irritated beyond control.

"George, my husband, and me and Ruthie and Aaron, my two children, were on the wagon train coming out here. I'd known a child was coming before we left Missouri, of course. I was pretty far along, but we couldn't wait for the next year because George had been hired on to be foreman on a railroad crew in Colorado and New Mexico. And he'd always talked about going somewhere fresh and living in some wonderful way with people who didn't try to outdo each other with money and fine things, well, like some of those religious societies, only George isn't very religious. But he sees the value in trying to live in some kind of peace, people just doing what they need to do to survive and care for each other. I guess it sounds foolish."

Robert nodded and then shook his head. "Maybe he would have liked to be Tinde."

"It was my idea to go out west in the first place. I guess we could've waited, but it was a good job, and besides, we might have waited and I might have been in the same condition the next year too. There was no sense in not going.

"It's a hard trip, you know, before the railroad came all the way out, but I didn't mind it much. I mean, I never did like having to look clean and neat, and on the wagon train people forgave you if you were rough and let things go. I could just have a good time with Aaron and Ruthie, and there were some wondrous things to see. Most of the other women complained a lot and wanted to go home. I guess I was lucky or something. I didn't have some of the trouble other women have with childbearing. And I didn't care about getting sun red or dirty. We had good luck, too, because it didn't rain much and the only Indians we saw were running a ferry across a river in Kansas." She was playing with the dirt on the ground, making little trenches as she spoke. Robert watched her hand as he listened. He let the comment about Indians pass. He had gotten used to people confiding in him about Indians, thinking he wasn't one anymore.

"My time came at night. It always did. But it went on into the next day and I knew something was wrong. I was feeling bad because I was keeping everybody, but George said that the men agreed that they'd made good enough time along the way, so it was all right to stop as long as we could go on the next day. But the baby wasn't coming, even the next night. I was so tired that I remember sleeping for a minute at a time dreaming about the pain. There was a Negro girl and a woman named Mrs. Delaney who helped me. The Negro girl sang hymns and was a comforting presence. She worked for a family a few wagons up and was always real sweet with Ruthie.

"It was almost dawn when the baby came, and I remember thinking that it was good not to make everybody have to wait another day. But then I realized that everything was real quiet. And the Negro girl said, 'Lordy, lordy. That sure is a beautiful girl,' and I was thinking that I couldn't name it Douglas after my father. And Mrs. Delaney touched my shoulder and said, 'God took her back to be with Him in heaven,' and I didn't know what she meant. I couldn't imagine what she meant. But I started praying and praying that the baby would cry, so that I could hear it gasping and sucking in air. I just prayed and prayed over and over. And the Negro girl knew I didn't understand, and she took my hand and said, 'She dead, Mrs. Pelham, but she's the most beautiful little girl I ever did see.' And I just stared up at the top of the wagon, up at the canvas, looking at the pattern the water marks had made there. I saw all kinds of shapes and prayed to each one of them to change what was happening, to make that baby cry. And Mrs. Delaney and the Negro girl were talking. They asked me for the christening clothes. I told them where they were and just lay there. I asked if Ruthie was being looked after, and they said that she was with George, all excited about riding with him. The Negro girl tried to lay the baby beside me, and I said, 'No. I don't want to see her.' Then they took her and washed her. I looked over once and saw one of her little feet hanging down, pale and bluish against the Negro girl's arm. And Mrs. Delaney said, 'Do you want to help us wash her? We'll wash her clean and dress her up all nice.' And I said that I didn't want to, that I just wanted to get some sleep. They took her outside and somebody on the wagon train took a picture of her."

Robert said nothing. The fire was just burning coals, and he looked into it. It seemed darker than ever outside; the rain had started up again.

"This night is never going to end," Eliza said.

Robert was thinking, and finally he said, "The cord that connects a mother and her child is very strong, like a magical rope that can't be cut. It's painful for one to be one place and the other to be far away. But I think there are cords that can be made between others, too, though it's rare. I think that some people send out these spirit cords, that it's their duty or their burden to cut themselves open and pull out these cords for people to hold on to. Like Mozart. When I hear his music, I feel the cord pulling me."

He touched his solar plexus with his fist.

"It is like Mozart is one of my mothers. But all the time I was in school I kept thinking about the mountains where my people came from, that they went back to when I was very small. I kept seeing particular trees and the line of a particular ridge and the feeling of my own bare feet walking on the ground there. When the train brought me back, I felt the cord pulling between me and the mountains; then I could see them in the distance, and I remembered stories and saw a horse falling on the ground and other things I don't understand. I felt that feeling, and I listened to the music in my head and saw the mountains in the distance, and for some reason the two went together even though Mozart never came out here and saw those mountains. I thought of when I was taken away and all the things I didn't know about and didn't care about. All I wanted was to stay. I can still remember why. But if I had stayed, I wouldn't feel so much, I don't think. There is a great sadness in the feeling. Partly I am sad because I am old enough to know that my mother sent me away to protect me, to give me some kind of power. And I am sad because I hated her and because I cried and made her suffer to see my crying. And because I think that she grew old that day and that everything grew old that day."

"Things don't seem right," Eliza said. It was dark and warm in the little cave. They looked at Bridie sleeping peacefully. Eliza touched her clothing and was glad that it was only a little damp. If the man wasn't there, she would have taken their dresses off and let their underthings dry too. It didn't matter that he had probably already seen them gallivanting around with their dresses off.

"Did you see us dancing and singing?"

Robert was lost in the thoughts he had been talking about. He readjusted his attention and said, "Yes."

"When you were looking at us…when we had our clothes off, did you want to do something?"

Eliza smoothed the hair back from her face. Robert's brow wrinkled.

"Do something," he repeated thoughtfully. "Yes, yes I did. I wanted to request a different tune. You sang the same one over and over. Very boring."

Eliza let her head drop back. "When I get home, I'm going to get into dry clothes and pour myself a drink. And I'm not going to do anything but be with my children. That's all I want to do is just be with my children." There was something else she wanted but couldn't put into words.

Then outside, a hoarse scream, a long, arcing scream.

Eliza stood up. Robert casually picked up a stick and peeled some bark off it.

"Did you hear that?" Eliza said. "It sounded like a child screaming. Dear God in heaven."

"Mountain lion," Robert said.

"It sounded like a scream, a child's scream."

Bridie put her hands up in her sleep as though pushing something away.

Eliza squatted down in front of Robert.

"You've got to go get them now. I'll go crazy if I have to wait."

Robert kept peeling the stick.

"I'll give you two hundred dollars, damn it. Or—I'll get them myself."

Stooping, her hair caught on a sharp corner of rock for an instant, Eliza stepped out. Robert shot out behind her and grabbed her wrist.

Eliza screamed, "You let go of me. I'm going to get my children. I'm going to walk up this damn mountain for a week if I have to."

"Go back in there," he said. Bridie was coughing in the cave.

Eliza twisted her arm away. She was getting drenched again in a renewed roaring of rain. She ran up the hill, sliding on mats of old leaves. Robert was behind her. She was screaming over the thunder of the rain coming down, "Ruthie! Aaron!"

It was completely dark except for stutters of distant lightning that made everything look blue. Eliza was slipping, sliding, pulling herself up the hill and screaming out her children's names. There was no piece left of her that did not want to scream out her children's names. Robert's hand came around her mouth and he said into her ear, "No wonder white people think Indians are quiet if this is the way you sneak up on somebody. Maybe you should scream a little more in case everybody in New Town didn't hear you."

She tossed her head violently back and forth until he released his hand. Coyotes wailed painfully, and some distance away the odd, hoarse scream could just be heard beneath the rain.

"She's moving away from us. That's good."

"Who?"

"The mountain lion."

Robert pushed Eliza's hair away from her face and said, "Come on. We'll go up to where his camp is. Just stay with me."

His tender gesture confused Eliza, sickened her in some way. If she'd known he was ever going to touch her like that, she wouldn't have said all those things about the baby. Was he going to rape her? Was she a fool to have left her children alone in New Town like Emily Schwartzchild had said? And was she still a fool to be running around in the mountains with an Apache man who pretended to be reading a book? How stupid of Bridie to think she was strong.

She walked further up the side of the canyon until she was on a small ridge; Robert was a shadow to her left. The shadow whispered to her, "There's a path here. Come here."

"I can't see anything," Eliza said. He took her hand and led her.

They walked on, Eliza's feet stumbling on sticks and rocks. They had to go steeply up for about ten minutes, then Robert stopped.

"Wait here," he said.

"Listen. The coyotes have stopped."

She could see his eyes in the dark; he could see the flat, streaked circles of her spectacles.

"Wait here. Just squat down."

She didn't move, so he pulled her down next to him.

"You should have brought your rifle," she said.

"Do you want me to go back and get it?"

"No."

Thunder rolled away, as though a tired child was dragging a toy over the mountains. Lightning still played with the sky, tickling the bottoms of the clouds. Eliza could see Robert's face through the rain streaks on her glasses—brown eyes, serious expression with some irritation in it.

"It's so quiet now."

She took off her glasses and tried to wipe off as much water as she could with her finger.

Robert moved away while Eliza was still squatting, biting her lower lip. In a moment he came back and picked up her fisted hand to pull her farther up the path. They stepped between some bushes that painted them with drenched leaves. Blue lightning blinked, and there before them was an abandoned campsite. It was littered with the headless carcasses of about fifty skinned coyotes in stiffened poses: light-colored lumps, visible in the dark as an afterimage with limbs akimbo, many of them small—the bodies of pups.

"Ruthie?" Eliza called out, and Robert's hand jerked to cover her mouth and then fell back in exasperation. Could she hear whining? The carcasses seemed to twitch in the stutters of lightning, imploring Eliza to find their heads, to find their skins and put them back together so they could flee into the rocks and never see a human being again. Muttering her horror, Eliza walked carefully around the sad, rubbery bodies to the overhanging rock. Underneath, on a small strip of dirt that the rain had been unable to soak, she saw a trampled ribbon, white or yellow, and a pile of human feces.

"Dear God in heaven," she said.

Robert said from somewhere near the center of the clearing, "Go on. Climb up the rock. Climb up and go down into the next canyon. You'll see lights there. Go on."

Eliza didn't move. She tried to see where Robert was.

"Go on!" he yelled.

A chorus of warped howling erupted all around her, and in a little tremor of lightning she saw Robert, but he was not alone; there was another man with him. It was Mr. Smith, the drummer, who was grinning and had a gun. He was holding it to Robert's head.

"GO!"

Eliza threw herself around the rock and against it. Grabbing and kicking at the side of the rock, she whined and muttered herself up to the top.

"Please," she wailed aloud, looking at the darkness in the direction where she had just seen the two men.

Then she turned to locate some path she should take. She could see nothing but dark shapes that went downward then up again. She sat on the rock and slid down, then pushed her way down and up the hill, struck by tree limbs, tugged on by bushes, grabbed by thorns. Then she heard gunfire behind her, one crack in the air that faded like smoke. She fell forward, whispering about her children and the coyotes, the gun and the rain. She stopped and listened for some sound to come from behind her, someone calling out maybe. She screamed, "Robert!" Nothing. Then, "Mr. Youngman," in case the drummer could hear, in case it would make any difference to the drummer that the man whose head he had held a gun to had a proper name. Nothing. "Aaron! Ruthie! You'll be all right. I'll get help," she called out so hard her voice cracked. Then she said to herself, "They'll be all right." She said this several times. She got to the top of a ridge and looked down.

There were indeed yellow lights at the bottom of that canyon. Heading down toward them, she fell and got up and then fell from tree to tree until she came to the slick, denuded opening that was a road around a sad assortment of ragged tents and cracked sheds. What did this remind her of? Why did her stomach turn seeing this? It was like the tents she'd seen as a child, in the field across from her school, the ones her father told her to stay away from, the tents the soldiers stayed in and called out to her from.

In the mining camp there were lights and shadows inside the tents. One of several shacks had light in its seams and shook a little with bursts of laughter and yelling.

⇒FIFTEEN⇐

*W*hen Eliza came through the crooked doorway, those inside the shack saw a woman made of water and mud, cuts and bits of mulch. They went silent. Eliza saw a small room full of sunburned white men and a few dark, serene men and women. In lantern light they were drinking from tin cups and glass bottles, playing cards or leaning on barrels. An old door placed across two barrels served as a bar on which a large, puffy, red-haired man leaned. On a bench against one wall a girl of about fourteen slumped, her smooth-brown face exuding fearlessness. She wore a Mexican blouse and a long, blue skirt which was hiked up over her knees, revealing bare legs and feet. Her hair was so dark it was almost invisible. She looked at Eliza as one slender hand brought a cigarette up to her lips.

A man with no front teeth said, "Lookee there!"

The girl narrowed her eyes as she drew on the dark cigarette, exposing the tan inside of her red-painted lips. She stared unwaveringly at Eliza.

"There's some trouble up there over the ridge. An Indian and some drummer from back east. My children are up there and a sick woman. I think somebody's been shot."

The man with no front teeth picked up a fiddle that was leaning against his chair and began to play a fast and merry tune, slightly out of key. One side of the smoking girl's mouth went up. The smoke had made her small corner of the room hazy.

The pudgy man behind the bar said, "For godssake, stop that racket, Rank." Then he said to Eliza, "Come on in, honey, come on in."

Tired faces watched Eliza.

"I've been looking for my children; they were taken and I think I know where they are. Up there, just over that ridge there. I need some help. Somebody needs to go on up there."

A card game between three Hispanic men resumed.

"There's an Indian like I said and a man with a gun and I ran down here. I need some help."

The card players said something in Spanish and laughed. The smoking girl smiled with one side of her mouth again and lifted her chin, still looking at Eliza.

"Is there a sheriff here?" Eliza asked her.

The toothless man pointed his fiddle bow at the man behind the bar and said, "Carter's the peace officer here."

"Yeah, I guess I am," he said.

Eliza looked around the room. Only the toothless man and Carter were paying any attention to her now. The card game and slow talk were squeezed into the small space. A man whose suspenders were stretched over stained longjohns and a pot belly was talking to the room about the problem with Texans. He couldn't see, he explained, much difference between the Texans and the Mexicans—both of them all fired up because they'd lost wars with the government of the United States. Both of them pretending like the wars weren't over so they wouldn't have to accept being losers—losers with guns, running around the territories, wearing hoods over their damn heads for one reason or another—that's what was wrong with the place—that's why people were getting shot all the time, some of them so stupid they shot their own selves in the foot, died of gangrene.

This monologue seemed to be familiar and tedious to the others in the room, who gave no response except to grin at each other, until the suspendered man turned to the Mexican girl and started a conversation with her in less public tones.

"Where are you from?" Carter, the bartender/peace officer, asked Eliza as he fingered the doorknob hole on the bar.

"What damn difference does it make where I'm from? I'm telling you that there are children up there with some crazy man. I'm from New Town."

One of the men playing cards looked up at her.

"I'm Mrs. Pelham. George Pelham is my husband. He works for the railroad."

The man who had looked up was eyeing his cards again, but he said to Eliza, "I know Señor Pelham."

Eliza turned to him.

"I need some help. I'm sure my husband would pay you."

The man lifted two cards out of his hand and put them on the table, taking two cards from the deck— the queen of diamonds and the ten of spades.

"I'm not in need of money," he said, and his companions showed their teeth.

Eliza leaned on their table and spoke into the man's face.

"I'm asking for help. Ayuda me, por favor—mis niños…"

They chuckled at her, and she swept the deck of cards off the table; some landed in the damp mud she had made by dripping on the dirt floor. The toothless man scurried from his table to pick them up. The men at the table kept looking at the cards in their hands.

Eliza stepped backward and slipped on the mud she'd created. She fell against the barrel behind her, and the toothless man steadied her with a hand around her upper arm.

Carter came from around the bar and said, "You want us to go traipsing around in the mountains you telling us some man's shooting people and there's an Indian up there? It's dark and still raining—we'd just git ourselves killed. Is that what you want?"

"I can't just leave my children up there," Eliza screamed. She was shivering.

"You need to go on back to New Town and get the sheriff there. I can't leave here to go wandering in the mountains. You got deputies in New Town. What're you doing out here by yourself anyway?"

"I wasn't by myself. I was with a friend and she and I met up with this Indian who was going to help…"

Eliza sank down onto a stool.

"Could I have a drink of whiskey or something? I'm shivering terribly."

"And you're turning this floor into soup here. You go on and get some dry clothes on. Go on in the shed next door. There's a tent right there with a shed built up against it. There's a woodstove in there and a cot. There's a trunk at the end of the cot. Go ahead and open it up and git out some pants and a shirt to put on. It ain't fashion, but it's dry. Now go on." He lifted her up by the arm and led her to the door.

"How am I going to get back to New Town? My horses have run off."

"Go on and change and I'll think it over. You go on and get out of those clothes."

Eliza shuddered and rubbed her own arms. She looked for the girl, but she and the man she'd been talking to were gone.

"Please, could I please have a drink of something to help me get warm? I don't have any money with me, but I'll owe you. My husband, George Pelham, will give it to you. You have my word."

Carter moved reluctantly behind the bar and poured her a small glass of brown whiskey with little bits of something floating in it. Eliza stood up unsteady like a newborn colt and got the glass off the bar. She took little sips, roiling the burning liquid around in her mouth.

"Go on now, honey. Maybe they're on their way home right now, or sleeping 'til morning when everything's gonna be all right. Jack's goin' into New Town tomorrow to pick up some supplies. Maybe he can take you on with him."

A man with a long, white braid down his back said, grinning, "Don't you go disturbin' Jack now, Carter." There was a general shifting of backsides and some snickering.

Outside, a few stars had come out. It wasn't raining. Eliza wanted to know how long it'd be before dawn. She looked for the moon and couldn't find it. Everything seemed to have slowed down and was about to come to a dry halt, and then fiddle music started up behind her as she went into the dark tent. Inside the tent, at the far end, a light came from the shed attached to it. A flap was partially raised to show the edges of crates and sacks. The faintest mist of white powder was in there and drifting around the open flap.

Eliza sat on the cot and stared. She quickly got up, remembering how wet she was. Her eyes were used to the dimness now, and she could see the trunk at the end of the cot. The slowness of the place had gotten into her skin and her brain, and she was unable to move with any decisiveness. But she took the dress off, slowly unbuttoning it and peeling it over her head. Her underwear was damp; she pinched at pieces of it and shook it away from her skin to dry it a little, to give herself time to think about what she was going to do next.

She could hear something bumping and didn't pay much attention to it until she realized that it was coming from the shed part of the structure. With her mouth partly opened she stood frozen and listening. The world seemed to have shifted absurdly— colors, shapes and noises that her mind couldn't digest, noises that she could only compare to the sound of rain and the one piercing gunshot.

She stepped closer to the flap and could hear now that someone was muttering. She kept walking, aware that her wet shoes made a slight squeaking noise. Near the opening she heard a man's voice. It said, "Is it too big, sweetheart? Is it too big?"

There was no answer to this question. Eliza put her hand over her heart and bent forward to see inside the shed. Again, the man said, "Is it too big?"

Eliza saw an ethereal cloud of pure white particles, a heavenly veil, and in the middle of it was the girl with the man who had been speaking with her in the bar. His suspenders were now lying on the ground around his ankles along with his pants. The girl was on her back on a pile of burlap sacks, her legs spread and her skirts lying across her flat belly. The man was standing between her legs and kept saying, "Is it too big?" as he rocked back and forth in and out of the girl. Her hands were gripping burlap sacks as the man started slamming against her. With every thrust, a puff of white flour shot up from one of the injured sacks.

The girl arched her back and moaned. The man laughed and said, "You like it; you like it big, don't you, little puta? Yeah, you like it big."

The movement became faster and faster, the breathing of the two seeming to spew out more of the white mist until they were like two angels riding through heaven, joined in holy intercourse.

"Damn big!" the man finally yelled, and then a "Yessir!" as he looked down at the place where they were joined.

The girl folded herself up and coughed.

Eliza backed away and heard the girl speak.

"You bring the food this morning. You tell my mother that I washed you clothes."

Pulling up his pants, the man said, "Honey, ain't nobody gonna believe these clothes have been washed."

Eliza kept walking backwards to the cot and sat down, shivering. The man and the girl walked out, leaving the lantern behind and paying no attention to her.

Eliza sat still, then shook her head, got up and opened the trunk. The cloud of flour slowly drifted from the shed toward Eliza. It was coming for her and would envelop her soon. She took out a pair of green pants and a brown shirt, exactly, she realized, like the clothes that man Carter was presently wearing. There were about three more sets of the same outfit.

She put on the pants, which were baggy and wide enough at the waist to fit another one of her in them. The shirt was also large, but she could roll the sleeves up.

She squatted in front of the trunk, feeling odd in the clothes. And she vaguely remembered that as a child she had worn pants to help her father with the horses. Yes, she remembered tying the pants on with rope and liking to jump down on the black horse from the fence, landing astride. She looked into the trunk, fishing for some rope or a belt of some kind. There was a packet of letters tied with a frail, brown ribbon. She held the bundle in her hand, turning it over, looking at the brown, spidery script on the envelopes. They were all addressed to Miss Caroline Carter. The letters seemed very important to Eliza. The weight of them, the unfamiliar handwriting of a stranger. And like a revelation in the midst of her exhausted, crazy mind, the curious thought occurred to her that other people had their own stories, their own lives that she knew nothing about but that must include some kind of pain, some separations, some wanting and not getting. She realized that Robert had told her something about his mother and Mozart, and that Bridie had talked about going home and yellow flowers. She put the letters back carefully, with gratitude for their having broken some kind of lock on her thinking. Her mind cleared a little for the first time since she'd come out of that cave. She even waved at the cloud of flour drifting around her and laughed about the ethereal fornication she'd witnessed.

She kept looking through the trunk, finding candles, several long, white candles connected in twos by their wicks. She slid her hand down one of them, squeezed it and then laid it back down. And in the bottom of the trunk, Eliza saw brown satin. She pulled out a dress, brown satin decorated with black brocade; the bodice was pleated and the sleeves great puffs that tapered into long, narrow tubes with brocade buttons at the wrist. Eliza held the dress up and in the diffused, white mist saw that it was made for a large woman. She folded the dress and put it back; she felt around more, under the dress, along the sides, hoping to find a gun. Then she closed the trunk and fell back on the cot. She was exhausted. She couldn't remember what she was like before coming into the mountains with Bridie. It was like her life before that had been somebody else's. Everything had changed—what she saw, what she felt, what she knew. She wanted to go back to New Town and find her children there, and George. And she wanted to take care of Bridie somehow, and she wanted to have another baby—a little girl. She just wanted to get on with things and stop wandering around. And she wanted to carry a gun. All the time. George would feel the gun on her when he held her, and George would laugh.

She tried to sleep, figuring that no one was going to do anything until daylight anyway. But she couldn't stop thinking about what she should do to make everything all right. Should she promise God that she would never have sex with Franz Schwartzchild again? That was easy. She couldn't imagine why she'd ever done it in the first place. Should she promise to go to church more often? Then the same old logic tangle came up—she knew full well that the women at the Episcopal church and the preacher, too, were not particularly virtuous, didn't have much in the way of inspirational integrity; but if God existed and He was moved by people like that just going to church and singing hymns, well, then she didn't have much respect for Him. Should she just try to be good and hope that if God existed He would help her? And what exactly did being good mean? If someone would tell her what it would take to be with her children again, safe, hearing their voices, seeing them, she would do it. If someone would tell her, but nobody would.

She would just get a gun and keep it with her. All the time.

"Christ almighty," she said.

Maybe she slept for a while. She didn't know where she was, when she felt someone shake her shoulder. There was no one there. She got up and rubbed her neck.

When she went back outside, holding up the pants with one hand, there was the dimmest grey cast to the world, a portent of dawn, coming as slowly as everything else. As everything became more visible, Eliza saw what a muddy heap the place was. Lean-to's, stained tents, pieces of chairs, old sacks, an empty tin of soda crackers were all stuck in the mud, derelict. A set of thin rails went to a black hole in the side of the mountain where a sad little cart sat just inside the opening.

In the makeshift saloon things were going on as usual, as though it didn't matter that the sun was coming up. The girl was back on the bench, smoking a cigarette. The toothless man looked defeated as he slumped over the table, caressing the neck of the fiddle. The three men were still playing cards, one hand lying out on the barrel top displayed a pair of queens.

Standing there holding up the pants, Eliza said to Carter, "Too big," and looked over at the girl, who laughed and coughed, holding the cigarette just beneath her eyes.

Carter got a coil of rope off the wall and cut it with a knife. He tied it around Eliza's waist and folded the top of the pants over it.

"It's getting light outside. I want someone to go on up and get my children. I can't just leave."

Jack, the suspendered man, spoke up. "Carter here says for me to take you on back to New Town with me."

"Can't anybody just go up there and see?"

One of the card players got up and stretched, careful not to expose the cards in his hand. Then he threw them face down on the table and said, "I'll take a look, Mrs. Pelham."

"Thank you," she said. "The little girl is named Ruthie, and the boy is Aaron." She repeated, "Aaron and Ruthie."

"You ready to go?" Jack asked.

She thought and then sighed. "I've left two saddlebags and a bunch of other stuff up there. I guess I'll never see them or those horses again. I guess I'll just get the dress, although it's pretty ruined."

The man said something to his friends in Spanish and took a few pennies from the table; then he said, "Jack, I want to have a word with Mrs. Pelham before you go."

He touched her waist to lead her out of the door.

When they were outside, the light had brightened and a group of little, round birds were pecking at the mud a few yards away.

Eliza now saw that the man was young, perhaps only about twenty, and he had a big forehead and heavy, dark eyebrows.

He reached in his pocket and brought out what she thought was a handkerchief.

"Their names are Ruthie and Aaron," Eliza said. "I thank you for going to look for them. Everything has gotten plumb crazy and I want them back with me."

He nodded and took her wrist and turned her hand palm up. He pressed the cloth into her hand and said, "Give this to your husband for me. Tell him he should perhaps wear it himself."

She looked down into her hand and the cloth unfolded; she held it up as the man walked away. It was an old five-pound flour sack with two eye holes cut in it.

When Jack was stuffing her wet dress into his saddlebag, Eliza got up on the horse and looked back over her shoulder at the ridge she had come down hours before.

"I don't know as I should leave," she said.

But she did, feeling certain that she could go into that place any time, day or night, and see the same people in the same places, the same card game, the same girl smoking a cigarette.

"Maybe they'll come down here for help," she told Jack.

But she had a feeling that if Ruthie and Aaron did come down the ridge and into the camp, they would pass through the tents and the people like ghosts, while the girl just kept smoking.

✦SIXTEEN✦

*J*ack smelled bad. Eliza was riding in front of him and was actually grateful for the comfort of his big belly, but the stains on the longjohn sleeves and the general odor of sour milk that he exuded made her angry. She was getting angrier and angrier as moment piled on moment and the horse seemed to be walking as slowly as it was possible to walk without coming to a complete halt.

Daylight made things seem better, less dangerous. What could be dangerous in the breezeless blue sky and the playful combination of trees, bushes and grass along the road? Bad things happened at three in the morning, not in singing daylight. Everything seemed to be humming, except for that nagging feeling that Eliza occasionally had to articulate to herself. She was without her children; she didn't know where they were or how they were. She couldn't do a damn thing to help them or Robert or Bridie. Then she wanted to turn around and push Jack off and ride the horse to New Town at a gallop the whole way. It would be easy to go fast wearing pants.

She kicked her legs against the horse's side and Jack said, "Hey, what're you doing?"

"I'm trying to get this damn horse to go faster."

Jack cleared his throat and spat. He made noises that were exclamations of things he was saying to himself. He urged the horse into a trot, but after a minute let it fall back into a walk. Eliza suspected that Jack was dozing. She kept seeing Robert with the gun to his head and kept hearing that shot. She was exhausted and everything seemed to be made of jiggling dots. She tried to imagine Aaron's face and couldn't make it appear unless she saw him as he'd been on the wagon train, coming into the wagon where she was lying after the baby had been born. And he just looked at her for the longest time. And she had gone over his face for every detail, including the little scars, the circles within circles that were mementos of the pox he'd had. He'd said, "It's all right, Momma, she's in heaven." She could imagine his face perfectly when she thought of him saying that. He wouldn't say that kind of thing now. He was growing up. She loved him as a baby, as a toddler, and she loved him now; she loved all the little boys he'd been and was.

A memory came to her of the time the wagon train was in Kansas camped by a brackish water hole that smelled like manure. All the wagons were looking dirty and crooked at this point; all the women's skirts were weighted down with mud hems. Hair flew out of bonnets in drifting tendrils. Noses and cheeks were red. There was that Negro domestic who'd attended the birth, a thin girl with reddish hair and a limp, who often amused Ruthie by calling her "Miss Gallivantin" and walking her fingers over the toddler's face and head. Eliza could see the woman's long, beautiful fingers, dark on one side and creamy, light skinned on the inside, and Ruthie's face, pale even then when everybody else's was sunburnt. Little Ruthie would just stand and giggle, squinching one shoulder up and pressing her cheek against it. Is this how Ruthie would be as a grown woman when a man, when a lover, tickled her? Or was Ruthie never going to grow up? Was Ruthie dead? Who was this man, this drummer who took away children? Why was she supposed to get out of New Town for a day? She thought, "I'd be willing to get out of New Town for a lifetime."

She shifted, sitting forward and subtly trying to urge the horse to go faster. But owner and animal seemed to have some bond— an agreement about not hurrying or working up too much of a sweat in life. Jack was talking about something, where he was from, why he'd come out here from Ohio, how he'd been too young to fight in the war. Eliza didn't listen. She was trying to justify a hope that everything was going to be all right. That in all this violence and madness her children were all right, and maybe she could just go to sleep for a long time, knowing that they were all right.

She and Aaron and Ruthie had after all made it all the way from Missouri; they'd been the best, least complaining family on the wagon train. Most of the other women had some complaint, showed their fear; some went almost crazy with grief and fear. When they got together, they fretted about getting sunred or ruining their dresses. They expected Eliza to completely fold up and pray all day and night when the baby died; but when she got up the next day and said she just wanted to walk in the open air, some said she was acting like a squaw, which was supposed to be an insult. That was all right; Eliza kept quiet. And it seemed that the whole Eliza only showed up when she was with Ruthie and Aaron; it was as though she'd hid the joyful part of her inside them. And without them?...What about when they grew up and went off on their own? What about if she never saw them again?

No, that couldn't be. It could not be.

Maybe Jack had some liquor. Maybe this damn horse was going to go so damn slow it would die and decay right in the road with them on it.

She kicked at the horse's sides saying, "Come on!" The horse skipped backwards a bit and Jack pulled her to a stop.

"What's wrong with you?" he asked.

"Nothing. Don't stop, for godssake. We're going slow enough as it is."

He shifted, making the leather of the saddle squeak.

"Well, I don't want to push her. I don't want to push her with all this weight on her back. I don't want her to get muscle lame."

"My daddy raised horses, and I think I know a little more about what a horse can take than you do if you think this one is going to go lame if it moves faster than an ant."

A bird screeched somewhere as though it had been pinched. Everything was still, waiting. A sagging, yellowing cholla on the edge of the dirt road was the only pathetic-looking thing in the landscape. Eliza wanted to get down and kick it.

The groaning man slid off the horse. He whipped up a tan piece of grass and put it in his mouth. Eliza sat back in the saddle and held the reins.

Jack didn't look at her but stomped at the ground in a concentrated way, as if he'd been hired to tamp down the dirt in various places along the road. This sight put a lethal hostility into Eliza. She sighed and adjusted her spectacles.

Jack looked up the road, squinting his eyes.

"Look, I haven't got time to sit around and admire the weather. I've got to get on and see about my children. There's somebody maybe murdered up there."

Jack laughed.

"There's somebody murdered all the time, two or three a day around here like I was saying."

"Fine. Well, I just don't want my children to get hurt."

"Like I was saying, Texans just don't want to admit they lost the war." He was off on his favorite topic, his reason for being, besides his big penis, as far as Eliza could figure. She'd already heard a piece of this speech in the mining camp.

"They want to keep on shootin' 'til they feel like they won. They come out to places like this where the law's a little loose and keep fightin', shootin' at anything makes 'em mad. War's not over. It'll never be over. They tell their kids about it so they'll keep fightin'. It won't be over 'til they're all dead, or they feel like they've won. They're even dressin' up like ghosts, runnin' around killin' niggers 'cause they're so mad about losin'. You got to kill people, wipe 'em out completely or let 'em win. You let the losers go, and the ones that don't kill themselves one way or another will keep on shootin'. If they admit the war's over, they got to admit who the loser is. Hell, I never met one Texan who'd walk up and say, 'Yessir, I'm a loser.' "

"What're you talking about?" Eliza said. "I don't have time for this."

He looked at her with pity, for being like the others who didn't have sense enough to know that he'd figured out what was wrong with everything.

"Same with Mexicans. It's been forty years since they lost, and they're doin' the same, pardon me, damn thing as the Texans. (Eliza got that to him the term *Texan* was synonymous with the term *Confederate*.) Still fightin', wearin' hoods over their faces like the Texans, only instead of hangin' niggers, they're shootin' white men—ranchers." Eliza remembered about the white hood the man back at the mining camp had given her to give to George. She thought of putting it on and shooting Jack. But getting his gun would be a battle, and she didn't see herself as the type of person to go around killing a man for talking too much.

"After a war's done there are a lot of guns around and people not wantin' to put 'em down. If I were a lady, I wouldn't live out here, I'll tell you that. I'd go back to Boston or Philadelphia and sit and make doilies. This place is where wars go when they're over somewhere else. It ain't no place for women and children, not yet. Look what it's done to you—sittin' up there dressed like a man, ridin' a horse like that."

"If I were to take your horse, Jack," Eliza said as calmly as possible, as though this might be a hypothetical point relating to his speech, "it wouldn't be stealing, because I would tell you that I'm just going to borrow it and you can get it later in New Town just asking for Eliza or George Pelham. And I'd take care of it for you and even pay you a little something for the use of it whenever you came to fetch it."

He looked up at her thinking, she was going to say more, because he wasn't really following her yet.

She leaned forward on the horse and it stepped back a few steps. Then she lifted her elbows and knees and kicked its sides yelling, "Come on!" The animal was startled and pranced back-wards; the man reached toward it with his mouth opening to say something. The horse went into a trot. The man yelled, "Hey!" Then the horse cantered.

"Hey!" the man yelled a few more times until he was very small and his voice was hardly as loud as the horse's breathing.

She sat tightly for a few minutes to make sure that the man was far behind, invisible, nonexistent. Worries passed through her mind, visions of trouble, such as Jack accusing her of horse stealing and getting others to come after her. Such as men shooting at her from a distance, unaware that she was a woman. In her foggy exhaustion her mind mused over each notion and got mixed in with some of the things Jack had been talking about. She figured that it was a huge privilege to be a woman in the sense that one was not shot at. So maybe whereas freedom to a lot of men was being able to have a gun they could shoot, to women it was being able to not be shot at.

She was exhausted and aching in her skin, wanting everything but the horse to stop so she could figure things out.

She heard her father laughing. She heard him as she passed under a tree and could swear he was up in its branches, shaking his fist in the air as a sign of defiant allegiance with her. He liked to see her riding that horse so fast, annoyed with the world. What was he doing here, she wondered. This whole experience could be unreal, she thought—Jack and all his talk and the mining camp all seemed like some kind of weird performance by actors or spirits playing a trick on her.

She was in a parable maybe—about a woman who is not a good mother—or maybe there was no moral, no lesson but that the world was nothing but one pain after another, chasing you down like dogs after a rabbit. The world and all its barking noise and chaos followed you no matter where you went, came crashing around the corner on trains and wagons, a raucous circus of dogs and people leaning out of windows, holding dollars, goods and trinkets spilling out of their mouths, out of crates and carpetbags.

She needed sleep. She told herself she'd better watch it in New Town, remain calm and sensible and not seem too strange. She needed food. It'd be nice to have a drink to stimulate her, help her think and soothe that ache in her skin. She slowed down the horse and patted the saddlebag. But she was already pretty sure that there was no liquor in it.

At one point, the exhaustion and heat met in a condensed desire for a hat that seemed more important than any other thought. Eliza remembered that it was like this on the wagon train too—little things becoming crucially important—a drink of clean water, a clean pair of knickers, a night's supply of dry firewood. There was an aliveness to living this way, to fully enjoying and celebrating the smallest thing. The hardship was okay as long as it didn't feel like punishment. And now it was a hat that had become the most desirable luxury in the world, because it would keep the sun from scorching the face and neck; it would shade the eyes. If she had a hat and her children and if George would stay with her a little while, she'd be all right. Everything would be so all right that she'd feel like singing.

Her father's ghost stood behind her on the road, his arms hanging sadly at his side, his clothes dripping water. The silence was a baby not crying, was a boy's mouth shot off so he couldn't scream.

All right, she wouldn't sing.

She turned up the collar of the shirt. The horse pranced now.

She thought—as she could no longer focus well on the land-scape, and as she started seeing the movements of lizards every-where—that she hadn't heard the children back up there in the rain when the gun went off. Maybe they'd been sent home. Maybe all this would be over as though it had never happened, and they'd be at home, sitting at the table.

She lay down on the horse who shook his neck a little, unused to such a feeling on his back. From a distance, to the left where the line of trees marked the river running parallel to her, Eliza saw someone walking across the flat land—a dark, striding figure—a woman wearing a black dress. She kept walking until she met Eliza and the horse on the road. She spoke to the animal soothingly in Spanish. Her shawl slipped from her shoulders often and Eliza saw how beautiful the woman's hand was when she pulled the black wool back up. Eliza didn't know how long the woman walked with her; she dozed and awakened occasionally when the horse jumped because the woman had suddenly laughed. When the road turned past the Apache plume bushes and ran beside adobe homes, the woman said, "Buenos días," and walked off.

⇢SEVENTEEN⇠

*E*liza could see the captain's walk on the top of Mrs. Fogharty's boarding house and wondered what ocean one could see from that walk, what sea captain, when the nearest ocean was a thousand miles away. Eliza slowed the horse to its comfortable walk and gave some thought to the order in which she would do things. She sighed deeply because the next few hours were going to require more energy. She would get looks because of the way she was dressed. She would get a lot more than looks from the sheriff when he noted that she was not riding one of his horses. At least her worries about her children had simmered to a necessary conviction that they were back home—that everything was going to be all right.

The first person she came upon was Clarence. He was sitting on the sidewalk in front of the depot, bent over and blubbering like a baby, his face soaked with drool and tears. Eliza did not want to acknowledge him and neither did the other people who walked past him, looking down in disgusted puzzlement. At least they weren't looking at her. She got off the horse and walked it up to the jailhouse, around the corner from Schwartzchild's store. She tied it to the beam that held up a flimsy overhang and started to go in, thinking of how she would break the news to the sheriff about his horses. But she was acutely bothered by Clarence's bawling. She took a step and almost tripped, because the sole of her shoe was coming loose and had folded back.

"Damn," she whispered, and her fist fell against her thigh. She walked up to Clarence and squatted in front of him.

"Come on, Clarence, get on up and go home."

He looked up at her with pink, watery eyes.

She put her arm around him to lift him up, but he leaned into her, sobbing. Her own tears got drawn out by his weeping. Someone walked by; she could feel the boards shake with the clomping, but Eliza stayed there, crying with Clarence and telling him, "Don't worry, Clarence. Don't you worry."

"Come on," she said, lifting him up. He stumbled forward, sniffling, and kept walking west.

When she turned the corner again, Deputy Salas was standing next to the horse she'd ridden in on and was shaking his head. There was a faint smile on his lips.

"Mrs. Pelham?" he said, raising his eyebrows at her. "You look like you've had an adventure." He pushed his hat back and smoothed his moustache.

"I'm not here to entertain you with stories, Mr. Salas, but I've had a very hard time, and yes, I've lost track of the sheriff's horses, and I came by here first to let him know and tell him I'll make it up."

He couldn't help but laugh.

"He's in the courthouse."

"I was up looking for Aaron and Ruthie, with Bridie—there was a man up there, too, an Indian who helped me. That drummer put a gun to his head and I had to leave."

Did her words make any sense?

She sighed and went on: "Bridie said something about somebody wanting me out of town. Do you know anything about anybody wanting me out of town and why?" She examined the deputy's face so hard that she stumbled forward. He caught her by the elbow.

"You ought to go home, Mrs. Pelham," he said. "The sheriff will be back and he'll know what to do. You just go on home. Maybe the children are already back there."

"I told this man at the mining camp…" she said, aware that the deputy's hand was still on her elbow. "He said he'd…maybe he got them." She pulled the cloth out of her pocket and dangled it in front of the deputy's face. "He gave me this to give to George. I'm worried about what bandits have to do with me and my family."

Deputy Salas's mouth was moving in an odd way, making his moustache twitch up and down. He looked around and said quietly, "Put that back in your pocket, Mrs. Pelham. You should go on home and wait for your children. I will tell the sheriff."

But just looking at the deputy and thinking about the sheriff and his long beard at the courthouse, Eliza knew that neither man, nor any official in town, was going to do anything helpful. It was as though she could see all their sullen faces, secretive, quiet, pre-occupied, lined up before her, motionless.

Eliza nodded to herself. She untied the horse and got back on.

The piano in Near and Anderson's started a tinkling tune, accompanied by bursts of riotous women's laughter.

"If you see George or the children," Eliza said, "would you come tell me right away?"

Salas squinched up his mouth and looked at the ground. "I will, Mrs. Pelham. I will come and tell you if there is any news."

Then he stepped back and nodded, "Con dios."

"When the sheriff gets back, tell him about the horses too."

The deputy laughed as he nodded.

She saw the sheriff coming out of the courthouse as she passed it, his long beard tilted and his face concentrated on a conversation he'd just left. Eliza was glad he didn't see her, and she kept riding toward home. She passed a woman from the church who knew her, and Eliza could now be sure that within five minutes the whole town would know that she'd come back alone, wearing men's clothes, without the sheriff's horses.

When she was within sight of home, her first perception was that things were very askew somehow. It took her a few seconds to realize what she was seeing; it came down to the fact that half of the house was burned down. The horse stopped, sensing that its rider was at the end of the trail. Eliza rocked back and forth in the saddle.

"God in heaven," she said.

The woodstove was just sitting out under the blue sky, waiting for the tender blossoming of the night's first, pale stars.

Eliza tied the horse to a small box elder about fifty yards from the house, wanting to approach it on her own, slowly. The outhouse was absurdly visible where it had once been behind the house.

The birds, interested only in calculations of territory and eating, chirped and glided, except for three crows who watched Eliza with bored attention.

"Aaron? Ruthie?"

Her children did not answer, and the horror before her was a new thing to contemplate and handle. She walked around, noting that, besides the fire, someone had knocked the charred adobe walls down. There was rubble and dirt and black mess everywhere. She touched a burned lump of wood that had once been part of a table.

"Cold," she said. She stood several minutes and moved her head to see what had been destroyed. "Damn," she kept saying, then, "I don't know. I just don't know."

The bedroom was still intact. The bed was still there. A bottle of liquor was still underneath it. She uncorked it, her hands so shaky that the cork fell to the floor. She started to get up and get a teacup from the other room. But then again, there was no other room anymore. She drank from the bottle, first putting her tongue into it and just feeling the warm sting. Then she drank in little sips, counting them, one, two, three, four, five—past twenty, until there was nothing left in the bottle but sighing fumes. The bed screeched quietly as Eliza lay down on it, draping one leg over the side, staring at the ceiling. She intended to think things through and then do something, but instead she fell into a very still, deep sleep.

When she woke in the middle of the night, someone was in the doorway that now opened onto the universe and the slow journey of stars. A black portion of this universe shaped like a woman broke away and came into the room. As she sat on the bed, she caused the metal springs to screech again. Eliza lifted her head and said, "Bridie?"

But the woman was black haired.

She took Eliza's spectacles from her face and folded them gently, putting them on the pillow beside Eliza's head. She stroked her hair and sang a song in Spanish, whispered it.

Drugged by the rose perfume in the woman's hair and the smell of cinnamon that came from her mouth with the song, Eliza could not move and fell back into sleep, fell with a violent twitch and then careened deeply into unconsciousness. She kept wanting to wake, to look for her children, to go back to the mountains, but at times during the night it was as though the woman was sitting on her chest and Eliza could not move.

✦EIGHTEEN✦

A crunching sound, mashing hard bits, steps that made a black and ashy sound—and her eyes opened. She didn't recognize her own legs, separately encased in cloth. She put her spectacles on and recognized the trousers. Then she moved on to the realization that someone was stepping on the burned rubble in what used to be the other room. It couldn't be the woman from the night before because the steps were heavy, plodding and coarse. If it was the drummer...

Eliza knew that if she tried to slide off the bed and sneak up on him, the damned springs would screech like a crow and he'd be in at her before she could kick. So she lay still and studied the room for a weapon. It came down to a choice between some toilet water on the dresser, that she could throw into somebody's eyes, or the stringless banjo. Quickly figuring that a woman wielding a bottle of cologne didn't look particularly dangerous, she decided on the banjo, even though she hated the idea of damaging it. The strings could, after all, come in any day now.

In a fast and smooth motion, Eliza bounced off the bed, grabbed the banjo and leaped to the doorway holding it like an axe over her head.

"George," she said, because her husband was standing there. He kicked at a charred tin and held his brown curls back with one large, calloused hand at the top of his forehead.

"What happened?" he said. He was sucking in his cheeks, that were bristling with two day's growth of multicolored whiskers. She knew this expression, this state of sucked-in cheeks, as one of supreme irritation, usually with her. This was the George she didn't want to see, especially when he looked so frustratingly much like the George she did want to see.

She had imagined that when she saw George again it would be a time of emotional reconciliation in the face of their mutual hardship—the absence of their children—and in consideration of her private decision to stop lying down with Franz Schwartzchild. She had seen them, in this picture, embracing, silently holding one another, passionately whispering their devotion. But they stayed at a distance like two cats.

"I don't know," she said.

"Why are you wearing trousers?" he said, as though he was weary with the amount of chaos that could occur without him there to control things.

Eliza felt that old weepiness that only George, too often capable of being the moon of her tides, could draw from her. She brushed her hair back from her face and over the top of her head; the banjo was hanging down in her hand.

"Is that all you're concerned about, George, what I'm wearing? Don't you want to know about Aaron and Ruthie, who've been carried off by some crazy drummer?"

"I just want to know what's going on." He picked up a piece of chair leg and threw it hard against the stove. The clang made Eliza's mind jump into a reverie on the past few days; and now her vision of herself was of a victim; seeing George, she now felt that she had endured unnatural and insurmountable discomforts and anxieties that no one cared about. And George was standing there looking irritated.

"What do you want to know?" she said a little shakily. "There's a lot to tell."

"Some drummer took them off?"

"That's all I know. I tried to follow them up into the mountains. Some Indian up there came on the drummer, and he had a gun and I had to run off. Bridie was up there too. I don't know what happened after that."

"What did this drummer have to do with Aaron and Ruthie?"

Eliza wanted to smash the banjo against the wall, so she let go of it to lean against the wall instead. She wanted to smell George's neck, too, to lay her face against it and have him stroke her back. But he was the inquisitor George.

"I don't know, George. I don't know. Emily Schwartzchild says he just wanted to take them hunting up there. I don't know."

"Sheriff says you lost his horses."

She looked up to the sky, seeing any hope of George comforting her floating away like cottonwood seed. "What happened?" she remembered him saying after the baby died. The wrong George was back; she was getting smaller by the minute.

Still she tried to defend herself to keep herself from shrinking down to nothing.

"I haven't done anything wrong, George. They're my kids too. I've been trying to find them while you were God knows where."

"I was working."

"You're always working."

They stood not looking at each other.

"What're we going to do?" she said.

"The sheriff and me are going to go up there where you said they went. We're going to go on up and see if we can find them."

How was it possible for her to now feel that everything, the fire and everything, was all her fault?

"I'm worried about Bridie, too, and that Indian. He might have been shot."

He finally looked up at her. The sun cut across his face and lit up one eye, making the iris look like brown quartz.

"You know what's odd?" she said. "I'm hungry. I forgot to eat for maybe two days. I guess I shouldn't be thinking about food with Aaron and Ruthie out there and I don't know what's happened to them." She squatted down and hit the ground with her fist; her braid moved in and out of the sunlight every time she pounded.

"I don't think I can live, George, I don't think I can live if they're dead. You don't know what I've been through."

He stepped over the rubble, crunching things again, and she thought maybe he was coming toward her, that he was going to circle her with his suntanned arms and she could breathe his smell as he stroked her hair. But he was walking away, out the door frame that had no walls.

Eliza followed him to his horse.

"What did I do wrong?" she wept. "Why won't you touch me?" She kicked the ground, furious at what she became with him.

He put his foot into the stirrup. He stopped for a minute, and the horse, confused, moved so that he had to hop beside her.

"They missed you, George. Aaron kept asking about you, when you were coming home." She was holding herself, rubbing her own arms as though she was cold. It was warm and still out, though.

As though she'd opened a drawer of other things to say, he put his foot back on the ground.

"What did you do, Eliza? Why weren't you with them? Were you drinking?" He spoke with his head cocked to one side and his hands on his hips. He was nodding his head up and down and then shaking it. She wanted to touch the hair foaming up out of his shirt collar.

She went to him. For a few seconds he kept his hands on his hips as she put hers around his waist and her face against his neck. His skin was warm and the smell familiar, yet she could never say exactly what it was, maybe a combination of sweat and cigarette smoke, but something sweet too. When he finally held her, he said into her hair, "I don't want anything bad to happen to them. They're just kids. So many bad things happen out here."

"I know," she said. "Maybe when we find them we should go back to Kentucky, or maybe up to Boston with your uncle."

"And things aren't going well for me. I mean, there've been some financial deals that are going bad. I've got enough to worry about already. I don't need this."

She parted from him, stepped back and crossed her arms over her chest.

"You haven't said one thing about what *I've* been through, George, not one thing."

She had the sensation that she and George had shrunk to crow size somehow.

"You're not the only one that has troubles," he countered, and they were separate entities again, suspicious, cautious.

"There was some man here from Mr. Catron's office in Santa Fe, talking about land buying and looking over everything."

"Oh, yeah. Yeah. That's just something…" He cleared his throat and took out a small tin with some worn orange lettering on it underneath a picture of a palm tree. He slid the top open and took out a hand-rolled cigarette. He put it in his mouth, looking around, assessing the fire damage calmly, as though this hadn't ever been any house of his. He took a match out of the same tin and tried to light it on the bottom of his boot. When that didn't work he just dropped the dead match on the ground and put the cigarette back in the tin. All this time Eliza just looked away into the breeze so that her hair didn't bother her face.

"You better give that horse some water and put it in some shade."

Eliza looked with him at Jack's horse, still tied up to the little box elder.

"I know, George. I know how to take care of horses."

"How did all this happen?"

"I don't know."

He walked out of sight back where the outhouse was. Then he called out, "Ellie."

She walked around and saw him squatting, the unlit cigarette between his lips again and another match in his hands.

"Did you see this?"

She came around and stood behind him. He struck the match against the wall and, narrowing his eyes, lit the cigarette and shook the match out.

He breathed out the smoke and pointed with the cigarette between his fingers at a cross with beams of light coming out of it drawn on the side of the house with a piece of charcoal.

"What's this?" he asked.

"I don't know," she said. "I didn't see it. I've been asleep since I came in yesterday."

He stood up and stretched, inhaling from the cigarette while still arching his back.

"Maybe somebody's trying to tell us to go to church," he said looking at the wall; then he looked at Eliza and grinned. "Come here," he said. And she put her whole body against his, pulled closer by his arm, at the end of which the cigarette smoked.

"I don't know why you're so calm," she said. "I'm feeling jittery about everything. My mind is like a hundred cats tied together."

"You look funny in those trousers," he said.

"I'll wait here. Maybe he'll bring them back here today."

"Well, I guess I'd better be going on. I don't think there's anything to worry about, Ellie. He probably just wanted free help with the hunting, from what I've heard. People are saying you just got too crazy about nothing."

"He held a gun against this Indian's head, somebody who was trying to help me. I don't care what he wanted. He took them off without telling me. That isn't right, is it?"

"They could have been here, Eliza." His face muscles tightened. "They could have been in the damn fire."

"I know, I know," Eliza said.

She watched him get on the horse and canter away and then went to the outhouse. Sitting in the dark she could see the cross through the cracks between the boards. It was well drawn, very straight lines—even the rays of light. It had not been done carelessly or quickly. She remembered about Manuel and Aaron getting into trouble for going into the morada. Then she looked into the corners of the outhouse and counted eight daddy longlegs before she ripped off a piece of newspaper. She crumpled it up over and over again, getting it soft. Then she threw it on the floor and got the cloth, the sack with the eye holes cut in it, out of her pocket. She wiped herself with it, a luxury, and let it fall into the hole. This seemed a defiant act to her; it gave her courage to admit that she was glad George was back and doing something.

Outside in a kind light, muted by wispy clouds, she got a bucket of water at the pump and took it for the horse to drink. She explained to the animal how fired up its owner would be if she let it die of thirst. She led the horse to the cottonwoods where there was some grass and tied it up there. It occurred to her that the black-and-white dog wasn't around. Was she in the house, burned up? Eliza didn't want to think about that. She undid the saddle, still talking to the horse about its owner, and just dropped the saddle and the blankets on the ground nearby, figuring if the man came for his horse, his gear would be right there. She went to take a look at the chickens, who were roosting in the coop; the rooster wasn't anywhere around. She threw some seed around on the chicken coop floor and left, saying they could keep their eggs for a while longer. Then she walked to town.

She took unusually long strides, aware of how walking was different, easier. Then she remembered that she was wearing pants.

"Damn," she said, because she didn't want to go all the way back to the house, so she thought about how she would say that all her clothes got burned up in the fire, although that wasn't true, since her clothes were in a box under her bed. She was also annoyed with her shoes, because the detached sole kept getting bent back as she walked. A few years ago maybe this disheveled version of herself could pass through New Town and be considered some necessity of the frontier—a wife left alone to do her own and her man's work. But since the railroad and the Episcopal church, there were fewer acceptable versions of a lady's appearance: baggy trousers and torn-up shoes were not one of them.

A man was selling cattle in the big livestock opening in the railroad yard. A crowd of about twenty was watching him as he leaned against one of the cows and spoke. Eliza saw George's horse tied up in front of the dancehall. That was all right, she thought. He knows what he's doing. She strode, taking the two steps as one, into Schwartzchild's store.

She stopped just inside the door which was held open by a big stone, painted blue. The tan dog that belonged to the bank manager but wandered around town all day lifted his head and thumped the floor with his tail.

The sense that she was the focus of a huge joke, of a joke so huge that it was going to explode and take the whole world with it, swept over Eliza like heat when she walked into Schwartzchild's establishment. Schwartzchild's humble store, the dank little place in which people got what they needed on credit, had metamorphosed. It had been transformed in three days by what? By elves? Prussian elves singing Prussian songs, wagging their little hats? More likely by a much bigger thing, by the train and by what came in on the train: things, goods, materials of civilization in neat and plentiful celebration of the miracle of American industry. Blessed bounty and amazing grace—there were things for sale that people had to take weeks, even months to make—things they had never even known they needed. A raucous plentitude of goods was in and on stacks of boxes, filling the once-pathetic shelves, in and on barrels—seven jars of multicolored candy where there had only been one jar of yellow; bolts of cloth that included wools and silks; tins with orange blossoms and smiling children's faces on them; whole, finished dresses gracing the fine figures of headless women; shoes, hats, caps, tinware, crockery; a petite Pennsylvania Dutch table with three kinds of writing paper on it and envelopes to match; tools, glassware; and a whole new display case with one thin crack across one of its windows, full of happy little bottles of perfume, medicinal elixirs and oils. To one side of the counter was an easel astride a box full of paints and brushes. And in the middle of all this, like a bug in the petals of a rose, was Emily, still dark and sullen.

As Eliza looked at all this, she had the distinct feeling that her children had somehow been traded for it, that if they returned the goods would disappear. Or, as in some eerie fairy tale, her children had crumbled into many pieces and been transformed into dry goods and sundries.

Seeing Eliza transfixed near the door, Emily did not move either, except to press her lips together a little more tightly as an expression of impatient pride.

The dog leapt up suddenly and chewed furiously at its hind leg.

The little steps going upstairs to the storage area creaked as Franz came down them and into the room. He had to bend his head down to clear the doorway, and he nodded to Eliza at the same time.

"Mrs. Pelham," he said. He looked around to see if anyone else had noticed this woman wearing trousers, but Emily was the only other person in there.

Eliza bought two apples and a tin of Dr. Peterson's soda crackers. Franz stood by his wife as Eliza handed her a nickel and two pennies.

"Who burned my house?" Eliza let the food she'd bought sit on the counter.

"Your house vas burnt?" Franz brushed at the counter with his hand.

"Tank Got dat your children were not in der," Emily said. Her liver-colored lips stretched out in a thin smile.

Franz threw up his hands and said, "It's doz Mexicans. I'm telling you, dey should have all been killed."

Emily put her hand out toward him but did not touch him.

He brought up a gun and wagged it at Eliza sideways.

"I am telling you, you should get a gun. Ya, I am telling you."
His face was getting red.

"It wasn't a Mexican who took my children."

Emily looked at the backs of her own hands and laid one on
top of the other on the counter.

"I tink dat whoever took your kids saved dem from a terrible
fire, Mrs. Pelham. God vorks in mysterious vays."

The dog's tail thumped against the floor.

"Things sure have changed in here," Eliza said.

Franz raised his chin and looked around.

"Ya. Tings haf changed. Ve're not so backvards in New Town
anymore, ya?"

Eliza took one of the apples and put it in her pocket. She
carried the tin of crackers and bit into the other apple as she
walked out. Franz followed but then just stood in the doorway and
watched Eliza walk away.

George's horse wasn't in front of the dancehall anymore, so
Eliza could stop in and pick up a bottle of liquor. Katie gave it to
her and asked about Bridie.

"She'll be coming in with Aaron and Ruthie," Eliza said, and
Katie nodded.

All the way home, Eliza had the sensation that somebody was
following her, but she turned and saw nothing but the bleak
landscape of the town behind her, and the vast plains where the
squat and twisted midget junipers could be mistaken for frozen
buffalo from a distance.

Jack's horse had wound part of the rope around its front legs.
Eliza untangled it, saying, "How'd you get yourself so tangled up?"
Then she heard a noise and stood up.

"Aaron? Ruthie?"

But it was only the noise of ghosts, spirits, wind or birds,
something oblivious and preoccupied.

When Eliza was sitting on the chair she'd brought out from
the bedroom and was finishing off the crackers, she saw, to her

despair, Clarence coming up the road toward her. His arms were slightly raised up from his side, and his fingers were moving as though playing flutes. She shouldn't have been nice to him, she thought. Now he'd dog her wherever she went.

He stopped a few yards away and began furiously picking his nose, making a real drama out of it, whining a little in frustration and finally flicking away whatever he'd gotten on his fingers and rubbing his hand on his pants. He took two steps forward.

"I was born in Missouri," he said to Eliza from a distance.

"Okay, Clarence."

"I got bad eyesight."

"That's okay, Clarence."

He took a coin out of his pocket and held it close to his face while he looked at it from as many angles as his fingers could maneuver.

"My daddy got shot right here." He put his finger on his forehead. "He was in the war. He got shot right here."

Eliza stood up.

"You better come on into town," Clarence said.

"Why?"

She caught sight of Deputy Salas riding up the road on a brown mule.

Clarence leaned on one hip, a pose he'd seen in an advertisement for men's hats, and said, "Mrs. Pelham, you better come on into town, Mrs. Pelham."

She brushed the crumbs off her lap, slowly following Clarence, who kept looking back at her and saying, "My feet hurt."

Deputy Salas met them on his mule. He said to Eliza, "Your children are back."

For a second this made no sense to Eliza.

"Where?"

"The girls at Near's are looking after them."

Then her muscles, her will, her senses wanted to bust out through her skin.

"Dear God in heaven," she said, and she ran past the deputy and Clarence, who was shielding his head with his arms.

She ran, saying over and over again, "Dear God in heaven." There was a crowd in Railroad Avenue, some were milling around the door of the dancehall; about fifty people in the street a few yards to the west were yelling and talking. The deputy's wife, Señora Salas, was there in the crowd, straining her neck to see something in the middle of the people; she wasn't saying anything; she was holding the cross she wore around her neck in her fist. Her son was beside her, picking up stones. She looked around and nodded when her eyes met Eliza's as Eliza ran up the steps and into the dancehall.

Manuel tapped frantically at his mother's arm and pointed to Eliza's trousered legs as they disappeared into the dark doorway.

"Entiendo, mi hijo," she said as she straightened his collar.

Many odd things happened these days. Many secret and odd things.

✦NINETEEN✦

*B*oth Aaron and Ruthie were sitting at a table near the door. Someone had gotten them mugs of sweet, brown soda. Ruthie was kicking against the chair legs in a rhythm that seemed to have everyone transfixed. Aaron held his glass in both hands but just looked at what was in it. No one was speaking. Amanda, one of the two sisters from New Jersey who worked there, was sitting at the table with them, bending toward them and staring at their faces; finally she said, "Are you sure you don't want something to eat, some bread maybe?" Little Ruthie looked at Aaron, who shook his head; then she shook her head. Eliza was standing in the doorway; two women in cleaning smocks who worked at the dancehall were watching her, leaning their backs against the bar. Mr. Near was holding an unlit cigar in his teeth; one hand was stuck in mid-gesture on his dark, thick hair.

Eliza, who had the power to undo the spell, took one, then another slow step toward the children. The Hispanic woman leaning against the bar nudged her friend with her elbow and nodded toward Eliza's legs. She took another step. Ruthie looked up; she narrowed her eyes, trying to figure something out. Aaron stood up, just stood up and stared at his mother.

Eliza went over and squatted next to Ruthie's chair; she laid her hand on her daughter's arm.

"Ruthie," she said cheerfully but softly, "I missed you so much. I was silly with worry. Don't go off again like that without telling me, you hear?"

Ruthie put her head down on the table. Aaron came behind her and grasped the back of her chair with both hands. They seemed to still be far away somewhere.

"Hey, Momma," he said, and he flicked his hair out of his eyes. Eliza stood up and put her arm around his shoulders.

"Aaron, I guess you had an adventure. You had me scared."

"Yeah."

The others in the room looked at each other.

Ruthie sat up and drank some of the soda. Everyone was watching her. Then she took a shuddering breath and whimpered, "Don't look at me." And she put her face down in the crook of her arm.

Eliza picked her up and Ruthie clung to her, wrapped herself around her with both her arms and legs like she was only two years old.

"Don't look at me," she kept wailing. Everyone was looking at her. Mr. Near lit his cigar.

Aaron stepped away.

"I want to go home," he said.

Eliza swayed back and forth with Ruthie, who was glued to her. Mr. Near dropped his head and rubbed his chin.

"Who brought them in?" Eliza asked him.

Mr. Near lifted his head and said, "They were with some Indian."

"Did you see him?"

"Sure, I saw him."

"Did he have short, kind of bristly hair and was wearing a vest without a shirt?"

"Something like that I guess."

Ruthie nodded against her mother's neck.

"Where is he?"

"Sheriff's talking to him."

"What about Bridie? Has anybody seen Bridie?" She looked at all the faces. They all shook their head, except Mr. Near, who let the women's gestures speak for him.

"Okay, well. I guess I better get them on home, what's left of it. What about George? He went to the mountains to look. He didn't come in with the Indian?"

Amanda stood up and said, "He didn't come back, Mrs. Pelham. They must not have crossed each other."

Eliza nodded. "Well, if you see him, tell him we've gone on home." She wanted to yell out, "What's wrong with everyone? Why are my children so quiet?"

Mr. Near stepped close to her.

"Maybe you ought to take them to Mrs. Boggs's or Mrs. Fogharty's."

"Don't worry, Mr. Near. We'll get on okay."

She carried Ruthie, who stayed affixed to her mother, quiet now. Aaron walked beside, sometimes running in front and whacking at chamisa bushes with a stick. There were long wisps of clouds in the blue sky, membranes from the spirit world, as though some ephemeral entities had shed their outer skins and left them in the sky.

"Why're you wearin' pants, Momma?" Aaron asked.

"I don't know," she said. "I'm sorry."

Aaron didn't look at her or respond. Eliza stared at her son and then put her nose into Ruthie's hair. She felt a panic coming over her, a terrible notion that these two children were not really hers. They were odd beings or ghosts who seemed to be Aaron and Ruthie, whose real essences were still in the mountains, perhaps turned to stone statues or wandering in helpless confusion and loneliness.

"What happened up there, Aaron? What were you doing in the mountains with that drummer?" Eliza's voice had a nice casual coating on it.

"Huntin'," Aaron said, looking at the stick in his hand.

"Why did you just go off?"

He raised his eyes so she could see them through the veil of blond bangs.

"He said you told him to go ahead and take us."

Ruthie lifted her head and stared at her mother's face as though to make sure it was who she was supposed to be.

"I never did say any such thing."

"Sometimes you don't know what you're saying," Aaron mumbled.

Perhaps her children's bodies were being used by demons, minions of the drummer.

"He had no business taking you and Ruthie off. What did you have to do up there for him? Did you have to help him skin all those coyotes?"

Aaron shrugged and ran ahead, making attack noises as he charged a bush.

Eliza's nose touched her daughter's skin and smelled the salty moisture there. Ruthie laid her head back on her mother's shoulder. Then they heard the wagon coming up behind them. It was driven by Manuel Salas, and his mother was sitting straight on the seat next to him.

"Mrs. Pelham," the woman said as her son stopped the wagon. "I have come to ask you to stay with me and my family at our house. I think it would be better for the children. I think that they have been through enough. We have many rooms. I have many clothes for them. I don't want you to think that because I scolded your boy that I do not have concern for him."

A thrush burst out of the grasses nearby. Ruthie lifted up her head to see it, her pupils growing larger, like stains spreading in her iris. Aaron and the Salas boy were at pains not to look at each other. Eliza lifted Ruthie up higher and shifted her own weight.

"That's good of you to offer. I don't know. I think we should be home. Maybe you could give us a ride the rest of the way."

Señora Salas nodded once and waited. Eliza put Ruthie between her legs in the wagon bed and made Aaron sit close to her. She was thinking she really didn't want to go back home, because it was a bad place to look at, a half-burned-down home, after you'd been lost and scared. But the bottle of liquor was there, and she wanted it. Of course, she could do without a drink. And if the children were with the Salases, she could go talk to Robert Youngman before he left. She needed to know about Bridie. And she wanted to see Robert without a hole in his head. She wanted to thank him, to give him some money. For some reason she felt eerie about being left alone with these children just yet. Eliza clutched Ruthie. She leaned forward, bending Ruthie over, and touched Señora Salas's shoulder.

"I think I would like to go with you to your home after all," she said. "If that's all right."

"Of course."

The Señora spoke to her son, and he turned the wagon around with some difficulty, catching Aaron's eye and laughing as he made an exaggerated expression of strain and said, "Come on you stupid horse."

They took the road across the wooden bridge that led to the northern fields on the other side of the river. There was a gathering of cows next to the river in the distance, slow, sleepy animals. Old Town materialized as boxes of adobe, formed from the earth the way Adam was made by God. Quiet and low, they sat at the end of the acres and acres of fields where silver threads of irrigation ditches gleamed.

The Salas house was a low rectangle of adobe surrounding a little courtyard. Its outer walls were obscured by trees of heaven, Apache plume and trumpet vines. It was a secret and ancient place. The walls surrounded an interior courtyard, where the old Señor Salas, Deputy Salas's father, was sitting on a blue chair under a cottonwood tree with a pile of newspapers on the ground beside him. He was reading the *Daily Optic* and looked over his reading glasses at Eliza; his lower lip stuck out. Several dogs, all of them black, were lying flat on their sides, sleeping even though flies walked on their faces.

Eliza was still carrying Ruthie; Aaron had stayed with Manuel in a lopsided adobe structure that was the stable, east of the house.

The man stood up, stretching stiffly and taking off his glasses. He was medium in build; his blue eyes were unusually bright in contrast to his sun-baked skin and his dark moustache. The rays of wrinkles around his eyes were white when he did not smile.

"Mrs. Pelham. I am so happy that you have your children again. I was just reading in the paper about the dangers from those renegade heathens. It is a parent's worst dream to lose a child."

"Thank you for letting us stay here. I'm just going to wait for George to get back and we'll go on home."

"You stay as long as you like," he said, waving his glasses. "There is plenty of room."

"I'll just get the children settled, then I'll need to go on back to town to tend to a few things. I want to leave word for George about where we are and speak to the man that brought Aaron and Ruthie in."

The man nodded and sat back down.

"Let's put the children to bed," Señora Salas said.

"I want to go with you," Ruthie said into her mother's neck.

"Oh, no, hija. You stay with us and have some milk and cake. You can stay in a nice room with pretty flowers painted on the wall." Señora Salas touched the child's back.

"I'll tell Aaron to stay with her," Eliza said.

Then, in a conspiratorial whisper, Señora Salas said as she touched Eliza's arm, "I can find something for you to wear, a skirt and a blouse. My dresses would be too small, but I can find something."

"No, no. I don't need to change yet. It's easier to get around in this." Eliza looked down at herself. The man raised his eyes over his glasses to see her.

"Dále el caballo viejo," he said, scanning the paper again.

"Sí, sí," Señora Salas waggled her hands in front of her at her father-in-law, a gesture of impatience he did not bother to look at.

"It's dark in here," Ruthie said when they got into one of the cool rooms off of the courtyard. There were two little beds with wooden frames painted blue, and a small table and chair. There was much cloth and other sewing paraphernalia around. On the wooden ledge over the small fireplace, several photographs sat in oval frames of different sizes, along with a retablo of the holy Niño de Atocha in a tin frame. Two wooden crosses hung on the white-washed wall, one over each of the beds.

"This is my older daughter's room." Señora Salas went to the mantel and picked up one of the frames. "My oldest girl, Carlita, is married and lives further south in the valley. She was named after my brother. He was killed at Glorieta."

She showed Eliza the man in the frame—a dark face that looked surprised about something.

Eliza sat on one of the beds and put Ruthie down beside her.

"He fought under General Canby. He was an officer." She put the picture back. Eliza said nothing, hardly looked at the picture.

Aaron came in and sat down next to Ruthie, while Manuel leaned against the door frame.

"You stay with your sister here for a while so she can sleep," Eliza instructed. "Maybe you ought to get some rest too."

"Manuel will get a horse for you." The Señora stepped out into the sunlight.

Before she left the room, Eliza went to the mantel and laid the picture of the dead brother face down. Then she put her hand on Ruthie's forehead, feeling for a fever. But the child's brow was cool and clammy. Ruthie turned her head away and put two fingers into her mouth, a gesture Eliza had never seen before. She backed up and then left the room.

She was about to mount the horse, a slightly swaybacked quarterhorse, when Aaron came running and stood in front of her.

He didn't speak, so Eliza said, "You ought to stay with your sister, Aaron." He didn't go, so she kept talking. "I've been on more different horses in one week than in my whole life, I think." She laughed, but Aaron still seemed mesmerized, caught in a little whirlpool of thinking.

"I don't think you should leave Ruthie. She's scared." He snapped up an old scrap of leather that was lying on the ground and started whipping it back and forth against the fingers of his left hand.

Eliza said, "I'll be back before dark. I just have to see some people."

"You're always goin' off somewhere. Why don't you just stay home, stay with Ruthie? She don't want to be left again. Why are you always goin' off and leavin' us?"

The horse's tail switched over its flanks at the flies.

"I want to find out what happened to Bridie. You remember, Miss O'Doonan. I want to talk to the Indian who brought you in."

"You mean Mr. Youngman?"

"Yes."

Aaron looked off to the right, squinting his eyes as though really focusing on something there.

"Don't you want kids? Don't you want us anymore?"

Eliza took a deep breath. A dizzy feeling in her chest rose up into her head; she licked her lips and took another sighing breath.

"I don't have to take this kind of talk from you, Aaron. I'm your mother. I do the best I can. I've been gone for days trying to find you."

"Mr. Smith said you didn't care about us, that you were trying to sell us. That he was going to try to find a good home for us. He said he knew about folks in Oklahoma would pay good money for a couple of kids."

"Where is he? Where is Mr. Smith?"

"I don't know. He ran off after Mr. Youngman took his gun."

"You don't really think I wanted to sell you, do you?"

Aaron studied her.

"No, I guess not. But I don't think..." His eyes filled up with tears. "I don't think you're careful enough about things." He wiped his eyes hard with the backs of his hands, but the tears just kept falling.

Eliza's hands contracted into fists. "I'm going to kill him. I don't care what happens to me. I'm going to kill him and walk on out and die myself." She pointed with her whole arm extended to some location that in her mind was the vast wilderness where people disappeared and perished effortlessly. "If there was a war against men like that, I'd be the first to join up. I'd shoot them all in the jaw."

Then Aaron struck her across the face with the piece of leather strap, stinging her jaw and leaving a little red welt there. He broke into heavier sobs, sucking in his lower lip.

Her hand touched the welt, and Eliza said quietly, "What did he do to you?"

"I don't know. I don't know," he sobbed.

"I better go, and you better get back to your sister."

Aaron nodded, letting the leather roll out of his hand. He would not look at his mother.

Still crying he said, "Mr. Youngman said he was gonna let me ride with him. He was gonna show me places where Indians used to hunt buffalo." He closed his eyes. He sounded much younger than twelve. He sounded like Ruthie used to.

Eliza put her arm out to bring him to her, but he stepped back. She took her boy's hands and held them palms up.

She had to clear her throat so she wouldn't start crying.

"I'm sorry I left you kids alone. You'll be all right here. Manuel's daddy is a deputy. You'll be all right for a little while."

Aaron tore his hands away and ran back to the house.

Eliza cleaned her glasses and got up on the horse. She looked back at the house, which seemed to be sinking into the ground as the trees and bushes bowed over to protect and conceal it. She fantasized that it was her house and that it was her father reading the paper with sleeping dogs all around his feet. Only then could she manage to go back to New Town, from where even now the hammering could be heard when the wind blew. And the truth was she wanted to be alone. She wanted to know that her children were all right, but more and more she just wanted to be alone. They made her feel odd, dizzy. And the air just didn't feel right if she stayed still. She had this itchy feeling that had gotten even worse since Aaron and Ruthie were back; she couldn't just sit and think; she would explode if she just sat and thought. And why not go by the house and check on Jack's horse and pick up that bottle?

As the hammering from New Town got closer and louder, not just one hammer, but three or four, Eliza asked herself, "What did I want after all?" And she remembered how she had envisioned life in the territories—how there would be quiet and just the fewest, simplest things and ideas to consider. But suddenly life was crammed with unwanted necessities: people to talk to, stories to unravel, goods to buy, deeds to sign. She had imagined her life in the West as it was in her father's mind—free, simple; humanity itself would be different. Didn't anybody consider that it would be better not to have the railroad bring in lawyers and old soldiers who still cleaned their guns every day?

But the railroad bonds sold like hotcakes. There was no holding back an idea that promised to make so much money, no matter how bad the idea was. And a railroad that would make a lot of businessmen very, very rich sounded so good, even to the common folk, who were sold, lock, stock and barrel, on the absolute goodness of having soap and cloth and tools and kitchen utensils just roll right up to their doors. At first people complained about the noise and the smell, but not much more. Everyone just assumed that some inevitable progress occurred the way the sun rose and set every day and that this force was more powerful, perhaps even wiser than they. People just assumed that they had all somehow decided together that progress was a good thing, only they couldn't remember exactly how or when they had come to this conclusion. The lawyers and politicians and salesmen had to constantly remind them of what they'd decided on and what they really wanted, what was good for them.

"We're all idiots," Eliza said. She was grinding her teeth and didn't know why she was so upset now. She had pretty much accepted everything since the baby was born dead, was rather proud of how calm she'd been in the face of a lot of unpleasant realities. She'd kept quiet, except with Bridie and Robert. And everything was all right now. There had just been a few incidents—her children being taken off for a few days in the mountains, her house being partially burned—but no harm done, no permanent damage. Worse things happened every day; someone was shot just about every day.

Someone was shot just about every day.

She touched the welt on her face and knew without a doubt that Aaron would disappear one day, go of his own free will because she had not figured things out in time. Maybe he would take a gun with him.

⇾TWENTY⇽

*R*iding from the fields to the north, Eliza could see New Town in its entirety across the little river—a small spreading construction with points and angles, the courthouse being the largest feature: a yellow brick rectangle that seemed stubbornly immovable but not rooted. She let the reins go slack and kicked the horse saying, "Hiya!" The horse was glad; he, too, wanted to run, fear-ing the closing up of spaces. He wanted to take the openness with force. He dug his back hooves into the soggy earth and sprang for-ward. Eliza almost could not hang on. For a few seconds she was thrown from side to side, until she crouched closer to the horse and its rhythm and she had the use of her thighs to hold on with. Then she could feel the speed and the distance and how one could not happen without the other. She was aware of an ecstatic relief that the children were back, that she knew where Aaron and Ruthie were. The force of her joy and relief surprised her. Never mind—she wanted to get that corn liquor just to have with her and to thank Robert Youngman and ask him some questions. She'd pay him for bringing the children back. What had they said before all the craziness? Twenty dollars? She'd give him thirty. Most of all, she needed to see him with his skull not exploded by the gunfire she could still recall, that one aching shot back in the dark and rain. His intact skull would add to a growing sense of potential she felt in the horse, the colors of the ground, the cottonwood tree under which Señor Salas read his papers, Aaron's face—bitter but alive—a blending of everything in one flowing current.

Robert's right hand gripped one of the three wooden bars on the small jail window. The wood under his hand had been worn smooth by the oil of many other hands that had done just as his was doing. They were the hands of men, and a few murderous women, who had looked outside and wondered what had brought them there and what would take them away.

Robert watched a dirt clearing in the alley behind the jail, where three yellow and orange cats crouched and stared at each other from the points of a triangle. One of the cats had a bad eye that it kept blinking. Robert heard a conversation outside the door of his cell but did not turn around. A few minutes later he was still watching the cats, and one of them sprang forward and then the others scrambled into a clump of bushes. Eliza's face appeared on the other side of the window.

"Robert," she said. "He wouldn't let me see you. What're you doing in here, anyway?"

He just looked down at her.

"I told him you helped me. Didn't you bring Aaron and Ruthie in?"

He looked away. Out on Railroad Avenue there was a terrible screeching sound and then a bang.

Robert moved his fist down along the bar and smiled. "I made the grave error of riding in on one of the sheriff's horses."

"What? You weren't stealing it, though. You were just using it." She said it like a question that Robert didn't bother to answer. "He should be glad he got it back at all. And it certainly means I'll be better off than if I had to pay for two horses. I'll tell him. I'll go tell him myself."

"What will you tell him that he needs to know? He lost his horses, and an Apache rode in on one of them."

"If you were stealing the horse, why would you just ride on into town?"

Robert laughed and spread his hand out on his chest.

"I am an Apache. Don't you know that you have been at war with the Apaches?"

Eliza kicked at the side of the building.

"What happened to Bridie...Miss O'Doonan?"

"I don't know."

"When did you last see her?"

He leaned against the wall so she could just see his profile.

"When I came back down with the kids, I saw one of the horses standing at the base of the canyon, so I left the boy and girl with the woman and got the horse. I took the boy and girl on the horse and told the woman to stay there. I left food for her. I told her I was going to look for the other horse and take the children to New Town."

"Was she bad off?"

"The fever was over, I think, the worst of it. She was not so bad. She could have ridden out with the other horse. But I didn't find the other horse. When I woke her up to tell her that I was going, she said, 'Father?' But she knew who I was when her head cleared. She gave me a narrow-eyed look."

The door to his cell opened and closed. He went away from the window and came back eating a tortilla.

"I'm hungry," Eliza said.

He got another tortilla and slipped it to her through the bars. They ate and the wind started blowing in forceful gusts.

Eliza bent down and brought up a bottle, holding it up to the window for Robert to see.

"Have some of this," she said. "Go on."

Robert put his hand up, palm facing Eliza, and said, "No."

She shrugged and uncorked the bottle. Robert watched her drink from it and said, "A little medicine for the nerves? I don't guess doctors and liquor salesmen would stay in business if it weren't for white women's nerves."

"I guess you're going to be a doctor, Mr. Youngman, seeing as how you were diagnosing Bridie, and now you're telling me about my nerves."

"As a matter of fact, I was encouraged to attend medical school by one gentleman—a teacher at my school. It was a ridiculous notion, of course. I don't think white women would allow a red man to examine their nerves."

Eliza stared at his hand, long tan fingers swept around the bar.

"Why aren't you with your children?" he asked.

"They're all right. They're with the deputy's family over in Old Town. I figured I owed you money. I wanted to see you before you went off."

"Well, here I am; no chance of going off."

"I meant to bring you the money, but the clerk at the bank says there isn't any in the account. I guess George…"

Robert nodded. He smoothed his hair back and sighed.

"I've figured out a few things," he said. "For one, I'm going to be hanged here." He looked around outside the window. "This is where I'm going to die."

"They can't hang you. You're not going to hang. You didn't do anything."

He laughed.

"Look," she said, grabbing the bar herself right where it was smooth, as though the spot drew hands to it. "George is bound to be coming back soon. I'll tell him and he'll know what to do. He knows people, lawyers and men who run things."

Robert was looking at the plate of beans sitting on the chair in his cell.

"Okay," he said.

The constant hammering sound turned to clanging as someone somewhere pounded on metal. One of the cats had come back into view and crouched behind Eliza with its ears back in fierce indignation over the noise.

"This place used to be quiet," Eliza muttered.

Robert stared at her.

"Before the railroad," she added.

"Before that," he said.

"I liked it when it was quiet. People always talked about how dangerous it was and how the territory needed to be civilized, but it seems to me the more civilized it gets the more dangerous it gets. Somehow I don't mind so much the idea of dying of a rattlesnake bite as I do of dying of a bullet in my head or some disease people get in cities." She drank from the bottle again.

Robert squinted his eyes at her.

"I guess the train brings in those liquor bottles, too, though. Seems that you don't want all civilization to go away, just the parts you can't swallow."

"You don't know what I left behind that people called civilized. You don't know what I saw—people dying and rotting from gunshot wounds—young boys coming home without legs, crazy and shaking, people drinking all the time so they didn't have to think about all the screaming and dying and the end of their lives—the end of everything they believed in. That's what Kentucky was like. Everything turning sad and poor. I know what a person looks like who can't put the bottle down for fear of what will come into his head. I've seen those ruined men, and I'm not like them—not even a little bit."

Robert stuck his lower lip out and said very seriously as he shook his head, "Oh, no. Not a bit."

"And now all that noise is out here, where it used to be quiet. At least people aren't massacring each other."

Again Robert laughed, this time putting his head back a little and regarding Eliza with a scornful light in his eye. "No sir, no massacres here—just us chickens."

"I want things to be quiet."

"White people like noise," he said. "It makes them feel like they're doing something if they're making noise. Massacres are very noisy."

"I don't like it. And why do you keep laughing? If you think you're going to be hanged, I don't see what's so funny. You ought to be banging your fist against the wall, screaming bloody fury."

"That would be uncivilized," he said. She couldn't make him snuff out the twinkle in his eye.

"Well, then, maybe you should pray."

His smile sank. "I have. That's about all I've been doing."

"You aren't going to hang. It just can't happen. You've been to school in Pennsylvania. You aren't a real Apache. They just have to be told, be reasoned with."

Robert grabbed the bars with both of his hands, gripped them hard. The glint in his eye had turned fiery. His face was trembling and he practically spat on Eliza, who moved back a step.

"I will tell you two things: I am Tinde or Apache or whatever you want to call it, and I will hang. I will be hanged by white men. That will make it clear who I am—Apache, Tinde—and that is what I am. That is what I came back to find out, and now I will know by hanging. I should thank them for recognizing who I am. I am their enemy. For a while I wasn't sure myself. I was liking Mozart too much."

Eliza said something quietly.

"What?" Robert spat.

"I don't want you to hang. Aaron said you were going to take him to see where your people hunted the buffalo." She looked up at him. "And what about your mother?"

He let go of the bars as though they shocked him, and he said loudly, wanting the sheriff in the other room to hear him.

"I admire the power of white men. They have certainly shown their power, and I respect it. I am in awe of it. I bow to it. I concede. I'm like a dog, a good dog lying on its back, like all of my people—called savage, when our only savagery is our homesickness and our hunger and a poverty we never knew existed. We comply. We understand who is dominant. We see it, smell it, hear it, feel it. Sometimes we think it is funny. But that's because if we didn't laugh we would go completely crazy. We would do nothing but get drunk. We like the guns, the clothes. We admire them and want to trade for them. We're not like some of these Pueblo people. We aren't soft. We like to fight sometimes. It feels good to fight and take a good horse away from a man who has been proven too weak to deserve such an animal. But we don't want to make things too easy, either. It's not satisfying if it's too easy. The white man who has power wants to wipe out everything that gets in his way. He wants things to be easy for him so he can buy and sell and make a lot of money without suffering. So he has to convert people, make them believe that he knows everything, that he can solve all their problems and make them happy—or he has to annihilate them. He has to even get rid of his own conscience when it fights him. His religion helps with that. He can say that God is on his side, or that God forgives him after he says certain words, or that Jesus has already paid for all the lying and cheating and killing. The white man who has power and money has made it easy for himself to do what he wants to do. I'm sure now that I am not a white man."

Eliza's face looked confused.

Robert laughed. "That is what my face looked like when my teacher was explaining geometry. You should go. You should be with your children. A mother should never let her children go far from her—not until they are looking for something."

"You can come to work for us. George is never around." She looked away, blushing, but kept arguing against the part of her that was blushing. "Yes, you should come work for us, help me with things. We need to build on the house. I can't do it on my own, and George, Mr. Pelham, is away all the time. And he's a good man. He came out west to get away from all the meanness and start a new life, a different kind of life."

Robert nodded. "Maybe live by simple farming, raising horses, share what you have, live with respect for the mountains, trees, water, game. Sounds uncivilized to me. Sounds like people who don't appreciate the American way of life. Sounds like Indians. Now why would your husband want to live like people who are being wiped out by his brethren for living that way? Very ironic, I'd say. Do you know about irony, Mrs. Pelham?"

Eliza hung her head.

"I'm grateful for your help. If I ever see that drummer again, I'm going to shoot him. My kids aren't acting right. He said some evil things to them, scared them badly and I don't know what. If I ever see him…"

"He's everywhere." Robert stepped back like an English thespian and spread his arms wide to indicate great expanses of space. "And more of him coming every day. And he'll sell you, and everyone who feels any pain over the way the world is going, all the corn liquor and rye whiskey and morphine you want. He'll make much money from that pain, and keep you quiet at the same time."

Eliza put her face against the bars.

"I'm not like that. I don't want to keep quiet anymore. I'll talk to the deputy. I'm staying at his house, and I'll tell him to let you go. I'll tell him you're going to come to work for us."

The plate of beans on the chair were illuminated by the sun.

"Beans," Robert said with a flourish. Then he pressed his face against the bars and said passionately to Eliza, "I love beans."

When Eliza got back to the Salas house, both Aaron and Ruthie were asleep on one of the little beds. Aaron's neck was crooked and uncomfortable looking, so Eliza moved his head and smoothed his hair back from his face. She lay down on the other bed, her feet hanging over the end.

That evening for dinner they had roast chicken, tortillas and squash and ate at the table in the courtyard. There were many people at the table. Manuel, Señora Salas, Deputy Salas and his father, of course, but also an old woman they called "Tia," two of Deputy Salas's brothers, a wife of one of the brothers and her three-year-old daughter, who kept banging her spoon against the table. They spoke with rapt attention to each other in whatever mood dominated, laughing loudly at times, or gesturing wildly and forcefully in anger and then returning easily to some joke. It was the freest collection of people Eliza had ever been with. Ruthie sat quietly in her lap, but Aaron exchanged comments and jokes with Manuel, sometimes speaking in Spanish and causing many at the table to raise their eyebrows and say, "Ohhh! So he thinks he's a man already!" to Eliza. This occasion, which to most at the table was just another meal, made Eliza forget her brooding. In Kentucky this crowd would have been called uncouth, too open with their emotions. Even Eliza had worried when one of them first raised his voice. She watched with open fascination as this family wagged fingers, or picked up each other's hands and kissed them, or leaned back in their chairs laughing, or crossed themselves in some mysterious momentary solemnity. It was another world to Eliza, an intoxicating validation that there were backgrounds different from her own, choices available as long as the industrious drummers and lawyers didn't annihilate those choices in the name of freedom. These were the kinds of ideas George would understand. She wished that George were there.

About eight dogs tried to fit under the table and occasionally fought each other for space; their vicious growling and twirling and snapping was ignored by the Salases, who seemed to have no fear that their legs would get bitten, as they had no fear that their theatrical threats to each other were real. Ruthie, however, was scared of the dogs and so ate her dinner sitting in her mother's lap, which was now demurely clothed in a dark brown skirt that came just a little too high above her falling-apart shoes. Aaron and Manuel laughed and gave chicken bones to some of the dogs.

Everything, even Ruthie's fear, seemed sweet and restful here, as Eliza sipped a dark red wine from a porcelain cup. The sunset was the color of watermelon and cantaloupe. Ruthie fell asleep on her mother's lap, as Aaron and Manuel walked down to the arroyo. Señor Salas and his son the deputy sat at the table speaking to each other in Spanish as Señora Salas and her sister-in-law came and went, making comments with playful haughtiness. The old woman sat in the chair under the tree, and the two brothers of Deputy Salas spoke seriously between themselves at the far end of the table. The old man banged his fist on the table to the amusement of Señora Salas who lifted up her father-in-law's plate before it could clatter.

Eliza sighed. There was the faintest smell of some sweet, pink flower in the air. She slowly pulled bits of leaves out of Ruthie's hair, content with the warmth of her little girl's body and the creamy colors in the sky, but aware of some huge sadness that was manifest in the coolness coming on with night. She shared a bottle of brandy with the men, glad to have Ruthie on her lap as an excuse not to get up and help the women. During a floating reverie her mind startled her with a bleak reminder that Robert was waiting to be hanged. She'd forgotten about that and had to order some words in her head to take care of the situation.

"Deputy Salas," she finally said when he and his father were silently glaring at one another. "I want to speak with you about the Indian who's in jail, the one who brought in Aaron and Ruthie."

Both the older and the younger man looked at her, the older man leaning on the table with a combination of weariness and interest.

"He didn't steal the horse," Eliza said. She was speaking slowly, trying to make her words very clear. "He brought it in, just like he brought in the children. If he was stealing it, why would he bring it right on into town?" She laughed, pumping her legs a bit and disturbing Ruthie.

"He didn't know who it belonged to," the deputy explained, as though he had read this in a book of facts. "He didn't think anyone would know whose horse it was."

"He did know who it belonged to, because I told him." She shifted Ruthie on her lap and sat up straighter. "He shouldn't be in jail. He didn't steal the horse."

"He's an Apache, Mrs. Pelham."

The older Señor Salas's eyebrows went up, and he began to tell the story of an atrocity concerning an Apache raid on his grand uncle's ranch in Raton.

"But he's just come back from school in Pennsylvania," Eliza said a little louder than she meant to. "He didn't steal anything. He was helping me. He brought my children back. Talk to Aaron and Ruthie. He knew what he was doing."

"He was going to try to get money for them," the deputy said, pulling at his moustache.

Eliza stared at him. "You are lying."

The old man waved one arm and spoke in Spanish to his son, and then he turned to Eliza.

"You do not know what these savages are capable of doing," he said. "They are the liars. They will steal your shirt and kill your children and then try to sell you a casket they took from the cemetery. I tell you, you do not know what they are up to."

"I don't believe all that. I think that the newspapers are full of these stories so they can kill the Indians and take their land."

"¡Oooo! ¡Diós! The woman speaks like the devil himself, like Eve in the garden, mi hijo!" The old man was very amused. He continued, "Do you think that I am lying when I tell you that my family has been killed? Three members of my family has been killed by those heathens."

"And your son-in-law was killed by Confederate soldiers. Should you jail every one of them and hang them?"

He leaned back, grinning and nodding his head vigorously, "¡Sí!"

The deputy waved his hand in front of his face and said, "Wait. We are talking about an Indian, about an Apache man who rode into town with another man's horse and another man's children."

His brothers had stopped talking and were listening.

"They were my children and I'm telling you that he was help-ing me. I'll go to court if I have to and tell the judge what I'm telling you."

All four men laughed.

"An Apache does not have the privilege of being defended in an American court," the deputy explained. "He is not a citizen."

"Sí," said one of the brothers. "It is only the privilege of the Mexican to go to American court and have his land taken away from him, no, Papá?"

The older man banged his fist on the table again, waking Ruthie, who gasped and sat straight up. Then there was a loud fight in Spanish between the four men. Eliza stood and said quietly to the deputy, "He just can't be killed. He was helping me. He's going to come to work for us."

"He'll just get a whipping or a while in jail and be run out of town."

"It's not right to humiliate him. He did nothing wrong. You're just making him hate you and want to kill you. That's how these things just go on and on. I'll talk to the sheriff; I'll talk to the newspapers; I'll get my own lawyer. I have had business with Mr. Catron himself."

She took Ruthie by the hand and went to find Aaron, who was sitting on an old stool by the arroyo, throwing rocks into the shallow trickle. Manuel was making jokes about the witch who wandered the arroyos, looking for children to drown. By now the sky had some pale stars in it, and Aaron was looking up at them as though he'd forgotten what they were.

⇥TWENTY‑ONE⇤

*T*he dream Eliza had while sleeping in the little bed in the Salas's home was vivid and nasty—like a terrible parable given by the God of the Old Testament. Her first view in this dream was of a vast and innocent-looking field, part of some farm in Kentucky with Queen Anne's lace and humming bees. But as she looked more carefully, she saw that the field was full of dead men and boys, disfigured, bloated, torn open, infested with maggots. She was aware of little movements that could have been the bees or a breeze weaving through grass and flowers and blowing the cloth on the corpses; but she became increasingly aware that the dead men were twitching. She told herself that this was just some stage in the bodies' decay and could even be disgustingly attributed to the movement of maggots in the carcasses. But one by one, the bodies, just as they were—bloated and bloody—rose and began to walk, all in one direction. They seemed confused, at first wandering; then they began to walk fast, then run, faster and faster, stumbling over a landscape that changed to prairie. They had guns in their hands. And her father, who was not dead, said to her, "They don't want to give up. They're going to keep on fighting." And Eliza wondered what role she would have. Would she fight, or could she hide somewhere or find a place where they weren't going and wouldn't make her join them? And then she realized that as a woman she had only one role: she would have to allow them to release their sexual desires with her; she would have to be the mistress of all of them, enduring their smell, their festering exposed intestines, the blood in their mouths.

One of them was bending over her; she opened her eyes up wide and saw George standing next to the bed. Aaron had woken up in the other bed and was propped up on his elbows.

George stroked his wife's face with the back of his fingers and said, "You didn't even take your spectacles off, Ellie. I guess you're a tired woman."

She hugged him around the waist, leaning against his belly, which was firm and alive, not decaying. George stroked her head.

"It's your daddy come back from looking for you," she said to Aaron.

"Hey," the boy said.

"Hey," the man said. And he reached out to jiggle Aaron's foot. "You look fine, son."

"Yessir."

Ruthie stood up on the bed and climbed on George, wrapping her arms and legs around him.

"We had chicken last night for supper," she said.

"That sounds good."

Eliza rebraided her hair and said, "It was real nice of them to let us stay here. It feels good here, like a nest away from everything that's troublesome."

"I guess," George said. "I just don't like being beholden to them."

"Did you hear about the Indian bringing Aaron and Ruthie back?"

"Yeah."

"Well, he doesn't belong in jail. He was helping us."

"I don't know."

"Well, I do know, George. He doesn't belong in jail. They might hang him."

"Come on and let's go."

A dog outside yelped and barked, then kept yelping. Ruthie gripped her father harder and started to cry.

"What's wrong with her?" George asked.

Eliza stood up beside him.

"I don't know. She's been real spooky ever since she got back. Something's wrong with both of them. Something happened to them."

"Tired I guess."

From inside the room Eliza could see a pot of coffee out on the table and some thick clay cups along with a pitcher of milk. A melon had a slice cut out of it, its orange seeds spilling out in a way that turned Eliza's stomach. Flies buzzed around and lighted on the sticky fruit.

Then the older man, Señor Salas, was in the doorway, like he'd crashed through something and was standing there with a long-barreled gun, pointing it at George's side.

"What's going on?" Eliza said.

George looked calmly in front of him and said, "Just come on, Ellie. Let's go."

Señor Salas spoke, moving his lips but keeping his teeth together. "Yes. You go. Go far away, out of my home, off my land, away from this territory where you don't belong."

Eliza peeled Ruthie off her father and walked with her out of the room into the courtyard.

"Aaron," she called in. "You get out here."

"I'm leaving," George said to the man as Aaron sidled past them.

"Your boy plays in the morada like it is a chicken house," the old man told him.

"I don't know anything about that."

"We will not let you take our land as though we were frightened women. We will not, I can tell you."

Señora Salas came into the courtyard with a bowl to put the melon in and Eliza said, "Your father-in-law is going to shoot my husband."

The Señora wiped her hands on the white sheet tied around her waist as an apron and sighed, looking into the room.

"Papá!" she scolded. "Don't cause trouble. Put the gun away before you shoot yourself in the leg. They are our guests."

He lowered the gun and said to his daughter-in-law, "The woman and her children are our guests. But this man and his friends have spit on us and our way of life, our way of sharing our land." Then to George he said, "You see. We are generous people. We do not take land from each other. We do not own land that everyone must use. And we treat you as guests; we offer you food. And you and the other ricos, even some of my own people who have been converted, you make big deals and go to your courts and we wake up one morning and all the land that we can see, that was given to us by the king of Spain—it is all gone, taken, stolen. You are nothing more than thieves who have documents instead of knives." He waved the gun toward the door. "Go. Go on! I cannot stand to look at you."

George walked out the door, and as he walked away with Eliza, the old man called after him, "My father built the house that you are living in. He built it with his brothers as a home for himself and his bride."

"Then why did you burn it down, you and your friends with sacks over their heads?" George asked with Eliza pulling at him. "I heard. Damn Mexican bandits—outlaws, nothing better than common outlaws."

"Get out. Get out of my house," the old man yelled, pointing the gun at him again.

George pulled his horse with Eliza, Aaron and Ruthie sitting on it. They went to town without speaking and then on to the burnt-out house. The children said nothing about what they saw, because their father was fuming and they didn't want any small movement or comment of theirs to spark him. Then he'd burst into flame too. Aaron poked around in the burnt-out room.

Eliza took Ruthie into the bedroom with her while she changed into clean underwear and her own brown skirt and white blouse, all creased from being folded up in the box under the bed. Aaron and George picked through the charred ruins and put anything not burned black outside in a neat pile—tins, pots, dishes, two candle holders and some other items. The chatted about this and that, Eliza feeling very glad about George being around, about his making jokes with Aaron about where the rooster went off to and how maybe he got roasted in the fire and the hens had a big party and ate him. But Eliza couldn't get rid of the feeling that Aaron wasn't the same boy. She stared at him and he looked back, empty in the eyes. She was afraid of him, afraid of her own son.

At midday George and Aaron went out hunting. Eliza lit the woodstove and tried to cheer Ruthie up, talking about how silly it was to be cooking out in the open on a woodstove. She found three potatoes and boiled them up, putting some dried parsley in for flavoring. She mashed the potatoes in a bowl for Ruthie, aware that she was babying her. Eliza sat outside on a chair, eating potatoes from a plate, talking to Ruthie, who sat on the stoop and said nothing.

"I guess your daddy'll build us a nice new house right onto this one, bigger and nicer." She eyed the corral posts just sitting out there like orphans.

Ruthie nodded and said very quietly, as though she was pretending to be a mouse, "I want some clean clothes."

"Well, baby, all yours and Aaron's clothes were burned up. But you know what I can do? I can get one of my nice blouses and make it like a dress on you. We'll tie a sash around it and it'll look fine as can be."

Ruthie nodded.

But when they were in the bedroom, Ruthie wouldn't take off her clothes.

"Just put it over these clothes, Momma," Ruthie said.

"Ruthie, that wouldn't make any sense. Now, come on."

"No, I won't. I won't get nekked. I ain't gonna get nekked."

She started screaming and sobbing so that Eliza felt like shaking her, but she took her on the bed with her and held her.

"Look, baby Ruthie, when I was looking for you and Aaron, I was with this lady named Bridie O'Doonan, the Irish lady from the dancehall, and we had the finest time taking all our clothes off, right down to our underwear, and got to feeling all fresh and nice. We even sang and danced like fairies in the woods."

Ruthie thought for a minute.

"Jesus saw you dancin' around in your underwear. He sees everything."

Eliza gave this some thought. She wished Bridie would come in just then and help her. In that flicker of a moment she convinced herself that she and Bridie would get together and find some place to live where they would help each other out and play music and sing and dance. She looked at the stringless banjo and sighed.

"I'd say that Jesus has seen a lot worse than me in my underwear."

"I'm all dirty on my skin," Ruthie explained.

"I'll tell you what—I'll heat a pot of water and clean you myself with a cloth, just nice, warm water and a cloth."

"Okay."

The steam from the pot of water clouded Eliza's glasses as she knelt before Ruthie and undressed her. The first thing she saw was the bruises, like fingerprints, on her shoulders.

"How'd you get these?"

"I don't know."

There were spots of blood on the baggy, woolen underwear, and when Eliza pulled it off, she said nothing. She just dipped the piece of linen into the warm water and timidly touched the marks on her child's thighs.

"Is this dirt?" she asked.

"I don't know. Ow, Momma."

"Criminy. Spread your legs apart a little bit, Ruthie."

"I don't want to."

"I'm just going to clean you off. It's nice, warm water."

Ruthie stepped one leg to the side, and Eliza could see the blue discoloration on the plump skin around the vulva.

She started humming and then asked, "How did you get hurt down there?"

"I don't know, Momma." She started to cry.

Eliza sat back on her heels.

"Let me get your face, Ruthie. You've got dirt all over it."

"Why are you breathin' funny?"

"I don't know. I just am."

Eliza finished washing Ruthie and got her dressed.

"Your hands are shaking," Ruthie whined. "What's inside your hands that's shaking them like that, Momma?"

"Don't whine, Ruthie." Eliza said this coldly because she wanted her daughter to disappear as she was then and return as Ruthie without bruises. Those marks on her daughter's thighs— she had a choice: see them or don't see them. Think about them or don't.

She went outside and paced up and down in front of the maimed house. "She fell," she whispered out loud to herself. "The poor thing fell, probably straddling some rock, or banged up on the side of the wagon, maybe when the wheel fell off. And that man didn't look after her. What kind of a demon would let a little girl hurt herself and not bring her right home, or wash her off? Well, I guess he was trying to be delicate with her." Ruthie just stood in the doorway, two fingers in her mouth, watching her mother muttering to herself. Finally she said, now like the smallest creature she could think of, an insect maybe, "I want to see Mr. Youngman," and tears came down her face.

"Did he hurt you, Ruthie? Did you get those bruises when you were with Mr. Youngman, maybe bouncing around on that horse?"

"I don't know. I got sore before that."

Later on, Ruthie was taking a nap and Eliza was hanging up the clothes she'd washed on a rope strung from the outhouse to a pole—Ruthie's clothes and the trousers, shirt and underwear she'd worn—when Aaron and George came back with a rabbit dangling from a rope over George's shoulder.

"When are you going back down to the crew?" Eliza was talking to George with her arms folded over her chest; she felt an overwhelming desire to fight with George, to get into a screaming argument—it didn't matter what about.

George draped the rabbit over the chair that Eliza had moved outside and rubbed his face with both of his hands. There was stubble all over it and down the front of his neck, which had gotten sunburnt.

"Well, I got some business here."

"Does it have to do with that lawyer from Santa Fe? Is it some land deal?"

"Take this rabbit on down to the arroyo and skin it," George said to Aaron. Then he said to Eliza, "I think I might be in trouble—some financial trouble."

"You've still got work, haven't you?"

"Yeah, I've still got work, but I bought into some deal and it's been caught up in court. And now the property's been burned so it's not worth as much…"

"I don't see as how it was ours to begin with."

He followed her to the house; they stopped and talked in whispers by the woodstove so as not to wake up Ruthie.

"Well, that was part of the deal. See this lawyer had a way of proving that the old deed wasn't any good, there wasn't really any deed, just some agreement about everybody using the land, and since we were on the property we were as good as owners."

"That doesn't seem right."

"Never mind that right now. I still had to put some money in, pay some fees so I could be part of this deal, see, that involves a hell of a lot more than this little plot—all the land along the river and down to this arroyo."

"What's somebody going to do with all of that?"

"Fence it in. Raise cattle. I'm talking about prime land for cattle ranching, access to the river."

"I thought everybody just let their cattle water along there, anybody could use it."

"That just doesn't make sense anymore, Ellie. That's not the way American laws work. Land just can't sit around for anybody to use. It doesn't make sense. And we're here at the right time to get in on these deals real easy. This land will go up so high in price you won't believe it. People coming in on the train will be wanting to buy up plots to build on for a lot more money than we paid for the whole deal."

"It sounds to me like the people who got this land in the first place don't want to sell it. How can you buy something somebody doesn't want to sell?"

George looked down and slapped at his thighs, raising dust.

"Well, you just don't understand these things."

"No, I guess I don't."

"Anyway some Spaniard took it from the Indians," George said. "This is just a better way of doing things. That's all. The lawyers are just straightening everything out."

"Well maybe we ought to ask one of them to straighten out what happened to your daughter in there."

"What do you mean?"

"I mean she's awful hurt, and that man kept her up there and didn't tend to her. She's just a little girl."

She leaned back, pressing her lips together, her whole face trembling. George looked down and shook his head.

"Have you been drinking, Ellie?"

"No, I haven't, and I don't see what that matters when I'm talking about our daughter being hurt and dragged all over the mountains like a dog."

"She just got banged up out there in the woods."

Eliza turned and got the pot of water off the stove and took it out to dump on the garden. The squash was wilted but salvageable. All the leaves had been sucked dry by squash bugs, flat, grey things walking around linked to each other in some kind of connubial stupor. The green beans were thriving. All the kale was dead, but it hadn't ever done too well.

That night they all four slept in the same bed, with the smell of rabbit stew coddling them. Eliza was between Ruthie and George, just barely sleeping, trying to figure everything out, to satisfactorily understand what disturbed her, so that she could try to dismiss it entirely. She kept thinking about the bottle of liquor under the bed and thinking about Robert Youngman in the jail cell. She needed to do something about that and about Ruthie and about the war and consumption, about her and George loving each other fiercely—but lost. There was a lot to go through— a complicated list of unresolved puzzles. She couldn't lie still. She was beset with an aching restlessness.

In the middle of the night George had one of the nightmares he had on a regular basis, the nightmares that he never remembered but that caused his legs to twitch and kick so that Eliza could never really sleep well with him. These nightmares came and went all night. His legs kept moving like he was always running away or toward something. Eliza used to wake him up and ask him to stop, but he said he didn't know what he was doing and how could he stop something he didn't know he was doing. When he wasn't away working, she used to get up and sleep on a cot with one of the children, but there was no other room anymore. She got up and spent about ten minutes carefully getting down on her knees and pulling the bottle out from under the bed without making any noise. Then she went outside with it and made a bed for herself out of saddle blankets. She held the corked bottle with both arms against her chest, like a beloved and comforting old doll. She imagined how welcome the liquor would taste, but she was waiting for a clear picture to come into her head, one that would elicit a long and revelatory, "Ohhhh, so that's what I'm bothered about." And then she could fix it, whatever it was.

As she was falling asleep, aware and angry that dawn was imminent, she indulged in a passionate hatred of George, conjured images of him as stupid and thoughtless, wanted to find Bridie and take the children to Mexico, leaving no note. Maybe George was what was wrong with everything. If he had woken up and embraced her, if he had said, "Make me feel good," in that way he did before they came out west…"Make me feel good, Ellie," he would say into her hair with a mischievous warmth, pulling her against him and slowly rubbing the small of her back. Just thinking about it made a wave pass through her belly. And then she heard laughter nearby, coming from the arroyo—a woman's laughter. Was it her own laughter echoing around at night? Or maybe it was some bird sound. She wished she could tell George about it, about the strange sensations she had sometimes. If George knew her, could see into her mind without fear.

She didn't want to think about it, because he hadn't embraced her, he hadn't wanted her. He had continued to sleep, twitching in some remote agony. It was better to despise something than to want it; she had practiced this often enough with George. But she was getting weary of that particular trick. Eliza had the uncomfortable feeling that her mind was being forced to shift by the weight of some trauma she was in the midst of. She had the sensation of having to hold on, to get ready for an internal quake that would end her ability to choose emotions according to what felt easy. She laid her face against the cool, green glass of the bottle, murmuring a prayer to whatever or whoever cared to listen. She gently took the cork out, wiggling it, as though George might be able to hear from all the way inside the house. "Go to the devil," she said to him. Then she wanted to taste Bridie, her feverish warmth and innocent righteousness—Bridie, no doubt disheveled and amusing in the Royene mining camp, coughing just a little. Eliza pictured Robert Youngman, too, asleep in the jail cell, and she told him, "You'll be all right." She imagined herself and George and the children and Bridie and Robert Youngman eating at a table like the Salas family table. They were laughing and eating and arguing like the Salas family. George was a euphoric preacher, holding the Bible; only it wasn't really the Bible, but a book by that Herman Melville. And then this became a dream in which all of them discovered bruises slowly spreading over their arms and faces.

❖TWENTY~TWO❖

*J*ack, the man from the mining camp, came early that morning to get his horse. Eliza was giving it some water and talking to it about the clouds in the sky and whether or not it was going to rain. They were big, blossoming clouds, white and gleaming on the edges of the horizons. George was in the outhouse, Aaron was throwing rocks against the house, and Ruthie was still sleeping.

Jack nodded at Eliza.

"I guess you weren't lyin'," he said.

"About what?"

"About taking care of my horse for me. That is my horse."

"I know. Go ahead and take him. I thank you for letting me use him. I'll pay you. I don't have money right now."

"Well, you ought not to run off with a man's horse like that."

"I do thank you and I'm sorry for any inconvenience." She looked toward the outhouse, hoping that George would come out.

"Big goings on in town," Jack said.

"There always are."

"A hangin'. You're lucky it ain't you 'cause he's hangin' for horse stealin'."

Heat went up and down inside Eliza's body. She knew. She knew as though a match had been lit in a dark room where someone had been sitting all along.

But she asked anyway. "What hangin'?"

"That Indian. I guess he's the one who stole your kids."

"He didn't steal anything. He didn't do anything but help me." She glared at him, trying to bore the truth into him as though he could alter what he'd said, take it back, make it not so.

"Well, I don't know anything about it except they're hangin' him."

"That drummer, that Mr. Smith took them. The Indian is who got them back and found that horse that had run off." She had taken Jack's arm and he backed off. Then she got up on his horse and kicked it hard. Jack watched this time without reaching out or yelling. He just scratched his eyebrow and shook his head, looking at the blanket and the saddle still on the ground. He had to admit to himself he admired a woman who could ride bareback like that.

Had she thought about it, Eliza too would have been surprised at her sudden ability to ride bareback, but she had no concern with present physical sensations other than the need to move forward. Everything pushed her forward, everything had hands—the sky, the trees, the cactus, the dirt—and pushed her and the horse. There was such terror in her that she couldn't feel anything else—no strain on her lungs or her muscles as she clung on to the horse and made it tear up the ground. She stopped at the bank on Railroad Avenue and listened, thought; then she cut west over the bridge to the Old Town plaza, where the ugly, brown, plantless space seemed dryer and paler than any place on Earth. And there was no way to lie to herself, to justify the vision she saw and dismiss it; it was Robert's body swinging from the windmill above the dry well in the bleak middle of the old plaza.

Robert's hands were tied behind his back, and his head was bent forward. The thick tufts of blue-black hair glistened and winked as the rope swung him in and out of shadows. He was high up, swinging from the top of the windmill. He'd had to climb two long ladders to get up to the little platform.

There was a crowd of over fifty people, Anglo and Hispanic, staring up at the dead man. A loud pop and a flash of light came from the front of the crowd where Mr. Cleaves, the photographer, took a picture. In that photograph one can see Robert's eyes, slits of polished brown, blind and no longer wondering, slightly opened and looking down. On the edge of the photo is a woman looking at the camera, her face out of focus, but a dark feather clearly in her hat. The most sharply focused feature of the photo is Robert's shoes, which are dangling close to the sheriff, who is sitting on the edge of the big platform in the middle of the structure. The sheriff's eyes seem all one darkness since his face, like the woman's on the edge of the photo, is not in focus. He can be recognized by his wide-brimmed hat and his long beard. In the background of the photograph is the Romero Brothers store, a long box with cold angles.

Leaving the horse to contemplate the complete absence of grass, Eliza saw many people that she knew, including Mr. Near and Emily and Franz Schwartzchild. The crowd was not irreverent nor flippant. They spoke, if they spoke at all, in low tones. The mood seemed to be one of bewilderment, as though they had come to see one thing but had seen something else.

A group of men were talking to the photographer, who was packing his equipment. As he bent down to pick up a bag, his bowler hat fell off, and the man who picked it up was the most outrageous sight Eliza had ever seen, because it was Mr. Smith, the salesman. The salesman with the beret was also in the group, and Franz Schwartzchild was standing there, too, as Emily Schwartzchild headed back to her store on the New Town side of the river.

Eliza cocked her head like a curious dog. She stood there a few steps behind the crowd and looked at Robert. There was a moving, billowing ball of something in her chest. She started to choke on it, sputtering and shaking her head like a frantic cat. She moved up to the front of the gathering, up to where the photographer was. She stood behind the salesman, breathing hard and noisily, breathing like a bull.

He turned around. There was a small smile on his lips, showing a pearly tooth.

"Mrs. Pelham," he said in his booming, theatrical voice. He removed his hat and fumes of lilac oil curled into the air.

She looked at Franz, but he turned away, crossing his arms over his chest and lifting his chin.

"It's you should be up there hanging," she said to the salesman. "That man didn't do anything and you know it. You took my children off. They could've gotten killed or lost. That Indian brought them back and you know it."

The photographer's face was red and he said, "Excuse me," and left.

The sheriff jumped off the platform and stepped up, rubbing his beard.

"You've hanged the wrong man," Eliza said to him. "This is the one that took Aaron and Ruthie. This man hurt my girl—I've seen the marks. You've hanged some good man who brought back my children and your horse, somebody who didn't do anything but help me." She dropped her head. "Dear God in heaven, what have you done?" She looked back up at the sheriff, wild with a fear that she could not live in the world after this day; her eyes were bloodshot and wet. "What're you going to tell his momma, huh? What're you going to tell his momma about why her boy is dead—hanged by the neck? Dear God."

The sheriff tried to put his hand on her shoulder but she jerked away. "Go get Doc Findley," he said in the direction of Mr. Near and Mr. Schwartzchild, but neither of them moved.

"You've hanged an innocent man. And now he's dead. His life is over. He doesn't have any more life. He's dead!" She shouted these last words feeling that these people didn't know what dead meant.

"Tell her what his last words were, sheriff," Mr. Smith said, quietly, with exaggerated regret in his tone.

The sheriff bent his neck and looked into Eliza's eyes. "He said, 'I'm your enemy.' He said that himself."

"Yes, he did," the salesman said in his booming voice. "I was here. I heard it with my own ears. He looked at the crowd like some proud wild animal, like a wolf, and said, 'I am your enemy.' "

"You made him your enemy. He was helping me. He wasn't my enemy. Did Deputy Salas know about this?"

The sheriff nodded. Mr. Near and Franz talked quietly to each other, and then Franz walked away.

The sheriff said, "I'll get her on back to George. Somebody tell Doc Findley to get on out here if he can."

Mr. Near nodded and said, "Gentlemen, I expect to see you in the dancehall later this evening. We're repeatin' the performance of 'The Victory of Love.' We need some good times, I'd say."

Eliza grabbed his arm. "Has anyone seen Bridie? What about Bridie?"

Mr. Near nodded toward Mr. Smith. "He said he took her on down to St. Vincent's in Santa Fe."

"I don't believe a word he says," Eliza said to the sheriff. "Somebody ought to go up there and look for her."

The salesman rocked back and forth with his hands behind his back and then said, "I swear on my own mother's dear life that I did no harm to those children. I was seeing to them because they'd been left alone. These are dangerous times, Mrs. Pelham, and children should not be left alone."

Eliza was staring up at Robert, mesmerized.

"Is anybody going to see to him?"

"You better get on home, Mrs. Pelham. I'll take you on home. You ought to be with your children now," the sheriff said.

The salesman cleared his throat and said, "Excuse me, sheriff, but I was wondering, since there are no other claims to them, if I could take the Indian's trousers, as a souvenir."

Now the sheriff's expression showed a startled reassessment of the man. Mr. Smith laughed, "Oh, now, I don't want you to think I'm peculiar or morbid. I think you'll understand that as a businessman I see the potential in cutting the trousers into pieces and

selling them as a sensational item to the folks back east who are so
thrilled with this sort of thing—a wild Indian hanged for horse
stealing—it's just the sort of thing they'll be thrilled to own and
hold in their own hands, show all their friends."

The sheriff's face softened.

"Well, I think maybe you should wait until he's not on public
display."

"I'd want a document from you, sheriff, to certify that they did
come from this hanged man. So many unscrupulous people have
made fraudulent claims about such things,...there must be enough
pieces of the true cross sold to build a whole town." He grinned
and touched the sheriff's arm.

Eliza stepped backwards, looking at the two men with dizzy-
ing horror. Tears tumbled out of her eyes. Everything, she thought,
has come apart. She climbed up the four steps to the first low
platform of the structure, then she grabbed the first long ladder
and started up.

Now there were only about ten people left in the plaza, and
the sheriff looked at each one of them before saying, "What are
you doing, Mrs. Pelham? You come on now and go on home." Mr.
Smith strolled away, expressing his thirst.

"I'm going to take him down."

"You can't do that."

"I'm going to take him down."

Then Deputy Salas walked up and asked what was going on.

"She's out of her head," the sheriff said. "Go get George."

But the deputy just stood there, and the sheriff yelled, "God
damn it, I told you to go get George."

The deputy looked at him lazily and then walked up to position her horse (Jack's horse) close to the platform.

"You come down and sit on the horse and keep it here," he
called up to her. "I'll bring him down."

She stayed where she was, poised on the ladder and looking
down.

"You let this happen, even after I talked to you?" Eliza said. The sheriff shook his head.

"You don't understand, Mrs. Pelham," the deputy said. "He said himself that he was our enemy. Do you know how many soldiers his people have killed?"

"He was in Pennsylvania learning geometry. He didn't kill any damn soldiers."

"I think you need to go to church," the sheriff said, pulling at his beard as he walked off toward the New Town bridge.

She came down and mounted the horse without bothering to sit sidesaddle.

"There's your wife and son in the wagon," she said to the deputy.

They both looked over to the Romero Brothers store, where Señora Salas and Manuel were getting off the wagon.

Eliza met the deputy's eyes. "There's no undertaker in this town will bury him right and no church that'll do it. You know what they'll do. They'll put him up for display, let people shoot at him. Aaron says there's some of you people take care of burying when there's no priest around. Can't you take him to the morada?"

Deputy Salas raised his eyebrows and shook his head.

"I'll take him home with me if you won't help," Eliza said. "I'll bury him on your father's land. I'll wash him and bury him myself."

"I'll get the wagon. You can take him to my home. I'll see what can be done."

❧TWENTY~THREE❧

*W*ith linen cloths, the three women washed the body: Señora Salas, Eliza, and the old woman called Tía. Eliza took off his shoes first, carefully untying them, slowly removing them as though not to wake the man. His feet were long and bony, with yellow callouses along the outside of his big toes. Señora Salas brought in a ceramic basin of water decorated with blue flowers. The old woman crossed herself often as she muttered prayers in Latin.

They washed the body slowly, meticulously, in silence except for the old woman's praying. As they wiped the skin, they could feel the body cool and harden, setting like a loaf of bread. Eliza looked often at the face. The cheeks were swollen, as though he had mumps. The pupils were still visible, staring down at something, though Señora Salas had tried to close his eyes. Without having to say so, they knew that it was the old woman's job to wash the genitals, the older the better—a woman so old that genitals meant nothing to her. But Eliza looked at them, the penis slightly erect, lying against his thigh. It was this view of the penis, a darker color than the rest of him, but so vulnerable, that made her feel more wretched than she had felt before. She washed his fingers, her eyes wide, not blinking. She wet the cloth and wiped each finger, wiped between the fingers as gently as possible. She raised the hand up to her lips and kissed the fingers. The other two women looked neither at her nor at each other. Eliza stroked her own cheek with the dead man's fingers, emitting a soft, short hum.

Señora Salas left the room, then the old woman. Eliza walked out the door into the courtyard and sat down at the table, where there were bunches of herbs drying. In a few minutes she stood again and carried the chair into the room. She sat beside Robert as the old woman was dressing him in black pants and a fine white shirt with billowing sleeves. Eliza sat there with him, holding his hand as Señora Salas oiled and combed his hair. Eliza stayed there beside Robert, holding his hand.

About three o'clock, when the light was in the west and the room very dim, Eliza could hear a conversation outside between Señora Salas and some men, the Salas brothers. They were whispering, and Eliza sensed that it wasn't so she couldn't hear. They were speaking in Spanish. It was so Señor Salas, wherever he was, could not hear.

Eliza stayed there with Robert, felt his hand grow cold, knew that the blood had collected in his back. She would stay there as he bloated and stank, stay there holding his hand, until someone did something. She would not be afraid. She would not turn away from him. She would not drink and forget him. She would not drink and fail to see things like this coming. Dear God, she would beg George to sit across from her and hold her hands to keep them from picking up the bottle. He would hold them until they ached, until he had to crush the bones.

Señora Salas came with a candle when it was dark. She said from the doorway, "You must come now. The men will take care of him."

Eliza didn't get up.

"What will they do with him?" she asked.

"They will take care of him. You must come. You must not see them."

"Where will they take him? To the morada?"

"I do not know," she answered. "It is not for us to know."

Eliza stood up, looking down at Robert for a last time.

"His mother should have been able to say good-bye to him, to hold him again, don't you think?" When she turned her face to Señora Salas, her eyes were smooth and glistening with tears. "Don't you think his mother should have been able to say good-bye to him, to kiss his cheek? It's still so soft, though he was a man." She saw them all as though she were underneath clear water.

"Come along, Mrs. Pelham. The men will take care of him. They will bury him somewhere."

Señora Salas led her by the arm to a room where a fire was burning in a little rectangular hearth. Two wooden rocking chairs with wicker seats were in front of the fire, and the two women sat in them, not speaking. They stared at the fire and could hear noises outside, men straining with a load, whispering instructions to each other. When it had been quiet for a while, Eliza got up and went out into the courtyard. She squatted down on the ground and put her face on her knees. When she looked up, she saw Robert's shoes in the darkened room, sitting at the foot of the bed.

✦TWENTY~FOUR✦

*T*he evening got older and more faded. There was an unusual silence—the town was weary, stunned maybe, but pretending to go along. Some slow music from Near and Anderson's waved around the still air. A woman started singing and Eliza stopped to listen, to hear Bridie's voice. But it wasn't Bridie's voice; in truth it was better, but Eliza imagined, knew, that the woman who was singing was not as pink or as ripe as Bridie. Eliza saw Bridie dancing in the woods, saw her smile—the one tooth a little crooked, but the face beautiful and rich as one of the pastries her mother bought in Louisville. Eliza tried to imagine Bridie in the hospital in Santa Fe, nurtured, mothered by gentle nuns who bent over her to feel her forehead. It might be nice to be there, to have someone wipe your brow—to just be taken care of like an infant.

Dark was sliding over everything, led by one crow in the sky who flew from tree to tree behind Eliza, flying quietly except when it took off in a flurry of wing sound. It followed patiently. Eliza kept looking back, kept seeing the slow, graceful splendor of wings, black as shadow, the eyes dark and shiny beads of determination. Eliza walked very straight—her posture was excellent, as her mother had always wanted it to be, warning that, though it was true her height was a deterrent to attracting boys, it was far more unappealing to be slumped over and sloppy looking.

"Maybe I should come home for a while, Mother," she said aloud. She would read the Bible with her mother, lingering over the parts about how thou shalt not ride horses like a man; thou shalt not make jokes at the dinner table; thou shalt not mourn too much, love too much, cry too much; thou shalt not like to have a man's hands on your buttocks.

The crow laughed.

One star shone very crisply; it was her father, she thought. Another star in the west but farther north—who was that? Some stranger; someone else's father. And all the stars in the sky could be the soldiers she saw whose bodies were so dirty, sons and fathers all who believed that they were dying for something important. And the star spoke to her, saying, "Whose side is God on, Ellie?" And she remembered his hands on her shoulders, holding her there, trying to explain why her mother called him a shameless coward, a traitor, a humiliation. Why a person was so often willing to explain the truth away.

"Whose side is God on, Ellie? There are churches in the North just like there are churches in the South, and don't you think that people in both churches pray to God to help them win?"

Eliza said, "I don't know. I don't know whose side God is on."

And wasn't "Daddy" the name that she called out to when the baby wouldn't come and she suspected that it was dead? Hadn't she called out, "Daddy," and the Negro girl wiped her brow and said, "Your daddy with you. He with you." But Eliza hadn't felt him and was very bitter. And she said to the girl, unkindly, "He's dead; he drowned in the river. He's all bloated and white."

"Tha's all right," she'd said. "He with you."

How could some people be so sure, so calm?

The star twinkled, winked at her. The crow still followed, sometimes sounding like someone lightly walking behind her.

Maybe George could tell her which side God was on. But the house was dark. There was no one there. What happened to that dog anyway? The grass whirled around in the breeze that finally put all daylight out. No light came on in the broken house; the substantial form of the woodstove could be seen in the open room. But everything else was empty, formless, ready to rise up and disappear like smoke.

Eliza stepped into the bedroom, wondering if this was the way her life would be from now on: her children always disappearing.

A page of Ruthie's workbook was on the bed. Eliza held it up to her face and managed to read the big lettering—George's handwriting, or maybe Aaron's. She wondered at first if George had left her, almost expected it. Who knows what people had told him about her and Franz Schwartzchild; about her and Robert; about her looking at Robert's penis.

But the note said:

We've all gone into town for the drama.

"All right," she said and sat on the bed. She looked around the room; everything was looking back at her, nervous—the dresser, the picture of her mother, the banjo, a button on the floor, the picture of the dead baby.

She stood up and sat in the corner of the room opposite the window and the dresser, hiding and watching. The subtlest shadow passed by outside. Then in the window she could see the form of someone pacing back and forth; just a form, a fleeting sensation of a person who knew she was in there in the dark, who was waiting.

She looked under the bed and located the bottle. But it was turned on its side and all but a few drops of liquor had seeped out around the loose cork. She looked hard at it—the prone position, the one swallow left glistening like collected dew, the ineptness of the cork—all taunted her. The whole day culminated somehow in the tragic details of spilled whiskey. She grabbed the bottle and held it up to see by moonlight that the little liquid remaining was a cruel tease. She laid it on its side and kicked it across the room. Its final rolling sounded like soft, jeering laughter.

"What are you waiting for?" Eliza whispered, holding her legs.

Then, preceded by the faintest whiff of cinnamon and roses, the woman—black, black, black—walked in and stood in the doorway, looking at Eliza.

She was beautiful—the most beautiful woman Eliza had ever seen except for Bridie; and the beauty was exactly the opposite of Bridie's: dark and slim. The woman's hair gleamed and moved like satin. The features on her face were sharp and noble angles, the lips small and soft. The woman's eyes were long, almond shaped, made narrower because they were squinting to see Eliza crouched in the corner.

"What do you want?" Eliza asked.

The woman didn't answer but moved around the room, touching things—a comb, a bottle, the picture of the baby.

She picked up the picture and held it to her ribs. She held it facing out so that Eliza could see it—the baby's translucent skin, the eyes shut, the lace cap a little crooked and much too big.

"What do you want?" Eliza screamed.

A pot fell off the woodstove and clanged. Something scurried over charred rubble.

The woman put the picture back and leaned against the dresser.

"I am curious," she said.

Eliza shifted her weight and put her legs straight out in front of her.

The woman laughed, her teeth so white in the darkness that Eliza could see traces of them in the air after the woman had closed her mouth.

"I don't like this world," Eliza said.

"Whose world? Your world? My world? Their world?" She flung her arms out, almost losing the shawl. Gathering it back, she said in a melodic Mexican accent, "You are feeling sorry for yourself, mi hija, a lonely woman who looks for the truth and fairness and finds only...¿qué?...trains, liars, killers, little gadgets that do not work as promised."

"I just want to die. Leave me alone."

"Perhaps you want to drown yourself from motives of delicacy."

"You don't understand."

"I understand that you want to be a woman of tragedy like me." The woman paced a little in front of the dresser. Eliza could see her dark reflection in the mirror. "You do not want to make love; you do not want to sit down at a table and eat with others; you do not want to tend to your child's constipation—you want to wail to the heavens that your tragedy is unique and that it excludes you from the mundane? You are special when you are the victim, no? Or perhaps it helps you to forget your own guilt if you make yourself the wounded one. What are you so guilty about, mi hija? You have not drowned your children. Not yet."

"The world is very ugly. My children have just begun to see how ugly the world is. Maybe they'd be better off drowned."

The woman walked over and noiselessly squatted in front of Eliza. How beautiful she was, her skin close up flawless and as smooth as porcelain.

"I think you are in love with the dead; I think you desire to become intimate with them."

She came closer to Eliza, and her warm tongue peeked out of her mouth and touched Eliza's lips. Eliza jerked her head backwards.

"Leave me alone."

The woman stood up and crossed her arms over her chest.

"What are you going to do then?" she said in a louder, more casual tone.

"I don't know. Maybe I'll sit here until people come, and I will kill them one by one."

"I have tried that. It does not work. There are too many people. They just keep coming and you get very tired. First they came in ships, then wagons, and now by the trainload. And anyway, you do not have a gun. And I cannot imagine you strangling one person after another with those skinny arms."

"Then I'll just sit here and scream and scream, and I'll tell them all what I think of them. They won't want to have anything to do with me because they won't want to hear the truth. Then they'll leave me alone."

"Including your children."

"Yes."

The woman nodded and then said, "Well, I am interested in hearing the truth. Why don't you start with me. Tell me the truth."

"The world is dirty."

"Yes. I already know this. What else?"

"People don't know what they're doing. Those who aren't too stupid to know what is right are too weak to do it."

Eliza got up on her knees; tears began to fall down her face.

"It is wrong," she said passionately, "to twist and gore and strangle and tear a young man's body. It is wrong to scatter dead boys all over someone's field. I know this. I'm not the only smart person in the world. Why do people act ignorantly? I don't want to see the world. I don't want to see any of it." She was hysterically crying, bending over, still on her knees.

The woman above her sighed.

"I can see that," she said calmly. "Yes, I can see what you are saying." She tapped her finger against her lips and thought for a moment. "But what about your children? That is the problem, ¿qué no? What about the children?"

"I don't know."

"It is painful, no, to see their little heads held beneath the water, unable to breathe? But if the mother herself can be only a victim, she must not be distracted by children. She cannot be dedicated to her victimization and her children at the same time."

Eliza looked up at her, breathing spasmodically but the tears no longer flowing. "Don't you have anything to drink? Some whiskey? Or some wine?"

"I told my children as I held their heads beneath the water, I told them almost what you have told me: 'The world is cruel,' I said. 'There is disease and guns and bad smells, preachers and people who are always trying to reach something by stepping on your backs. I am saving you,' I told them, 'from much suffering.' I told them, 'I am saving you from the suffering I must go through.' Oh, how I pitied my own suffering."

A tear fell from her eye onto Eliza's hand.

"Really I just wanted to get rid of them so I could be with my lover. Who is your lover? I think you have many. I think you make love to your own thoughts and to whiskey and to dead boys."

The woman squatted again, holding her shawl and looking closely at Eliza's face. She took both of Eliza's hands, and their faces were inches apart.

"I can offer you a place in the world. Are you listening?"

"Yes."

"You can come with me. You can walk at night with me and we will moan together—two women, victims of this horrible world, victims finally of our own actions and despair. We can wail and weep together, strolling arm in arm along the arroyos, perhaps as a warning to others, perhaps because we feel like it—I do not know."

She stood up, pulling the shawl back over her shoulder.

"You cannot be weak, though. I will tell you that. This life is not for the weak. I do not want to have to listen to your complaints about your feet hurting or your throat getting sore." She clutched her own throat. "I am good at it. It is my calling, and I have not made this offer to all the women who think that their suffering is profound. Oh-la, let me tell you. There are thousands of them, all over the place, perfecting their ability to suffer. If every woman who felt that her suffering was worthy of public attention walked along the arroyos to wail with me, we would not have room to move; we would be walking into each other all night saying, 'Excuse me. Perdón, Señora, Señorita.' "

She walked back to the dresser and leaned against it as she had in the beginning. Eliza sat back in the corner, her arms resting on her bent legs. She watched the woman, the witch, the saint, the mother; Eliza listened, though she wanted only to sleep.

"Or you can let me take care of the wailing. Let me do what I do well for you, and you get on with other things."

"What other things? The world will go on with its noise and greed and lies no matter what I do."

The woman pressed her thumb against her fingers and put them near her mouth as though tasting something.

"The truth is not all sweet or all bitter. It is like a meal with different tastes. I am the sad one. I am the bitter one. I will suffer for you."

"Why?"

The woman raised her head haughtily. "Because I like to; because it makes me feel important. And I am at least as good as Jesus Christ. The difference is that I do not just die for one's sins, I express the guilt. I am guilty for you. Jesus gets to sit on the right hand of God, but I must walk along the arroyos, expressing my remorse and guilt."

Eliza looked at her through glasses speckled with tears. The woman laughed and came next to her, sitting beside her on the floor. Eliza leaned against her.

"I am so tired," she said.

"Entiendo, mi hija. Entiendo." She stroked Eliza's hair, and the smell of roses was strong on her clothes. Her hands felt like water rolling over Eliza's head. Eliza wept hard, relieving the feeling in her stomach that she had carried around for days, years maybe. She called out for her father, for her dead baby, for Robert, for George.

"Mi hija," the woman kept whispering, and she, too, began to weep, so that her skin smelled like damp, dark earth.

Eliza fell asleep in the woman's arms, aware that at some point the woman gently slid away, saying, "Buenas noches."

When Eliza opened her eyes again, she saw George in the moonlight, holding Ruthie, laying her on the bed. Aaron was leaning against his father, complaining about being tired.

George looked over and saw Eliza lying on the floor in the corner. He said to Aaron, "Go on and get in bed, son."

"I need to go to the outhouse first," the boy answered.

Squatting down beside her as the woman had, George asked, "What are you doing down here on the floor, Ellie?"

And all kinds of habitual thoughts lumbered wearily through her mind about how George would be irritated with her no matter what she said, that he would be especially annoyed and cold if she acted weak and weepy, that he blamed her for all her own problems and most of his. He blamed her for the baby dying, and that's why she didn't call out for him; he blamed her for the children being taken away. And why shouldn't he?

But in a strange instance of lucidity, she decided that the George who chastised her in her head was a trick—whose trick, she didn't know for certain. But this beginning awareness compelled her to lean against George as she had leaned against the woman.

She wept. "They killed him, George—that young man is dead, hanged." She could hardly say the words without choking on sobs. He sat down with her, held her hard, harder than the woman had held her. He rocked her and didn't say anything.

"He's dead," Eliza sobbed. "And I washed his body."

George sighed and rocked her. When she had calmed down, he lifted her hand to see what she was holding. It was the picture of their baby, smiling, dead.

When Aaron came back in and got in bed, George and Eliza were sitting together on the floor; later they both lay down right there in the corner. The next morning they were still there, asleep and tangled together.

The picture of the baby had fallen out of Eliza's hand. Aaron found it on the floor before anyone else had woken up. He put it carefully back on the dresser and went out to sit in the arroyo.

✦TWENTY~FIVE✦

*I*n the grass plains to the east there were dark hillocks on the horizon, a group of them slowly moving. A few people stood around at the edge of New Town, just east of the railroad tracks, watching, pointing: two workers from the railroad, a father holding his three-year-old boy and pointing. An old man stared, a little lost, and then asked no one in particular where his Sharpe's rifle was, the one he used many years ago to fell buffalo.

"Mister, it could put a hole in one of them, blow his whole head off," he said aloud. Women were chatting with each other, their arms crossed over their chests, children clinging to their legs, wrapped in skirts that the wind blew over them.

One of the many drunks accumulating in New Town tried to panhandle a few of the reverent watchers, but they shooed him off.

The people whispered, although the buffalo were perhaps a mile away and could not hear them. The grasses also made a delicate whispering sound and bent in arcs in unison, becoming more orange in the last light. People wandered off reluctantly, except for the old man, who wondered what it was he was thinking twenty years ago. He forgot, but he was sad; he had made a mistake, but he was not quite sure what it was. Certainly, God would tell him when he died. He looked at his hands for a clue— they had become a landscape of dry riverbeds and treeless valleys.

A younger man's hands were fumbling with the cloth buttons on a woman's dress. "It's been a long time," he whispered. The breath of two people made a rhythm, enhanced by the woman's humming sighs. One hand cupped a breast clothed in yellowed cotton.

The old man walked back to the edge of town; he stopped to grab a hitching post and get his breath. He looked around and didn't recognize anything, didn't remember all those buildings, didn't like the sound of the hammering. What was that mistake he had made and meant to correct?

George, lying on top of Eliza, held her buttocks and pulled her to him with the same rhythm he was pushing into her.

"Slow," she breathed.

The old man looked back; only a few people were still standing there talking and pointing; one of them, Mr. Near, was chewing a piece of grass. The small herd of buffalo seemed to be looking back at the town, and then, elegant in the twilight, noiseless like spirits who wanted to taste the moisture and substance of this Earth one last time, they moved on—out of sight behind a copse of young elm.

The old man wanted to go with them, but even he didn't understand this desire. A man waved at him from the door of a hardware store; the old man looked up stiffly; he did not wave back, but whispered, "Scoundrels," to himself. And two of the women from Near's, who were smoking little Mexican cigars in front of the dancehall, laughed at him.

Eliza touched George's back with her fingers, moving down his skin from his shoulder to his waist. She was thinking of Bridie, seeing her breasts beneath the wet camisole, seeing her pretending to have the ecstasy. Should she do this for George? Should she pretend? Would he not leave her so often if she did?

George lifted his face, sweaty and red, his eyes drooped with effort. He balanced himself on his elbow and looked down at Eliza's sweet nipples, which showed through the cotton. He started to move his lips, but didn't say anything. Then he rolled on his back with his arm bent over his eyes. Cricket sounds sharpened around them as the first star in the west was lit.

Then George got up and put his pants on. Eliza brought the edge of the blanket they were lying on over her and watched George roll a cigarette. He looked up toward the house and said, "We have to move on from here."

"Is that what you were thinking about?"

George didn't answer, so Eliza said, "I thought you were going to build on, fix it up and build another room on like you said." She sat up as he lit the cigarette.

"I can't afford to." He spat out a little shred of tobacco.

"Why can't we just stay?"

"It isn't ours anymore, Ellie, that's why."

"It belongs to the Salases."

"No, it belongs to Franz Schwartzchild mainly. He's in with a group of men, including that lawyer and Mr. Near."

"What?"

"Franz called in the credit, and this place wasn't worth much, being all burnt up like this." He pointed with the cigarette.

Eliza looked down at the ground. She shook her head, laughed, and lay back. George muttered to himself saying "damn" a lot. Eliza sat up again and put her hand on his leg.

"They cheated me. And those damn Mexicans burning this place down. I haven't got anything left," he said, coughing and sputtering, unwilling to allow room for any sobs that might be collecting. Eliza stroked his hard calf and said, "That's all right."

"He called in the credit like he's been doing to those Mexicans," George said incredulously, "like we were just some Mexicans."

"We never owned this land in the first place," Eliza whispered.

George stepped away, angry, threw down the cigarette, and obliterated it in the dirt with his bare heel.

"You don't understand. You don't understand anything and you never will. I *had* the deed. The lawyers drew up a deed—it had my name on it." He poked himself in the chest. "They didn't have the right papers," he pointed to the west with his arm, toward Old Town. "It wasn't theirs; they couldn't prove it. That's the way things are now."

"Why can't we still live here? Franz has a big house in town."

"He wants to lease it to us—says it's worth a lot more to let people graze their cattle here, but he'll lease it to us for a hundred a year." He glared at his wife.

She lay back laughing again, and George pulled his boots on, fuming as he hopped around on one leg and then the other getting them on.

"I remember when you used to talk about how you wanted to live," Eliza said.

"What?" George was angry.

Eliza spoke up: "I said I remember when you used to talk about how you wanted to live, maybe start a society like the ones you read about."

"Why do you mention that now? Are you trying to make me feel worse than I already feel?"

"I just don't understand—"

"What don't you understand now?"

"How things could change so much—how a person could change so much. How a person could live with himself, pretending he never wanted something."

"And just what do you think I should do, Ellie? I can't help the way the world is; I can't help that I'm surrounded by scoundrels and a wife and children that have to eat. You think somebody pays a man to dream?"

George walked up to the house.

"I'm going to stay out here for a while," Eliza called out as she put her glasses on.

She watched the stars clarify and thought about Bridie, waiting for her in that hospital in Santa Fe, probably getting the nuns all in a dither. She'd go down and get her; they could live like sisters and help each other and amuse George. She would never leave George. What else could she be but George's wife? And she still loved the smell of him, remembered the honest, innocent times when they weren't afraid of each other. She wanted to have his baby, a living baby. What else was there to do? He hadn't had the ecstasy this time when they made love. But he would, and maybe even she would, and they'd have that baby, alive and squalling. But first she'd have to go to George and ask him please not to go away again. She'd have to not be proud. She'd have to admit that she wanted to be with him and be loved by him. Bridie had said she was a strong woman. What did that mean? Did that mean not needing a man around? She surely didn't need Franz Schwartzchild; it made her face hot to think of what she'd done for no good reason. She needed George, though, in order to feel right. And she knew that George needed her to feel right, no matter how deranged he acted sometimes.

She found her bloomers and started getting dressed.

And besides, her old brain had caved in, like the rotted loft in an old barn, when she had to see Robert hanged, dead. Old liquor bottles and the dust of dried-up ghosts had fallen out of her head, useless. It was hard to know what to do now. Ruthie needed her, and Aaron, too, in his own way, so she couldn't entertain any notion of going crazy or flopping down like some rag doll. But she didn't want to be strong alone. She wanted to be strong with George, because they had once been completely honest and foolish with each other.

When she got to him, he was lying on the bed next to Ruthie, who was snoring a little, like a cat.

"She sleeps all the time," Eliza whispered, standing in front of the dresser. "She doesn't chatter like she used to and even wet the bed a couple of times."

"Yeah," George whispered, looking at his sleeping daughter. He pulled the quilt up to her shoulder blade.

"Where're we going to go?" his wife asked.

"I don't know, Ellie," he said impatiently.

"What about Mexico?"

George looked at her and laughed meanly.

"Why do you hate me so much, George? Is it because the baby died?"

"Keep your mouth shut, Ellie. We've got enough to worry about."

"No, you keep your mouth shut." Why wasn't she on her knees, telling him how dear he was to her? She tried to change her tone. "My mother'll send us money. You know we aren't going to starve."

"Where'll she send it? I don't even know where we're going to be."

Eliza thought for a minute.

"She can send it to Schwartzchild's store, and we'll be able to come and get it."

"From Mexico?" He looked sideways at her.

"I'm just tired of this place. I don't like how things are going."

"What do you mean?"

"I mean all the killing and death and noise."

"You think Mexico's better?" he scoffed at her.

"Is the railroad down there?"

"If it weren't for the railroad, I wouldn't have a position. I'd be hog-tied."

"So, you're going to keep on working with the crew?"

He lifted his head up and made his whisper as much like a yell as he could. "Hell, yes. What did you think?"

"I just thought we could go out and farm somewhere. Why not do what you talked about?"

"There's no more cheap land available. People have bought it all up. Besides, you don't like making butter. How're you going to work on a farm? You never seemed much interested in my plans, anyway." He lay back down and closed his eyes.

"Damn you, George, can't you even listen to me? Can't you even give me a chance?"

He pointed his finger at her. "Don't you talk to me like that."
The air began to feel nauseating to her.

"I want to be with you. Don't you remember how we used to talk about being different from everybody else?"

He sat up on the edge of the bed, rubbing his face. Eliza walked to him, and he held her and put his face against her belly.

He stood up and held her, his palm pressing her head against his shoulder.

"This isn't how we thought it would be, is it?" he said.

"People don't like me here. I'm not like these people."

"How do you know that they don't feel different too?"

"They're better at hiding being different. I can't seem to hide it for long."

"Maybe if you didn't drink so much you could hide it. You just don't act right all the time. It gives them ideas. You can't just go off with some Irish whore and come back wearing pants and think nobody will be bothered."

"Then why did we bother to come out here if we're going to end up the same as if we were in Kentucky, worrying about what the Baptists and the Methodists think? They do wrong things all the time, worse than I do. I don't hang people that tried to help someone. I don't steal people's land. Why am I being called the bad one?"

"I'm not calling you bad, Ellie," George said. He took her head and held her face up to his. Ruthie said something in her sleep, so George waited. Then he looked right into Eliza's eyes and she saw in the intricate quartz of his irises how lonely she was.

"I know you, Ellie," he said as quietly as air. "I know you."

"Is that why you stay away so much?"

He closed his eyes and took his hands away from her head.

Eliza said to him, "Why can't we just go somewhere and make a home together without burned-out rooms and drummers coming around? I *will* make butter, George, and sew and cook, and maybe do other things when I get a notion, because too much goes on in my head for just sewing and cooking. I want to talk to you about things. I want to be held by you every night and do things with you that the dancehall girls know how to do. I want to have six more children, your children. I want my body filled with babies made by me and my husband."

She looked straight into his face, shameless.

"Why do you talk so much, Ellie? Why do people talk so much? Why can't I just do my work, get paid, make a few deals, and sit back when the day's over? Why can't people just stop talking so much?"

"I feel so sad," Eliza said, "and I'm scared that's all I'll be for the rest of my life—sad."

George walked out to the other room and stood with his back to the woodstove, looking at the sooted rugs, partially burned up. Eliza followed and stood with her head bowed over the stove. There was a little light left in the day, enough so they could still see the pale parts of each other.

Then he was behind her and lifted up her skirts. He slowly pulled down the bloomers, as though he was peeling away the skin of a grape. Eliza stepped out of them, her loose sole making her stumble a bit.

"You need some new shoes, Ellie," George said, as though they were strolling along somewhere, but his breathing was noisy.

Eliza backed herself against his hips, rolling her buttocks against the stiff erection in his pants. "All right," she was saying in her head. "All right. You'd better be ready, George. You'd better not be a coward." He backed away and looked at her naked bottom, then rubbed it with his palms, making her move back and forth with the rhythm of fornication. "You're my husband," she whispered, as though it was a lustful, delicious word. She laid the top half of her body down on the cold iron stove, indulging in the feeling of grit and old grease on her face and arms.

With one hand George moved stray hairs away from Eliza's face. She heard him unbutton his pants; one of the buttons flew off and made a pinging sound somewhere in the charred mess. They both laughed. Then Eliza moaned, "Oh," as she felt him go into her, fitting snugly as a solid warmth that compelled the bodies to move against one another.

"You are my Ellie," George said, "my fine Ellie."

"Yes," Eliza said. She was staring at the stovepipe and thinking how good George smelled, how much she loved his voice and to lie on his chest and hear his voice inside there like a drum in a church.

"We know each other, Ellie. Don't be afraid of me. Don't be afraid."

He spread his legs apart and bent his knees a little to get deeper, to come up inside her hard. Her pelvis was up against the stove, grinding into it through the cushion of her wadded-up dress.

"Don't be afraid of me, sweetheart," he said. And her eyes opened wide looking at the stovepipe as he moved so tenderly against her. Eliza couldn't think of what she was supposed to be afraid of in George. It wasn't this George who scared her at all, but the one who wouldn't touch her. She wasn't afraid, but transfixed by the power of his penis, a godlike power to put a child inside her, an act of divine trust in her willingness and ability to be mother. Still staring at the stovepipe, which had transformed into an icon, Eliza was taken over by the involuntary tightening and loosening inside her where George had rammed himself and stayed deep, saying, "You feel so damn good, Ellie." She imagined the ecstasy of his explosion inside her, so deep that her belly would instantly grow, and when she stood up she would be able to feel the child moving inside her. She made a slight squeaking noise as she breathed. She wanted to tell him all about the feeling and how wonderful it was. How wonderful it was that they could please each other as husband and wife after all these years.

George lay down on her back, careful to keep some of his weight on his arms. He kissed the back of her neck and she laughed.

"I can't believe what we're doing here. I've got dirt all over me." He stood up, pulling her with him, swaying with her in his arms, her back against his chest. They stayed like this for many moments until it was very dark.

"I'm so tired, Ellie. I've been so tired for so many years."

Liquid fell out of Eliza, tickling as it slid down the inside of her thighs.

"I want to have another baby," she said. He kissed her in the curve of her neck and nodded with his head still nestled there.

"I want to get strings for the banjo and make up songs on it like I used to," she went on. "I want to ask Bridie O'Doonan to live with us."

George let her go. She turned and stood before him with an intent expression on her smudged face that he could barely see.

"She's a dancehall girl, Ellie. And she's got consumption."

"I don't care. She was like a sister to me, and I haven't always treated her decently. She thinks I'm strong. I want to be strong, George. It'd be a help to have somebody around who already thinks I am."

He studied her.

"They say you've been seeing Franz Schwartzchild, lying down with him upstairs at the store."

She didn't say anything. Ruthie sighed audibly in her sleep. They stood still until there was a growing sense that the closeness had become awkward for both of them and they moved apart. George walked to the doorway and stared at her. She stared back. Then he walked out.

Still Eliza didn't say anything. She was thinking about going after him when Ruthie screamed in her sleep like a baby mountain lion. It was an inhuman sound that made Eliza's skin freeze. When she got to her, Ruthie was sitting up; she had wet the bed again.

"I don't want to be anybody's wife," she said.

Eliza looked down at her child and felt barren and old. She was sore between her legs. It was the juxtaposition of Ruthie's outburst and the soreness Eliza felt between her legs that caused her to suddenly feel extremely nauseated, like the shredded remains of a dead animal were being propelled up through her. She threw herself down to the floor and crawled halfway under the bed to get the whiskey bottle. Facing Ruthie again, she said, "Do you want some whiskey?"

"No."

"I didn't think so. Here I'll put some worn-up old sheet down. Did you get that nightshirt wet?"

"No."

"Take off those leggings, then, and get on back in bed."

Such small movements the child made, the legs so bare and skinny. Eliza didn't see how she could keep her solid, keep her from disappearing.

"You go back to sleep now," Eliza said; then she went out of the room and stared at the woodstove.

She waited in the demolished room, holding the bottle by the neck like it was a dead chicken, until Aaron came in and asked her what she was doing standing around in the dark. He told her about the nickel he'd gotten for helping Deputy Salas and Manny whitewash the jail. He asked where his father was, and when Eliza said, "I don't know, but Ruthie's wet the bed again," he sighed and went outside.

"I'm sleeping out here on these blankets tonight," he said.

And Eliza, still standing in the dark by the woodstove said, "All right."

Aaron, whom Eliza could only see as a lump some feet away in the night, finally said, "You want me to get you something?"

And this made Eliza cry and tell herself she was crying far too much. She smelled her hands that smelled like George.

"That's all right, Aaron," she called out in a loud whisper. "I just have to figure something out."

⤳TWENTY~SIX⤦

*H*anging out washed sheets in the brilliant morning, Eliza
wanted to use them as sails to take her into the sky; child's
leggings flapped on the line, kicking in tantrum.

Eliza took a clothespin from the canvas bag Aaron was holding as he walked beside her.

"How did your sister get hurt?" she asked, as though mildly
curious about an insignificant event.

"I don't know."

"Didn't you see her fall? She must have fussed. Ruthie doesn't
let a chance to fuss go by. What did that drummer do when she got
hurt?"

"He read from the Bible."

"Oh, I see. Did he look to see if she was hurt bad or not?"

Aaron looked at the kicking leggings.

"He read to us out of the Bible every night. He said he was
going to teach us things boys and girls should know." He threw
one of the clothespins at a tree.

"Don't do that. Why'd you do that?"

"I don't know."

"What do you know?"

Aaron shrugged.

"Look at me, boy. What do you know?"

Aaron leaned toward her, giving her his full and dangerous stare.

"Nothin'!" he yelled. "I don't know nothin'!"

"What did he do?" Eliza yelled back, walking him backwards to the house. "What happened to Ruthie?"

"He said he was going to teach her."

"Teach her what?"

Aaron held his face up to the sky and closed his eyes. Then he screamed, "Teach her to be a wife! All right? All right?"

Eliza dropped the laundry basket, a dry wicker thing, already splintered in places. She couldn't blink. Aaron's face was trembling as he looked back at his mother.

"Ruthie didn't like it. I told him she didn't like it, and he said a girl needed to be taught certain things and I'd be glad of it when I had a wife'd been taught those things."

Eliza's mouth moved.

"Stop," she whispered.

Walking away, she stumbled over the dropped basket, splitting its dry reeds on one side. Aaron just looked down at it lying there, mute and useless.

TWENTY-SEVEN

The newspaper the next morning had two articles in it concerning Indians, one about the desperate need for the federal government, which seemed to have forgotten its territories, to send more troops to fight the renegade Apache and Ute who were constantly conspiring to commit mayhem. The editor hailed the valor and skill of the soldiers who were trying with all their hearts to quell the spreading danger. Never mind that the biggest medical problems at Fort Union weren't battle wounds but syphilis and alcoholism. The article harped on the need for more funding to the military installations in that area so constantly harassed by nomadics who simply did not understand the civilizing character of the American reservation system.

The other article was about the hanging some days ago of a brutal Apache who had stolen a sheriff's horses—there was an exclamation after this fact and a reference to the Indian as a shameless scoundrel. In light of the editorial mission of that day's newspaper, the article on the hanging concluded, "If we must rid ourselves of these scoundrels one by one, we will eliminate them from this now civilized territory." It supported this approach over the reservation idea for, it said, "It is a shame to waste good land on Indians who don't know how to profit from it."

The newspaper also mentioned the dance being held in one of New Town's newest dancehalls, owned by a gentleman from Ohio. The dance was to feature Dr. Findley's band, with Dr. Findley on piano.

Deputy Salas could hear Dr. Findley playing "I Dream of Jeannie with the Light Brown Hair" as the former rode his newly acquired quarterhorse out of New Town to the river's edge. He wanted to go down to the ejido—the common land where the cattle of five families watered and grazed—before the sheriff found something for him to do. He'd heard an ugly rumor he wanted to check out. He could hear the mourning doves cooing and luxuriated in the smell of pine coming down from the nearby mountains. His thoughts were on a number of things and drifted to Eliza Pelham, who bothered him, but he didn't know exactly why. He couldn't quite settle in his mind the hanging of that Apache; he didn't like that he had had a name—Robert Youngman— and that Eliza had talked about what his mother would think about his being hanged. Burying him had just made Deputy Salas's discomfort worse, because it was the beginning of an admission that maybe this Apache, this Robert Youngman, shouldn't have been killed. That hanging seemed to relieve the town temporarily—like the lancing of a boil that was getting chronic. But one thing had disturbed him about the actual incident: the dignity with which the Indian had said, "I am your enemy." He couldn't just feel sorry for the Indian, or hate him; he had to feel some respect for him, because Salas too was, after all, the enemy of the Anglos—sometimes. When he wore the deputy's star, he was everybody's friend. When he wore the sack over his head, that was another thing. And that look on Eliza Pelham's face when she came up to them at the hanging—she was looking at them all like enemies—every single one of them. And he had to respect her too. Poor Eliza Pelham—she was an odd one.

It was sad, Deputy Salas was thinking as he rode along pleased with the horse, that the Americans who came here from the East were so alone—few abuelas or tías who could console and keep someone, like Eliza, in line and tell her how to behave so people wouldn't talk so badly about her, even rumoring that her father had refused to fight in the war. Still, he wondered if she had seen the buffalo last evening and had the strangest notion of riding out and asking her.

About two hundred yards from the river he thought his eyes were tricking him. He trotted the horse up and stopped it short at a fence, an ugly new kind of fence, skinny wires with knots on it and mean, sharp points coming off the knots—a vicious-looking thing which at first reminded Salas of the wreath of thorns the cofradías, who held their rituals in the morada, wore around their heads to imitate the suffering of Jesus. He did not participate in these secret rites, though he had been let in on the fact that his brothers and his father were members of the cofradía. Perhaps it was because he was a deputy, upholding American law. Perhaps it was because once when he was drunk he had told his mother he no longer wanted to attend mass.

Salas sat in the saddle, puzzled, and looked up and down the edge of the river. About twenty cows ambled up closer to him, stopped before the fence, looking stupidly at the water beyond, waiting for the man to do something. A sign on the fence said, NO TRESPASSING. *Private Property.*

Salas got off the horse and stood with his hands on his hips. He kicked at one of the posts. He kicked and kicked at it, turning around and going at it like a mule, cursing. The post fell down, laying the barbed wire on the ground. The cows moved slowly, shouldering each other, mooing and passing through the opening to their usual watering spot. Salas bent over and got his breath and then turned around to see his new horse cantering off. He spent some time pulling the sign off and jumping up and down on it while the cows watched him.

About this time Eliza was outside, smashing the banjo against one of the larger cottonwood trees next to the house. She'd already broken the neck, so she was now whipping the round part of it to splinters. Aaron, who had returned from town with a burlap sack of potatoes, was watching his mother.

"What are you doing?" he finally asked.

She stopped long enough to wipe the sweat off her upper lip and say, "I'm playing the banjo."

Aaron nodded. "Nice tune," he said.

⇥TWENTY~EIGHT⇤

*I*t was the part of summer when the rains came every evening. You could smell the rain first and see it sometimes trailing across the plains in dark, blue-black veils. Eliza had to go into town to do some business. She wanted to get some more crates from Schwartzchild's store for packing, and she wanted to finish up a deal to sell the woodstove to Mr. Gordon, whose family had just moved into one of the new Victorian houses on the northwest side of town near the new Presbyterian church. Poor man, it was rumored, had been a Mormon and had had three wives, two of whom died. That was the rumor. But whatever his past, he was becoming well respected as the assistant bank manager.

As the three, Eliza, Ruthie and Aaron, started off to town, Eliza held Ruthie's hand, and Aaron walked ahead whacking at plants as usual, chopping tall stems in half. He had taken to reading dime novels bought at the pharmacy in town—novels about gunfighters, men who killed for the sake of honor and justice— never money. If they killed for money, they were always outlaws who got their punishment in the end in some ugly way—that's how the books presented it. Aaron was pretending to whip transgressors and cowards, men he had caught who had hurt women and children and were tasting the sting of his manly justice.

About halfway to town, where the big cottonwood pontificated about the majesty of nature and scorned the boy's feeble stick, Eliza stopped and pointed.

"Well, will you look at that! It's that dog! Come here, dog!"

The black-and-white dog, looking thinner than ever, walked up sheepishly, tail wagging, head lowered. She pranced, crossing one paw in front of the other.

Eliza bent down and said, "You're a good girl. Where you been? Huh? Where you been?"

The dog kept walking up.

"Well, look at that," Eliza said. She held out her hand. The dog walked all the way to her and sat down. Eliza patted her head and rubbed her neck. "Look here, Aaron. She's letting me pat her."

He stopped his drama with the plants and watched. Then he put his hand out for the dog to sniff and patted her.

"I wonder why she changed," Aaron said.

Eliza started them walking again, the dog following close behind.

"She must be hungry. We'll get her something to eat in town."

Aaron walked with the dog, touching her and talking to her.

In town, Deputy Salas was standing in front of a trio of miscreants: a drunken man, a woman, and a man waving a gun around, claiming to have been the victim of pickpocketing on behalf of the woman. The woman was a notorious prostitute who, people said, lured young boys into her crib behind Near and Anderson's when they were on their way home from school. It seemed unlikely to Eliza that the woman, whose hair was falling out and who had sores on her mouth all the time, could lure anyone. But the newspapers had printed a letter said to have been from her to one of the young boys, inviting him to come around any time.

Sets of people had stopped to watch the fray, which got loud when the woman began to scream indignantly. Clarence was dancing in the street in front of the deputy, a sweeping waltz that took all his concentration but seemed to have as its music the tones of the confrontation. Eliza stood beside two men from the county clerk's office who were muttering about the need for places to put "these people." As the town and the territory were clearly growing and becoming more civilized, there was increasing talk of the need for the three institutions of a civilized culture: a university, a prison and an insane asylum.

Deputy Salas sent the couple off and ended up shaking the alleged victim's hand with a friendly warning to avoid such characters. Then he turned and saw Eliza standing with Aaron and Ruthie. They stared at one another with the intimacy of two people who together had freed a dead man from his noose. Finally, the deputy touched his hat and nodded.

Eliza told Aaron to take Ruthie on into Schwartzchild's and get her a peppermint and then went to speak to the deputy.

"I guess I haven't thanked you and your family for the help you gave. You were the only people who did anything for us here, I guess."

Deputy Salas looked off into the distance behind her and then down at the sidewalk boards.

"Town's getting wild," Eliza said to relieve his awkwardness.

"Yes, it is." The deputy laughed.

"Too many people."

They both breathed heavily at the same time and then laughed.

"I guess I also wanted to say that I was sorry about your land getting sold out from under you. I don't know exactly how it happened, but I guess we got run off too."

"Oh, my family did not suffer so badly, Mrs. Pelham. Others did worse, those who counted on watering their cattle like they'd done since they came here. They had to sell. But we still have our home. We will always have our home, Mrs. Pelham."

She looked off and blew air noisily out of her mouth.

"There's just a lot that's wrong, and I'm trying to figure out what to do about it. I guess I've seen things so bad, I'm not afraid to look anymore."

Deputy Salas wiggled his hat brim, adjusting his hat, and got a thoughtful look on his face.

"Sometimes even if you know it will not change anything, you have to do something for your own dignity."

Were people watching them? Eliza felt uneasy. The black-and-white dog lay down beside her.

Not looking at him, she said, "Is that why my house was burned down? Somebody was doing something for his dignity?"

Deputy Salas stood still and said nothing.

"You know, I was thinking about this the other day. When I was up in that mining camp, a man gave me something to give to my husband—a Mexican man. I never showed George. It was one of those masks." She moved her hand in front of her face. "Made out of a flour sack. Isn't that what Mexicans are wearing when they go out at night causing trouble? I guess I understand your feelings, but me and my children, we didn't do anything. I was the one kept telling George we didn't own that land. I guess maybe since Aaron and your boy went up to the secret church or something, maybe you think we don't have respect for your family..."

Deputy Salas leaned over and said to her, "I want to give you some advice, Mrs. Pelham. Do not believe everything that you hear about people, especially when the information comes from those who want to take something from the people they are judging. Do you understand?" He did not look like the deputy at that moment, but like an enemy.

Eliza's face reddened and she took a few steps backward before turning and walking to the store. Before she got in the door, she could hear her daughter's aching screams. Three elongated howls. She then saw her daughter being held by the drummer, Mr. Smith, who had come in on the stageline from Santa Fe sporting a leather cowboy hat and a light green suit. His big face and thin curls were the same, though. And his voice boomed in the same old way as he announced to the people shopping, "Oh, she just doesn't remember me. I'm your old friend, Mr. Smith. Get her a peppermint."

Ruthie had gone silent and her head was lowered, almost fused with her chest, as she was still held and the peppermint came to her at the end of Emily Schwartzchild's thin, grey hand. Ruthie shook her head. Eliza could not move. Aaron simply threw an apple up and down.

"Mrs. Pelham," Emily said. "Look who has come back to town dressed like a cowboy!" She laughed. Eliza had never seen her so ebullient. Yet even when she laughed, one could not see her teeth, only a cavernous darkness rimmed with thin, brown lips.

"This place has been the source of much prosperity for me," the salesman said loudly, so that everyone in the store smiled or nodded. "Why, do you know how much I made on those coyote skins? Well, it's gauche of me to say. I'll just humbly admit to skinning a few Philadelphians in the transaction, a little business I put together down in Santa Fe. I didn't even have to go back east."

His audience chuckled, even those who went on examining the objects of their interest, dazed by the store's multiplying goods.

He put Ruthie down. She had not taken the peppermint and did not move the position of her lowered head by so much as an inch. Finally Eliza could move. She walked, shaking, to her daughter and took her hand. It was cold and sticky.

"Well, I think I'll go on down to Miller's and get one of those steak and biscuit lunches that have gotten my clothes so tight." Again the people in the store chuckled, but with more tolerance than enthusiasm now.

As he walked out, Emily said, for everyone to hear. "He's a good man," and the shoppers nodded.

Franz came in through the door, carrying a sack of chile peppers.

"I was wondering if I could have a few more crates," Eliza said. She heard her own voice as a distant sound.

"Sure, sure," Franz said, dropping the sack. "Sure, dey're out back der. I got maybe two or tree. Maybe you let da boy go out and get dem vit Rutie and ve look for dem banjo strings. I tink some came in yesterday."

"Momma don't have a banjo no more," Aaron said, grinning. "She smashed it up against a tree, smashed it to smithereens."

The others in the store eyed her, cloth poised between their fingers, fingertips resting on the tops of milky glass bottles. It was only in this silence that Eliza noticed Ruthie's whimpering—a terrible beaten sound, like an animal dying in a trap.

"I'll get the crates later," Eliza said, sweeping Ruthie up in her arms. "Come on, Aaron."

"She's too big to be carried around like a baby," Emily Schwartzchild clucked.

Franz followed Eliza out and watched her go down the street to Deputy Salas, who was pulling at his moustache in front of the depot.

The deputy waited for her to speak, looking cautious. It was obvious she had something specific to say. She first spoke to Aaron as she lowered Ruthie down. "Aaron, you take your sister over and show her the livestock pens where the calves are."

"But Clarence is over there," Aaron said, holding his sister's hand.

"Clarence won't bother with you. Go on. Just for a few minutes."

Alone, except for a man's bored face in the depot window, Salas and Eliza looked at each other.

"He's back in town as though nothing happened."

"Yes, ma'am, he is. He hasn't broken any law."

Eliza crossed her arms over her chest. She was fighting hard not to just go on over to Near's and get a bottle; but lately she'd smashed up whiskey bottles like she'd done with the banjo, throwing them against the adobe wall the cross was drawn on.

"Do you believe that I'm an honest woman, Mr. Salas?"

"Yes. You are an honest woman." With some effort he managed not to show any embarrassment but kept staring into her eyes, as if there was some contest going on between them.

"I know people say I drink. My daddy drank; I think he might have been drunk when he drowned, come to think of it. But I can tell you that I'm cold sober right now. And so you listen and I'll tell you what Mr. Smith did to my Ruthie—a five-year-old little girl. He touched her, Mr. Salas, between the legs, so she bleeds down there. There's bruises all over her little legs." Her voice shook, so she cleared her throat and raised her chin. She looked over to see Aaron trying to lift Ruthie up onto a sawhorse. Deputy Salas looked at the children too.

"You don't want to know, do you? You don't want to think of such a thing; nobody does. She wets the bed because she keeps herself from doing her business for as long as she can hold it in. She says it hurts, it stings. I had Dr. Findley out, and he shook his head, went pale at first, so I almost felt sorry that he had to see it. Then you know what he said? He said, 'This happens sometimes.' I said, 'Dr. Findley, she's been brutalized,' and he said, 'You see this sort of thing every now and then. Children don't understand, though. They forget all about it after a while.' He patted Ruthie on the cheek and told her she should be a good girl. He asked about George and how the chickens were laying. I guess he didn't think much of me, because I said he should go to hell. That I never knew a doctor to do anything useful except provide morphine."

The deputy's face was dark red.

"She's five years old, Mr. Salas. If Robert Youngman hadn't gotten my children away from that drummer, I don't know what. I might never have seen them again. Mr. Youngman is dead, hanged, his young face ruined by maggots, and that drummer is thriving, wanted to take the pants off a dead man to sell back east. He'd dig your grandfather up for his gold teeth, and you know it. You know you hanged the wrong man."

The deputy's moustache was quivering slightly. He parted his lips but said nothing. The face in the window was gone.

"I asked you. I asked you not to let him hang. And you didn't do anything to stop it, while Mr. Smith sells this whole territory, coyotes, trees, land, water, children, whatever he can get, and gets rich. The wrong man got killed and you know it. I know you know it because you're a good man. You and your family are good people, able to rise above what's sweeping through this sad country. I don't see any justice in any of what's going on. I guess I'm just a woman, Mr. Salas, amongst all you men who know better."

Deputy Salas pulled her farther away from the depot wall and said, "If you want justice, Mrs. Pelham, you're going to have to kill a lot of men."

She held up her finger. "One man," she said.

"I want you to kill one man. I want you to kill that drummer. You do it and we'll be settled—you'll pay me back for your people burning down my home, and you'll pay Mr. Youngman back for his life being over for no good reason."

Now Deputy Salas looked away, down at his own toe-worn boots, and shook his head. "You do not understand, Mrs. Pelham."

"I'm going to Miller's Restaurant now. I'm going to talk to Mr. Smith."

She waved her arm at Aaron and Ruthie and the three walked off. The black-and-white dog trotted happily behind them; Clarence strolled after them, playing with a frayed piece of rope.

At the end of the row of businesses, before the alley alongside the restaurant, four ladies from the Episcopal church were standing, all wearing fine hats. They watched the length of Eliza's journey to them. With every step toward them, Eliza had the growing sensation that her feet were going to explode and she would collapse, crushing Ruthie beneath her. They were the last obstacle in what now seemed some Herculean task that had begun with the view of a young boy dead and disfigured in her father's office.

"Good afternoon," the sleek-feathered lady said.

The little silk Chinese hat said, "We're all so glad your children are safe. Such a heartache—and you caught out in the mountains in that storm."

The sleek feather said, "Well, I think public hangings are disgusting and uncivilized. I would have stopped it if I could." She put her hand on Eliza's arm.

"The children don't know," Eliza said.

"Oh." All the hats looked at Aaron and Ruthie.

"Well, we're all missing your peach bread, Eliza," yellow hat said.

"I'll try to make some. I'm right busy now, getting all packed up." The women looked at each other; one popped a parasol open.

"I wish I were moving back to Richmond," she said. "I truly do."

"Oh, Beth, don't get weepy again," sleek feather said to parasol.

"I'll see you ladies," Eliza said, moving along.

Aaron saw Manuel sitting on the railroad tracks.

"Can I go be with Manuel?"

"No. You wait until after we've seen Mr. Smith."

"What're we seeing him for?"

She didn't answer, but lifted her chin.

"You don't think I know about that Indian being hung?" Aaron said.

Eliza put Ruthie down and stared at Aaron.

"Mr. Youngman. Didn't you used to call him Mr. Youngman?" she said.

"I guess."

The smell of hot meat fat hung around the doorway to the restaurant, a very small room with only five tables in it. The salesman was sitting alone at the table closest to the counter where baked goods were displayed. A young woman poked her head out of a curtained doorway, and Eliza said, "We're just visiting Mr. Smith here." The girl nodded and pulled her head back.

Mr. Smith had his hat off. His hair was oiled back without a part, ending in puffs of curls at his collar. His cravat was bunched up, looped over the light green vest. He was hot, wiping sweat off his face with the napkin. He watched Eliza and the two children walk up, the napkin touching his mouth. In front of him was a plate with part of a steak on it; pink watery juice with dots of oil in it spread out to a spoonful of greens. Biscuit crumbs danced around the plate on the red-and-white-checkered tablecloth when Eliza pulled out one of the empty chairs and sat down.

"Hello, Mr. Smith." she said. Aaron tossed hair out of his face and held on to the back of a chair. "I hope you don't mind if I sit down."

The salesman didn't move; the napkin was still in front of his face. Ruthie climbed into her mother's lap and leaned against her, her fingers in her mouth.

The napkin slowly lowered, and Mr. Smith pushed his plate away from him, sucking his teeth. Then he smiled.

"It's good to see you taking care of your children, Mrs. Pelham."

"Ruthie hasn't been the same since she was with you, Mr. Smith. She's like a baby. Can hardly do for herself."

Ruthie sat up and fell back against her mother hard.

The drummer leaned over and patted Aaron on the cheek.

"Why, I'm their friend and took good care of them, didn't I, son?"

Aaron tossed his hair.

"Did he, Aaron? Did he take good care of you?"

"I guess so."

"You guess so."

"Yes, I guess so," Aaron looked at her the way he'd looked before striking her face with the strip of leather. He said to the drummer, "But you aren't my friend."

Ruthie turned her face and hid it in her mother's blouse.

"They've been through some kind of tribulation, Mr. Smith."

"These are rough times. Hard times."

He patted his mouth with the napkin. The complacency of the action caused Eliza to get hot and shaky.

"I know who you are, Mr. Smith. You harmed my child. You did something so bad to her...something even an animal wouldn't do. I don't care who they hanged at the well. I know who should have been hanged."

"I don't like you," Aaron said to him. "You're a liar."

Mr. Smith took in a breath and held it. Then he let it out with theatrical patience.

"I don't think you raised these children right, Mrs. Pelham.

My mother would never have allowed me to speak like that to an elder." He leaned back a bit and smiled indulgently. "I realize these are hard times and that this country is wild, but that's when righteous folk have to stick, madam. We must raise children with a firm hand." He clenched his fist in the air in front of his face. Then he looked behind her.

Eliza turned around to see Deputy Salas sitting at the table nearest the door, watching them.

"You be brave, Ruthie. You be strong and brave," she said into her daughter's hair. "It's all right. You have every right to be angry and sad, but don't be weak, all right? You be strong with me. I'm not going to let anything happen to you. But you can't keep quiet, not when bad things happen and you know they're bad. So you tell me something. Did Mr. Smith hurt you?"

It was very quiet now except for the small sound of silverware being put away in the back room.

Ruthie sat up stiffly, arching her back, and with her eyes closed she said loudly, "Yes!" with an exaggeration of dignity.

Eliza glared at the salesman.

"Why did you hurt her? I want to know."

"She's just a child," he said, looking at the deputy. "I don't have to listen to this. You should be a better mother, Mrs. Pelham. You're exposing your children to harmful thoughts." He looked at the deputy. "I gave them some attention when they were being neglected by a drunken mother."

"I just bet, Mr. Smith, that you'd be the first man to sell me the whiskey if I asked for it, wouldn't you?"

Eliza stood up, letting Ruthie down to stand up beside her. Ruthie looked at Aaron and smiled mischievously. "I don't like you," she said as her older brother had said it. "You're a liar. You hurt me down here." Bending her knees, she clutched herself between her legs with both hands.

Mr. Smith leaned back in the chair, smiling. He eyed the deputy. "Clearly the asylum has not been built in time. I am completely and utterly shocked at what dementia you have visited upon your own child."

Eliza pulled Ruthie against her leg and held her around her shoulders.

"I want to know what happened to Bridie," Eliza said.

Mr. Smith shook his head.

"That dancehall girl who was with me up there," she explained.

"Oh, that Irish whore. Yes, well, I'd tell you, only I don't think the children should hear. They already seem so confused."

"Then let's go out back. Tell me out there."

When he stood up, the back of his coat had a line of wetness down it. He threw the napkin down on the table, where a corner of it fell into the plate and absorbed some of the reddish meat juices. He picked up a canvas bag that was under the table.

Aaron touched his mother's arm. "Can I go see Manuel?"

"Go ahead. But take your sister."

He rolled his eyes but took his sister's hand and led her out past the deputy, who was pulling at his moustache.

"Don't you go messing around that morada this time," she called out and exchanged looks with Deputy Salas.

She walked in front of the salesman down the side alley and around to the back of the restaurant, where the plains were in view, making the little cluster of New Town buildings seem flimsy and temporary. They could hear the sound of the young woman washing dishes in the back room of the restaurant. She occasionally muttered either to someone who didn't speak or to herself.

"It's easy to breathe out here," the salesman said, putting the bag down and then his hands into his pockets.

"What did you do with her?"

He looked at Eliza and scowled.

"I can't believe you would keep company with a common whore, Mrs. Pelham."

"Why don't you just tell me what happened to Bridie?"

"Now don't you get hysterical, Mrs. Pelham. Maybe you're going through hard times, with your husband away and all, spending money God knows on what down there in Santa Fe, that sink of vice. I tell you what, dear, I'll give you a little cash—a gift. I hate to see you so distraught. A little money should smooth everything over." He bent down and fumbled in the bag and brought out five twenty-dollar bills. He held them out to her. "Go ahead. We'll just forget all about everything. You won't have to pay me back a cent."

In an instant several scenes passed through Eliza's mind in which she easily paid for a number of things. Her hand went up, and then she looked at the drummer's face, swollen with nervous fear and mysterious, private desires. She thought about Robert's shoes and dropped her hand. Mr. Smith shook his head and put the money back.

"Well," he said, calmer than before, happy, "after that Indian assaulted me and took the children, I went looking for them, of course. I found Bridie in that cave, sick, awful sick. The pitiful thing, as sick as she was, asked me...well, I want to put this as delicately as possible for you, Mrs. Pelham. She said she needed money to go to one of the sanatoriums to get some help for her consumption. She said that she would entertain me for a certain amount that it's not important to disclose."

"Where is she now?"

"Well, of course, I refused her offer. I'm a Christian man, and I certainly didn't want to risk infecting myself with her tragic illness."

"Where is she now? In Santa Fe?"

"Well, she was so desperate for money, and I saw that she had a most valuable asset, so, well, let me show you." He opened the bag and lifted out something covered in tissue paper. Unfolding it, he displayed a hunk of orange hair, glistening hair. He moved his hand up and down as though weighing it.

"You can just imagine how many old dowagers in Boston would pay a pocketful of coins for this as the basis of a wig."

Eliza stepped forward. She touched the hair and whispered, "Bridie. I plaited her hair."

"I've already had eighty-four coyote pelts shipped to Philadelphia. This has been a most prosperous venture, and my business partner is on his way out right now. This is a land full of promise for those willing to stick, yes it is. If I was a younger man, I'd be in the mines." He put the hair back.

Eliza said, "Is she in Santa Fe?"

"Well, yes, yes. I took her on down to Santa Fe as a gesture of charity. It's a charity hospital; she wanted me to take her to Albuquerque, but I'm a capitalist, not a philanthropist, Mrs. Pelham. A free hospital for the poor is good enough."

"I think you are evil, Mr. Smith. I think you are the evilest thing I ever knew about. Her hair was so beautiful. She wanted that pair of gloves, just a pair of gloves."

"If you knew how much money I intend to help the people of this good town make...I have been involved in some of the land dealings. If you knew..." He winked at her.

"You're telling me you took Bridie to St. Vincent's?"

"Well, yes. That's right—where the nuns could look after her."

A man then came quickly out of the back door. He was wearing a sack with eye holes in it over his head. Mr. Smith laughed as though being engaged in a prank. The masked man held out the salesman's new hat, which he had left in the restaurant. Puzzled but amused, Mr. Smith took the hat, revealing a gun in the masked man's hand, which was pointing at him. The eyes in the mask looked briefly into Eliza's. They were dark; even the whites in the shadow of the sack seemed brown. In a moment he had taken the salesman by the elbow and was running him across the grasses to the arroyo.

They looked absurd to Eliza, two men who had suddenly become very small and distant, quirky marionettes with their strings tangled together.

She stood there for a while until there was nothing to see except for grass; the air was very still, very hot, waiting on tiptoes for the coming rain. There it was in the distance—a dark, delicate curtain, sliding across the sky. Only a few grass stems moved when grasshoppers jumped from them. Eliza looked down and saw the bag. She stared at it, then picked it up and walked back to the restaurant where there was no sign of anyone. The black-and-white dog, however, was trotting down the street with a steak bone in its mouth.

✥TWENTY~NINE✥

"*W*e saw him, me and Manuel saw the salesman and the man with a sack over his head. We saw them going along the arroyo and end up down at the bridge by the river. They waited in the trees and didn't see us. The man with the sack over his head had a gun—a 'Peacemaker.' We kept after 'em, though, across the river. They walked on across, gettin' their pants legs wet, and come up the other side near the place where the cattle come to drink, over there near where we found the dead calf that time. And so we saw them go up there, and we kept following. Manuel said they were going to the morada, and I said I didn't want to get caught there again, but we kept our distance and kept going. Then we saw them go into the morada, and Manuel and I waited for a long time. Manuel wanted to know what the drummer had done to us, and I said it weren't any of his damn business, so we ended up talkin' about the new pool hall that was bein' built and how the man who owns it looks like a chicken 'cause he ain't got no chin. And Manuel was sayin' that the new hotel goin' up is gonna be five stories high. I was glad that we'd made Ruthie go on back to Schwartzchild's, 'cause she was startin' to rankle us some with her talkin' on and on again like she used to. Anyways, it got late and we forgot what we was doin' there and we snuck on around the morada, but there was no one there and I saw where there was a picture of Jesus with thorns around his head and then both of us at the same time heard somebody comin' and we ran off and it was a woman who told us both to get on home or somethin' bad was gonna happen to us. And so we ran, Manuel on up to his home and I came back down here. And when I was comin' across the river, I saw three men with guns; one of 'em looked like Mr. Near, walkin' back and forth in front of that same place where the cattle come to water. They didn't see me, though, because I came on back to the other side of the bridge, where I swim all the time, and that's how come I'm all wet."

A dark, small space. Lantern light showed the features of Eliza's face; there were two small replicas of the lantern in her glasses. She was sitting in the outhouse, her bloomers around her ankles, her skirt bunched up and falling in front of her between her legs. She was leaning over, taking out the contents of the carpetbag in front of her.

She laid the tissue paper–covered hair on the seat beside her. She took out a box and opened it. There were three pairs of ladies' gloves in it; she put one glove on and admired her hand. She stood up and pulled up her bloomers. Then she took more things out of the bag—a packet of papers, some kind of stocks and deeds. She looked at one and saw that it concerned the part ownership of a section of land that was numbered and described according to certain features on the landscape—a tree, an old sheepherder's hut. There were three ledger books bound in black leather, one full of orders. Another had dates and appointments listed in it. The third was blank and had some pages torn out of it. Eliza pulled out a stack of envelopes tied together with one of Ruthie's ribbons; she untied the ribbon and opened the first envelope. There was paper money inside—five twenty-dollar bills.

"Jesus, Mary and Joseph," she said.

She opened the next envelope: more money. She threw the things she'd taken out back in the bag and left the outhouse with it and the lantern.

"Aaron," she called. He was sitting outside on a chair, patting the dog. "Come here and help me. You've got to do some adding for me."

She got out one of the ledgers and handed it to him.

"Add up the orders and prices in here for the things where it says 'paid.' "

She had to explain it to him again.

"I don't know if I can do it without a pencil and paper."

"Well, go on in and get a pencil and paper."

When he came back out he saw his mother sitting cross-legged on the ground, counting a pile of money in her lap.

"Criminy," he said.

"Shush—I lost count. Go on ahead and add that up for me."

They sat with cricket sounds and the lantern light. Eliza finished and said, "Your sister still asleep?"

"Yes. Now don't bother me. I'm almost done."

"Don't talk to me that way."

He muttered numbers to himself.

"People paid him fifty-four dollars and eighty-seven cents."

"Is that all? Are you sure?"

"Yeah."

"How many people?"

He counted aloud and got to twenty-eight.

"We got to give this back—the bag and these ledgers and the money that goes with them."

"How much money?"

She looked at him; she smiled and held the stack of money under his eyes.

"Four hundred and two dollars."

"Criminy."

They looked at each other.

"Give me the book. We've got to put things back. Wait." She took out Bridie's hair. Then she put one of the envelopes back with five twenty-dollar bills in it. Aaron was watching her, puzzled; then his eyes brightened and he grinned.

Eliza said, "I'm going to buy a good horse, maybe two, and a wagon. What are you going to buy?"

Aaron grinned more. "Me?"

"Yes, you. Your share is twenty dollars."

"Criminy."

He thought for a minute.

"I know what I'm gonna buy." He tossed his hair sheepishly out of his eyes. "But I ain't gonna tell you."

She narrowed her eyes. "I guess you're too young for getting into too much trouble. I don't have to worry about liquor and women with you yet, I guess."

"No!" he yelled out.

"Shhh!" She put her finger to her mouth and laughed. "Now look," she said, trying to be serious. "This isn't stealing. Well, yes, it is stealing. Okay, look. I don't care about taking money from some drummer who does harm to people. He doesn't give a fig about helping people—none of them do. They just take the money. They'll sell anything. It's these kind of people your daddy talked about—remember those railroad tycoons and how they treated those poor Chinamen? Same thing. Now, I can't rightly explain this to you, but I wouldn't do this to somebody like that drummer who wears that silly little French hat. He's too pitiful already. But I figure as how Mr. Smith and a lot of other men getting rich off selling things people don't need and taking things they do need owe us. So, I'm going to give part of this money to some of the poor folks in town that don't have the gumption to do for themselves."

"You think you're Robin Hood?"

"Hey," she said, standing up and pointing to herself. "I'm keeping most of this for me, don't you worry."

"What if he comes back?"

"I'm going to take the bag into the sheriff, everything in order, nice and undisturbed, and tell him he ought to give the people's money back, and, well, I just don't think we'll have to worry."

She thought.

"I guess I'll have to pay the sheriff for his horse before he sees me buyin' my own." She laughed and twirled around. "You know, Aaron," she said more solemnly, "I guess I'm smart, smarter than most people. I guess if I put myself to it I could do pretty well."

She put her arms around Aaron and said, "I can go get Bridie and give her some money for that sanatorium in Albuquerque."

"You already gone past the money you got, Ma."

Up in the mountains, in the canyon just north of the Royene Mine where men were playing cards, a kestrel's sharp cheeps echoed all the way from the sky down to the stream. A mountain lion was dragging something out of a cave. She pulled and pulled, then stopped, panting. She pulled again, looking suspiciously around, growling a little should any other animal think about sharing this booty. What she had was the pale, naked body of a human female, the legs and arms flopping stiffly as the body was dragged. The face was blotched with black and blue marks, one side purple and red where the blood had collected. There were bits of leaves and dirt on the head, a pixielike head of cropped red hair. The mountain lion spent a long time pulling the body out and then lay across it, slowly licking one arm, closing its eyes and licking the arm with deep patience and satisfaction.

⤳THIRTY⤲

*E*liza stayed outside, too excited to sleep. She lay back on a blanket and thought about Aaron and Ruthie being safe in the bedroom. A little burrowing owl started its strange barking sound in one of the cottonwoods. Behind Eliza a man peered over the edge of the arroyo and could see her painted in the light of the lantern.

When she stood up to go inside, the man got up and waited by the doorway to the burned-out room as the lantern light moved to the bedroom window and flowed out yellow.

She came back out to put the carpetbag in the woodstove and saw that part of the darkness in there was shaped like a man. She stopped, put the bag down and said, "Who's there? What are you doing?"

Deputy Salas walked past some partially packed crates and showed his face to her.

"Is that his bag?"

Eliza looked down at it. "I guess so," she said.

"That is not what I am here for. Do not worry."

"Well, you might as well take it. I was going to take it into the sheriff's office in the morning anyway."

"You should take it in. I do not want anything to do with it."

Eliza could smell tobacco and horse on him, and the smell of cooked cornmeal.

He handed her some papers he'd been nervously rolling into a tube.

"I want you to look at those," he said.

She got the lantern from the other room, casting a shadowy light on the chaos of the burned-room, the yellow wood of crates and the black of the charred things.

With the deputy standing there, Eliza unrolled the papers and started to look them over. They made no sense to her at first.

"This is more business about land. I don't know anything about this."

Salas nodded his head toward the papers in her hand and said, "Keep looking. Look at the notes about the property's value."

Eliza read aloud from some little pages torn from a notebook and written on in pencil: "Pump, outhouse, arroyo, some old cottonwoods, old wagon road into town—well, I guess this is about this place. I remember when that man was out here from the lawyer's office making these notes."

"Keep reading."

"Where'd you get this?"

"Clerk's office. Keep reading."

Her eyes swept slowly down the little pages, which she turned over until, in the middle of one page in big letters and underlined twice, she saw the words FIRE DAMAGED and beneath them a measurement of the distance between the road and the arroyo and then some other notes concerning the sandy quality of the soil.

She looked up at the deputy. "There hadn't been any fire when he was out here."

The deputy nodded and took the papers back.

"Then how did he know?" Eliza asked.

"Your boy was back up at the morada," Salas said. "You must tell him to stay away."

"I'll tell him."

"Don't believe everything you hear about Mexicans, Mrs. Pelham. When people win they are called heroes, when they lose they are called bandits. Why would we want to burn down a house that is ours, that was built by our grandfather? It is a smart plan to lower the price of something you want to buy and at the same time make those you are stealing from look like the bandits. I just wanted you to know."

"We ought to do something."

"We *have* done something, Mrs. Pelham. It is done."

He stepped out, knocking against one of the crates.

✦THIRTY~ONE✦

*E*liza could hear the wooden floor creak outside the confessional. The air seemed to swirl around in dark eddies and eruptions. Eliza didn't want whoever was out in the sanctuary to hear what she was saying, so she leaned in closer to the grille. On the other side another woman's face, veiled in black lace, also came close and listened.

"I have sinned," Eliza whispered.

The other woman's head nodded.

"I have committed adultery, and I have caused the death of a man."

"Only one man?"

"Yes." Eliza paused and then said, "Maybe two. I had a man killed, and another, who helped me, was hanged. He could have walked on, disappeared forever in the mountains, but he brought my children back. I was going to pay him; I didn't believe they would hang him. But I *wanted* the drummer to die. I wanted to see it; I wanted to do it myself." She put her fingertips through the latticework of the screen and looked into the woman's mink brown eyes. "I'm no better than the others. I wanted to put a gun in his mouth and make him taste the metal before I exploded his head."

Eliza became absorbed with the amazingly beautiful sight of the woman's eyes behind the black veil. They drew out confessions.

"I have sinned. I have made mistakes. My children might've been killed. And now I don't know what I've done, how many deaths I've been responsible for. There was a young boy…many soldiers, boys…"

"Do not exaggerate your importance, mi hija. Why don't you just go have a drink?"

Eliza sat back and licked her upper lip. She closed her eyes and sighed.

"I don't ever want to not look straight at things again. It's a hard life to choose, looking straight at things, but maybe that's the difference between me and somebody who'd shoot a man in the head or let their children die."

The veiled eyes closed and opened again, moister.

Eliza looked into them. "My father drank," she said. "He didn't want to see things. He didn't do anything wrong, though, except for drown. Maybe if he'd been bitter or if I'd asked him to stop drinking…"

The woman waved her hand in front of her face, the same gesture Eliza had seen Senora Salas use to dismiss her father-in-law's prattling.

"Do not waste my time. There are others waiting."

Eliza looked outside the confession box through the grille-work but could see nothing but the empty sanctuary.

"We are alone. There is no one else."

"Never mind. Are you asking for absolution?"

"Yes."

"Have you prayed to God?"

"I've asked for forgiveness, but I don't hear anything but the wind outside at night."

The veiled woman made the sign of the cross.

"What will I do?" Eliza put both hands on the grille; she was now so close to the woman's face that she could see that the skin had dark rainbows in it like a pool of oil. "I don't want to drown. I'm tired of the dead talking to me, pulling at me, looking down at me from trees. I don't want to think about what's over and done with and can't be changed."

"If you don't want to think, mija, you have several choices," the woman said, leaning in conspiratorially and whispering as though her superior might hear her and punish her. "For example, you could become an idiot. I could perhaps arrange for someone to drop a rock on your head while you are sleeping. Then you will see nothing but your shoes and the food on your plate."

"How could I take care of my children?"

"Eeee, you are asking me? Well, if you think that you can be an idiot, you get rid of the children, for their own protection, of course."

"All right. I don't want to be an idiot. Just give me absolution and I'll try to go on. What should I do? Tell me what to do."

"If I tell you, you will not like it. It is not easy."

"Help me. I don't know what to do."

"Here, mi hija. You must take this and wear it until you do not need to any longer, perhaps forever. Perhaps you will, for the rest of your life, have to put this on at times. That is the first thing you will have to accept." The woman opened a little window in the latticework and pushed through a mass of black cloth, a completely black dress with rustling petticoats. It was then that Eliza realized that those who were waiting outside were various dead people: the boy from Kentucky, her father holding her infant daughter, the drummer, and Robert.

"Go on," Robert said, nodding toward the dress. He seemed infinitely patient and forgiving. His hand was resting on the drummer's shoulder.

"Go on, Ellie. It's all right," Bridie said from behind Robert.

"How odd," Eliza muttered.

The dark woman tapped on the grillework to get Eliza's attention. "As for the adultery, I will tell you what to do. Do several Ave Marías with your husband between your legs."

Her sweet and girlish laughter went flying around the church so that the walls cracked.

When the train came in, it held more people than made sense. It stopped and exploded with passengers, some tired, some excited. Four men in very expensive suits and silk cravats got out and stood moving their heads around, looking at everything, but mostly looking at the sky: it was so huge some weren't sure they could live under it. Eleven Catholic nuns stepped gingerly down onto the platform and became one huge black-and-white flower, the black petals moved by the breeze. Other women and men, holding their hats, holding their bags, standing on their toes and searching the crowd, talked or coughed or waved. Children stood still next to their mothers' skirts. One little girl held on to her father's hand as he laughed at a joke a drummer told. The train sat, enormous and hot beside them all, the blackest thing around. It waited, letting soiled, sweating men take things off of its freight cars. Six men straining every sinew in their arms were taking out a huge woodstove, the biggest woodstove ever seen in the territory. It was for Fogharty's Restaurant, "promising the finest in fresh-baked trout and mutton stew." Mr. Fogharty, an unusually tall man with a long, red moustache and thick features, watched the men handling his prize and chewed on the ends of his moustache.

"Don't worry, Mr. Fogharty," one of the bearers said. "If we drop it, it will make a hole big enough for your grave!"

The onlookers laughed. Mr. Fogharty smiled, but his eyes kept serious vigil over the progress of his stove, a luxury that was soon to cause the famous New Town fire, in which every single structure except the courthouse was burned to fine ash.

"Why is it called a banjo, Momma?" Ruthie asked. "I don't like that name much, except for if I had a cat maybe I'd name it banjo. Banjo sounds funny to me, so the cat would be a funny cat. Do Chinamen eat cats, Momma? Mrs. Bradley said that Chinamen eat cats."

"Mrs. Bradley doesn't know anything about Chinamen or cats," Eliza said. She was busy at the woodstove, standing in the burned-out room, taking bread out of the stove, wearing a black dress with black pearl buttons up the pleated front.

"Momma sometimes I think I have weasels in my mind. Can people have weasels in their mind?"

Aaron, standing and looking out the door, said, without turning around, "You are a weasel."

"No, I'm not," Ruthie said.

On their way out of town, Eliza and her children were atop a horse-pulled wagon all packed up with crates and a second new horse tethered to the back—a fine brown one, the texture of satin. They stopped by the sheriff's office, where Deputy Salas was sitting outside on a stool, cleaning his gun with his son Manuel. Aaron jumped off the wagon and whispered in his friend's ear.

"I'll be right back," he called over his shoulder as he ran down the sidewalk with Manuel.

Ruthie continued to administer some kind of medical care to her new doll, which involved some serious cajoling and prodding.

The sheriff stepped out to go over to the courthouse.

"You leaving so fast, Mrs. Pelham?" he said on his way.

"I want nothing more to do with this town," Eliza said.

"Nothin' wrong with this town," the sheriff said angrily, stopping to answer this affront to his domain.

"Listen to all that hammering. It makes my head hurt. And everything's starting to smell like that train, metal and smoke. I don't see how anybody can stand it."

The sheriff's eyes narrowed.

"You always wearing that black dress. You in mourning, Mrs. Pelham? Somebody in your family die?"

"I'd say so, sheriff. And so did some ideas I had about how things were supposed to be. I guess a lot of things died. Maybe that's why this town smells so bad."

"I don't suppose you're in mourning over some Indian, are you? People don't want to have anything to do with an American who'd be in mourning over some Indian."

"I guess they wouldn't. I guess there's several Americans I wouldn't want to have anything to do with."

Deputy Salas laughed openly, blowing a piece of grit off the gun barrel.

The sheriff stalked off to the courthouse, his beard trailing behind him over his shoulder.

Eliza held out an envelope for the deputy, who carefully stood up and put the gun barrel down on the stool on top of the cleaning cloth. Her hand was shaking a little.

"This is a letter I'd appreciate you posting."

Ruthie sighed because the porcelain face of the doll had taken on a very petulant and snooty expression despite her sincere efforts to help the creature.

"We better get going," Eliza said. "I've got another favor to ask you, though. I know you won't like this much, but I'd appreciate it if you'd take this down to the Episcopal church for the dinner tonight." She twisted around and got two loaves of bread wrapped in cheesecloth. "This one's for the church and this one here's for you and Mrs. Salas—Senora Salas. Don't let the sheriff eat it."

Aaron came then, walking up to the wagon with a grin splitting his face and both hands behind his back. Manuel was behind him, sheepish and languid.

"I went down to Clementi's Music Emporium," Aaron breathed. "And I got this."

He held out his hand, a brand-new, smiling banjo hanging from it. It was an S.S. Stewart, strung and all, busting with pride, showing off its silver plate inlaid with a flowering vine. It looked for the sun and darted a fat ray of light right in Eliza's eyes. "Yessiree, Bob, I am one hell of a banjo."

"You!" Eliza said. "Why, you boy. Did you spend everything you had on that?"

"Almost."

Eliza drew it up to her, laid it in her lap, where it might have hummed all by itself like a lost lover come back. She strummed and that banging, sweet tin chord seemed to quiet the whole town like a blessing.

"He paid himself," Manuel said.

Ruthie plucked a string.

"Isn't it the finest thing you've ever seen, Ruthie? I'll teach you to play it. I'll bet you could make up some fine tunes yourself, about cats and dogs and all kinds of silly things." She hugged the instrument to her. "I sure do thank you, Aaron." She was getting tears in her eyes, so she said, "I guess we better go on now."

Salas handed one of the loaves of peach bread to Manuel.

"And there's this dog out there, a black-and-white dog," Eliza said.

Manuel nodded. "I know. I'll see to it."

Eliza stayed for a minute, wondering if Deputy Salas was going to say something before she left. Then she felt foolish and said, "Come on, Aaron. Let's go." She laid the banjo carefully down in the wagon, putting blankets over it. Aaron got up beside, her and she said, "I can't believe you did that. You are sure a wonderful boy."

"No, he isn't," Ruthie said.

Deputy Salas watched them go and then put the bread on the sheriff's desk. There was a good chance the sheriff would eat it if he left it there, so he told Manuel to stay and keep an eye on it while he went to take the other loaf and post the letter. How he'd come to do errands for a woman he didn't know? But he did know it wouldn't happen again. There were several things he was bound and determined wouldn't happen again.

The letter was addressed to Miss Bridie O'Doonan at St. Vincent's Hospital in Santa Fe. It said:

Dear Bridie,

I hope you get this letter before I come for you because I don't want to give you a shock. I came into some money and wanted to go on down with you to Albuquerque to the

*sanatorium there. Aaron and Ruthie and I are moving out
of New Town and are joining up with Mr. Pelham to start
farming. He doesn't know that yet, so don't say anything to
him if you see him. He was put out with me for matters I
think you understand, but I believe that when he sees all the
money I got he'll forgive me and we can start anew. I guess
I like the idea of George keeping me warm at night. (Don't
let those nuns read this letter!) You will be more than welcome
on our farm, as a friend and a sister, as soon as you are done
at the sanatorium. We will talk about all these matters when
I see you soon. I am happy about seeing you again and I
wonder how sweet you look with your hair all cut off like a
fairy's. You will be most surprised when you see that I have
your hair with me and we can find a wig-maker to fix it up
for you to wear yourself while your own is coming in.*

*Somehow I feel that you will understand everything I have
to say, and that is a precious thing in this world. Sometimes I
think I will live my whole life without anyone knowing how
deep my thoughts go.*

I am surely glad to be leaving New Town.

Your dear friend,

Eliza Pelham

On the road, just past a mountain people called Hermit's
Peak, Eliza listened to her children talking.

"What if we were cockroaches instead of human beings?"
Ruthie asked.

"I don't know," Aaron said. "I guess we wouldn't think much of it one way or the other. We'd think we were the most important thing. We'd think human beings were big bugs."

Ruthie looked down at her hands, confirming that they were not an insect's claws.

"I won't never be a cockroach," she said. Then she stretched her young body.

And they continued along the road, having reached that point when a process must continue and cannot be reversed.

Set in BASKERVILLE
Designed by John Baskerville *(1706-75)*
who desired a more progressive typeface,
one less florid and well-suited for business.
Championed by Benjamin Franklin,
the strict, vertical *rationalist* axis embodies
what we now consider *neo-classical*,
reflective of State Capitol Buildings
built out of similar emphasis.
The italic has a crow quill scratch
like handwriting, rather than
the nib script flow of Renaissance faces.
This version by Monotype
feels slightly gazette.

•

Book design by J. Bryan

Kate Horsley was born in Richmond, Virginia. In 1977, she moved to New Mexico, where she obtained a Ph.D. in American Studies from the University of New Mexico. She has done investigative journalism and now teaches college English in Albuquerque. She lives in the South Valley of Albuquerque with her husband, her son, her husband's garden and various non-human animals.

But often, in the world's most crowded streets,
But often, in the din of strife,
There rises an unspeakable desire
After the knowledge of our buried life;
A thirst to spend our fire and restless force
In tracking out our true, original course;
A longing to inquire
Into the mystery of this heart which beats
So wild, so deep in us—to know
Whence our lives come and where they go.

from THE BURIED LIFE
Matthew Arnold, 1852